Advance Praise for *Hollywood and Sunset*

"This is a rare thing—a truly entertaining novel with soul."
Tracy Kidder, Pulitzer Prize–winning
author of *Mountains Beyond Mountains*

"Like D.W. Griffith, the pioneering auteur whose *Intolerance*
(1916) provides the shooting stage *Hollywood and Sunset*, Luke
Salisbury conjures a wondrous pageant of intricate design and
rare beauty. With a gimlet eye for cinematic detail, a sure grasp
of narrative drive, and a grand sense of epic sweep, he takes the
reader on a spellbinding excursion through the back lots of
embryonic Hollywood—and into the heart of a man who is himself caught at the crossroads of myth and history, starry-eyed
romance and harsh reality. An A-level production from title
frame to end credits, *Hollywood and Sunset* is a work of wit,
warmth, and boundless fascination."
Thomas Doherty, associate professor of film studies,
Brandeis University, and author of *Pre-Code Hollywood*

"With *Hollywood and Sunset*, Luke Salisbury dishes up a wicked,
wacky, ribald dream of a novel. The mightily unheroic Henry
Harrison blunders through Lotusland on an unholy Pilgrim's
Progress that rises to a breathtaking climax. You'll laugh and
you may cry, you'll cover your eyes and yet peek through your
fingers as the Golden Age of the Silver Screen comes back to
outrageous life."
Kai Maristed, author of *Broken Ground*
and other novels

HOLLYWOOD AND SUNSET

Also by Luke Salisbury

FICTION
The Cleveland Indian
Blue Eden

NONFICTION
The Answer Is Baseball

HOLLYWOOD AND SUNSET

Luke Salisbury

Shambling Gate Press
Hyattsville, Md.

Published by
Shambling Gate Press
3314 Rosemary Lane
Hyattsville, Maryland 20782
301-779-6863
www.shamblinggate.com

Front cover photograph of the Babylon set from D. W. Griffith's film
Intolerance courtesy of Photofest.

Design by Cheryl W. Hoffman

Library of Congress Control Number 2005928944

ISBN-10: 0-9679728-2-5
ISBN-13: 978-9679728-2-4

Printed in the United States of America

Printed on acid-free paper that meets the American National Standards
Institute Z.39-48 standard.

To
Barbara and Ace
and
the memory of Ilona Karmel

Acknowledgments

A book has many fathers. I received much help in research and editing, not to mention encouragement and inspiration.

Paul Adomites went to Los Angeles with me to look for Griffith sites and read every draft; David Adomites provided a place to stay; Carlos Bauer guided us through "the Nickel" and photographed places in Hollywood; Dick Beverage accompanied us; Holly Posner edited and encouraged and brought her fine sense of language to the manuscript; Leslie Epstein criticized, suggested, and remains a model of excellence; Martin Espada pointed out the abyss between form and content in Griffith's genius; Jean-Danny Joachim always believed in the book, and parts of it were read at his City Nights Readings series; Cappy Gagnon provided details of Los Angeles. Many thanks to George Fifield for insight, Jake Shearer for decades of conversation about film and Griffith, Robert Knox for a lifelong dialogue about fiction and for reading early drafts, William Brevda for signs and Americana, Ace Salisbury for common sense and for designing an early cover, and Barbara Salisbury for everything. The summer afternoons spent with Ilona Karmel discussing the book were glimpses of paradise. Special thanks to Cheryl Hoffman and Lawrence Paulson of Shambling Gate for bringing their remarkable intelligence and critical skill to the manuscript, and for publishing it. Any historical mistakes, anachronisms, or false steps are solely mine.

I

CHRIST ON SUNSET BOULEVARD

LOS ANGELES

April 2, 1916
5:30 a.m.

1

Head high, eyes scanning the hills, Jesus Christ drove Henry Ford's Universal Car out of the east. I squinted. It was Howard Gaye, the English actor who played Robert E. Lee in *Birth of a Nation* and Christ in D. W. Griffith's new motion picture. I'd heard Gaye liked to drive his Model T around Los Angeles looking for women while dressed in Christ regalia. Another day the Wonder of the Ages driving the Wonder of the Age down Sunset Boulevard would have made me laugh. Today I was numb.

An hour ago my wife told me she was having an affair. I said, "I'll forgive you."

She said, "I don't want to be forgiven. I want to leave."

∾

I walked through the shroudlike, mysterious Los Angeles dawn. Mist hung like phantoms—strange, ghostly, pale—call it angels at your own risk. The light looked put down from another world.

I was going to interview D. W. Griffith. Trust your wife to leave on your most important day.

∾

The white figure braked, stopped, and in a posh accent said, "Do you require a lift?" I got in. Jesus was surprised I wasn't surprised. He sniffed, a slender hand gripped the polished wheel, and we were off, with robes and cowl billowing at ten miles per hour.

"Take me to Babylon, Mr. Gaye." My voice cracked.

"Call me Jesus. I try to stay in character. All of us could stand to be more like the Nazarene."

Gaye was the full image: white robes, gorgeous hair, neat brown beard, penetrating blue eyes, sandals with leather thongs that wound up hairy legs like a double caduceus.

"To Griffith," I said, getting control of my voice. I'd waited weeks to see Griffith. I had to get control of myself.

"The public can't get in."

"I have an interview." I held up my briefcase. "Harrison. *The Atlantic*."

Jesus' face lit up. "Not Henry Harrison? Not the Harrison who wrote 'The Man Who Gave *Birth*'? You dislike the Master more than I do!"

I nodded. I didn't feel like Henry Harrison, Harvard man (H '94; Law '96), relation of two presidents, author, owner of the Rochester Hustlers baseball club.

Cuckold.

"My good man! I'm delighted." Jesus shook my hand; his sleeve touched my leg. "No wonder Griffith didn't send a car! Does baloney reject the grinder? Harrison, you've taken the measure of this 'genius' hacks call 'the Shakespeare of the screen.'" Jesus leaned over. "He'll keep you waiting. Griff wants you buggered with anticipation.

"Then the Master will take you aside and say the photoplay is ushering in a new world. It makes men see so they think and act differently. The New Millennium. Pictures. The universal language. Griffith thinks human nature will

4

change. He thinks he can stop the world war. The fool thinks because *Birth of a Nation* got Americans to riot and hate niggers, this new monstrosity will stop the killing. Ridiculous! *I* am the New Millennium."

"Jesus Christ?" I said, bitterly.

"Art. The theater. The medium of Shakespeare. The real one!" Jesus shouted, robes flying as Our Lord's must have when he ejected the moneylenders from the Temple. "The flickers art? A photoplay director Shakespeare?" Jesus swerved to avoid a dog. "The theater is art. The genius failed at that. Miserable actor. Failed playwright. Failed poet. Failed husband. God help us!"

"Griffith made a fortune attacking the Negro race," I said. "I despise him."

"The Master thinks he can do anything." Jesus ran both hands through his mane. "He's too damn bloody rich. Too many girls. Too bloody independent."

I wanted to scream. Edith! Why?

"I can help you," said Jesus.

I thought of Michael X. Murphy coming to our house with his plain wife, prating about family and service, looking at everything with eager eyes. My God, Edith had to teach him table manners!

"Harrison, why are you so upset?"

"What?"

"Either you stole that suit or you killed someone. You look awful."

"Who lacks a reason to be angry?" I said.

"For God's sake, hide it better."

"My wife just left me. I hit her . . . another man . . . I don't want to talk about it."

"Who lacks a reason to hit his wife?" said Jesus.

∾

We went west on Sunset. The few bungalows were dark. Mist hung in the road like ripped gauze, not angels. It would take less than an hour to reach Fine Arts Studio at the corner of Hollywood and Sunset. I was supposed to see Griffith at seven thirty.

"I've never hit anyone," I said.

"What will you miss most about your wife?" said Jesus, suddenly.

The hills looked greener as the sun climbed over my shoulder. The fog and strange milky light would be gone soon. "Her body," I said, attempting sarcasm but the words broke.

Jesus raised an eyebrow. "Harrison, you're sentimental. That's a disadvantage."

"What?"

"Women are never sentimental."

"Why do you care?" I said.

"I don't. I merely want to know if this is going to derail your book. You are writing a book? That's what frightens Griffith."

"I am. For Houghton Mifflin."

Jesus extended his arms as if on the cross. "About your wife. No one forgives. All you can do is get even." Jesus ran a hand through his luxuriant hair. "Stick with me. I'm an expert at getting even. Is that suit English?"

Why? Why didn't I see? They were always together.

I imagine them covered by a single sheet. Murphy hears me and jumps up, throwing off the sheet. An erection points crazily at the ceiling. I've got a baseball bat. A heavy Louisville Slugger. I smash his shin. Murphy hobbles, grabbing his leg. Edith screams but no sound comes. I hit him in the crotch. I hit again and again until bone cracks. He rolls to the floor, begging to be spared for his children. I tell him to beg for the man who f***ed Edith. Beg for his best. I pull back the bat and aim for his skull.

∽

At six a.m. she said, "I have something to tell you."

Maybe it was Edith's tone, her best lace dress, the enormous, purple-feathered hat, but I knew this was about Michael Murphy, whom we hired to run the baseball club we own in Rochester when I started to write. Man does not live by baseball alone.

"I'm in love with Michael," said Edith. "We've . . . "

"You've what?"

"We've cared about each other for three years."

"Three years?" I said, as if trying to pronounce words in another language. I knew we'd drifted apart. Hadn't made love in months, but the idea of Edith and Murphy . . . Edith and anyone . . . it was impossible, obscene, insane.

"Thank you for telling me the day I see Griffith. It's

only the culmination of two years' work!" I looked at Edith. One of us wasn't real.

"I can't lie anymore. Thank God, it's out." Edith looked at me carefully. We had rented a Queen Anne beside Angels Flight, the three-hundred-fifteen-foot funicular railroad that runs up and down Bunker Hill, one car pulling and balancing the other.

Harry, our six-year-old, was on *Olivet,* which rose as its twin, *Sinai,* went down.

I sat down on a purple-fringed orange ottoman in a red and yellow room, presided over by a silver cow skull and wagon-wheel chandelier. Edith called the room the "Bordello." It was her joke. My wife has a marvelous sense of humor.

"Michael wants me to make up my mind. This weekend."

"He's here? In Los Angeles?" I barely knew what I was saying. I was two people. One in this room and one in a hallucination. The room expanded and contracted—the joke expanded and contracted. The cow skull seemed to grin, the wheel was turning. The room was black and white and moving like a jumpy flicker. Edith gestured, hands and lips moving, and I dumbly waited for a leader to say it was all a test or a joke for a foolish husband.

"Michael wants to see Griffith. He has an idea for a scenario."

"How convenient! I see Griffith, Murphy sees Griffith. How original."

Edith looked at Angels Flight. *Sinai* was coming up, *Olivet* going down. "Henry, you're not intimate. Harry and I irritate you. The most important person in your life is you."

"When did it start, Edith? What month? What day?"

"Does it matter?"

"I want to know when it started because I know when it ends!" My face was inches from hers. "Tell me!" Spit flew. A tiny piece landed on Edith's cheek. She didn't wipe it.

"September. Three years ago." Edith didn't back away. "Nineteen thirteen. The year your mother died and you stopped running the ball club."

"I was finishing the Cleveland novel!"

"You stopped running the team. You let me do everything. I had to oversee the books, check the gate receipts, talk to reporters. See that broken seats are repaired. Even make sure the sausages don't poison the customers. A dozen things every day, Henry. Running a baseball club isn't just sitting in the stands and drinking with the manager."

"That's what we hired Murphy for!"

"One of *us* has to be responsible, and it isn't you. You're busy. Money doesn't interest you. Baseball doesn't interest you. Only your novel and D. W. Griffith." The spit gleamed on her cheek. "I worry about the club, Henry. Money, Henry.

"Remember when I started waking up at two or three every morning? You were no help. No comfort. I wanted you to wake up. Just for a little while. Just to say it was all right. But if I woke you, you got angry. You had to sleep.

9

You had to be fresh to write. I started going to the office early. When Michael learned I was coming early, he came too. He made my life easier. Michael takes care of things."

"Because you couldn't sleep, you took up with the hired help?"

Edith stepped back and looked at Angels Flight. Harry was climbing down out of *Sinai.* "You're selfish Henry. You wanted a child. A son. I did it for you. But once he was born, you didn't have time. You don't take care of us."

"We had nurses. Maids. My God, Edith!"

"You don't understand!"

"Where is he?" I said. "What cheap hotel?"

Shouting connected the two parts of me: one in the room with the cow skull, one in a hallucination.

"Michael loves me," said Edith, with weary satisfaction.

"We're finished, aren't we?" I had the urge to hit her, but I had never hit Edith. No matter the provocation. No matter the joke.

"I stayed because of Harry. I felt sorry for you, and sorry for us, but I'm tired of your anger. Tired of your obsession with D. W. Griffith. You don't need a family, Henry, you need an enemy."

"My obsession is truth, and *Birth of a Nation* is full of lies!"

Edith stood by the wide window looking at Angels Flight. She was too well dressed for Saturday morning. She was too prim and puffy sleeved. Her lavender dress and hat were intricate, complicated by hidden folds, crimson ruches—a subtle suggestion of secrets. I'd known this woman since childhood, been married for sixteen years, and she was an utter stranger.

Neither of us moved. Edith was right in front of me. All five feet purple seven inches. So Calm. Proud. Challenging.

"This won't stop me," I said. "I will interview Griffith and finish the book. We'll deal with your little farce later."

"It's no farce," said Edith.

"You know something?" I said, suddenly very sad. "I never stopped loving you."

"You never stopped loving *you*," Edith said. "Writing is more important than Harry or me."

"You're jealous of my book!"

"I'm not, Henry. I'm lonely. I'm tired. We have a child, remember?"

"You used to be honest," I said, quietly. "You were the most honest person I ever met."

Edith sat down in a high-backed black Chinese chair. "God, this is awful."

"I never cheated," I said. "Never."

"There are other ways of cheating." Edith shook her head slowly. "You stopped paying attention to the club, then me. Worse, you don't pay attention to your son. Hating D. W. Griffith is more important."

"It's better than sneaking around with a little Mick!"

"Michael's a hard worker and a fine man."

"Ask his wife about that," I said.

"You live in your head, Henry. It wore me down."

"This book is important! My father almost died at Antietam. Griffith rewrites history and makes money with lies! It's immoral! It has to stop!"

"You used to hate the cruelty in the world, Henry. Now you hate success."

"I hate bigotry," I said, "and I hate you." The room was an unreal dance of red and yellow, glistening skull, wheel topped with melted blue candles, serapes edged with silver bangles—nothing is as unreal as vulgarity, and my wife was the most vulgar object I could imagine.

"How could you, Edith? In God's name? With that self-satisfied bootstrap? His father's a railroad conductor."

"Don't be such a snob, Henry."

"Better a liar! Better an adulterer! But Michael came to the office when you couldn't sleep. How convenient. The early bird and worm."

"You're blind to everything. Even your son."

"I'm glad you said *my* son because that's exactly what he's going to be! I will interview Griffith and take Harry to Boston."

"Before you leave, will you take him boating, like you promised? Or don't you have time?"

"You think you're in control, don't you?"

"Henry, I haven't made a final decision."

"Yes, you have," I said, thinking what a hideous charade the last three years had been. "Do it in public. Do it in the road. Just don't do it in front of my son. You may live with whom you like, *he* may not."

"Henry. Henry. If this is the end, let's be civilized."

"Be civilized with Murphy. I'm sick of you."

"I'll tell you what I've decided tomorrow night."

I hit Edith with the back of my hand. Her cheek was hot, solid. She stood there and dared me to do it again. Triumphant. Spit gone. Victory complete.

"There," I said. "I've made it easy for you."

～

The sun stood higher. Beyond the low buildings dotting the hillsides, through the last morning mist, by orange and lemon groves, the electric sign at Coronado Livery blinked at the last of the dawn. Beyond rose the towers of Babylon, Griffith's fantastic city of a set. Huge, secret, gaudy as adultery. We saw the ten-foot-high fence Griffith erected to keep the public out. Above the fence were scaffolds, massive columns, spidery wires, cables, and hawsers that held up the largest set ever built. The great hall was a quarter mile long. Publicists said it was three-eighths of a mile deep. The walls were supposed to be three hundred feet high, above which Griffith had anchored a balloon we saw floating in the clouds. For free, the public saw only the angular, wired, scaffolded back of Griffith's spendthrift kingdom. D. W. and cameraman Billy Bitzer shot between 10:00 and 11:00 a.m. The perfect light.

"All it is, is big," said Jesus. "Like the United States. Have you been inside?"

"No."

"It's unbelievable," said Jesus. "Hundred-foot

columns support forty-foot plaster elephants that salute the sky with serpentine trunks. Pillars! Balconies! Courtyards!" Jesus held out his hands, palms to heaven. "Winged gods, beasts with the heads of men, men with the heads of beasts, and not one, but two Trees of Life! And Ishtar! Good God, Harrison! There's forty feet of bare-bosomed Ishtar, great goddess of Mesopotamia. She's so big a six-foot plaster man at one breast appears the size of an infant. How does Griffith get way with it? Raw, naked paganism in California? Alas, Babylon! Every inch has been painted, sculpted, carved. Reds, yellows, orange, purple! Some puff design it? None of this color—all prepared by Italian artisans, from Italy, not San Francisco—will appear on film, but the Master has to have color!

"The public gawks all day at the walls and the bloody balloon. They'll line up at the box office. Shrewd hawk-nosed bastard."

"I don't think the word 'bastard' appears in the New Testament," I said.

"Today they rehearse the Shot," said Jesus. "'The Shot' he calls it. Griffith's attempting to photograph the whole bloody set."

"The most ambitious shot ever attempted in a motion picture," I said, sarcastically.

How did Murphy have the nerve to touch Edith? Was he drunk? It must have been the greatest moment of his life.

"The arrogant bastard," said Jesus. "D. W. tried an aeroplane and the balloon. The plane shook, and Bitzer puked in the balloon. The real problem, according to Lillian Gish, is that the balloon won't take orders."

"Griffith always tries something new," I said.

"Griffith makes money," said Jesus. "What's new about that? Allan Dwan suggested putting an elevator in a tower and mounting it on railroad tracks. Sixteen men push it. Then Pharaoh rides on top with Bitzer and Gish. If the Shot fails, it becomes part of the legend. Don't you see? Griffith'll say his set was so big it couldn't be photographed. Damn Yankee huckster.

"Harrison, the Shot is an excuse to have naked women dance. It's an orgy. The girls call Griffith Mr. Heinz because he likes fifty-seven kinds."

I looked up at the scaffolds and towers and, thinking how Edith and Murphy wouldn't have to hide now, bit the inside of my mouth.

"Harrison," said Jesus, "if you kill them, you'll never write that book."

∽

The Model T slowed to a perusing crawl as we went down a hill. Jesus spotted an orange cat by a bungalow tucked neatly into a vine-covered hillside. A white door, peeling, with rusty hinges, was open under a sagging portico, behind posts badly in need of paint. Jesus put his finger to his lips, parked, and whispered, "Never underestimate the power of motion pictures." A redheaded woman with a sunburned face and bright freckles across the bridge of her nose and tops of her breasts—visible between the lapels of a chenille turquoise robe—reached for the cat.

Jesus managed to move, then stop, arms out, palms up like a plaster statue, and made walking look like a series of appearances. The woman was round-faced, a bit heavy, sleepy, thirtyish, ordinary in every way except for the ratty ball of turquoise clutched in her fist and frozen look of amazement on her face. The cat scooted into the house.

The actor's luxuriant hair touched his shoulders. He seemed to float. He was a walking image and the woman was transfixed. Jesus glided up two steps to a little porch under the sagging portico. He extended his hand and spoke. I didn't want to watch but it was fascinating, repulsive, bitterly satisfying.

Jesus talked softly. The woman couldn't stop looking. She didn't notice me; the orange cat peeped out the door. Jesus took her hands and she went to her knees. Was it this easy for Murphy? Jesus stroked her unruly red hair and she looked up, hands shyly touching his garment as if testing its temperature. He spread his arms and his robes opened, hiding all but the top of the woman's head. Wild red hair disappeared behind gorgeous white folds, reappeared, disappeared, reappeared. He trembled; she moved. Robes shivered. Jesus clutched her head through white fistfuls of robe, so the woman labored in a shimmering, makeshift tent, which hid everything but her pink ankles.

I got out, my white suit gleaming in the morning sun and the Model T humming in neutral.

I was faithful. I thought it was a deal.

I went up a green hillside sprinkled with azaleas and stones, wanting to drop my pants and desecrate my marriage just as my marriage had been desecrated. Quick. Impersonal. Like putting a bullet in a gun. Jesus waved me back. I stopped as his face turned to bliss; he winked, and the robes fell—white curtains sagging at the end of the performance— hands dropped, cowl drooped, red hair sank, ankles turned in, toes relaxed. The woman saw me, grabbed her ratty robe, and ran into the house.

Back on Sunset, Jesus said, "I told the woman I'd get her into motion pictures. I told her you were a producer. Harrison, you're a good-looking man. Tall. Slim hips. Nice hair. I bet women like you, but you've got to be patient."

"I'll learn," I said, bitterly.

"'This people honoureth me with their lips but their heart is far from me.'"

"John?" I said.

"Mark. Griffith made me read the whole damn New Testament."

࿙

After a mile of exposing his chest to the sun, Jesus said, "No one has any idea what Griffith's up to! We've filmed four different stories. They cover forty-two centuries and have nothing to do with each other."

"Who's mocked?" I said. "That's what Griffith does best."

Jesus shrugged. "It's the fall of Babylon." He looked at heaven. "Never so many women, so few clothes. And the story of Christ—the only reason this bloody flicker will be remembered. And the St. Bartholomew Massacre. Nasty, but nice clothes. And a modern tale. A dreadful meller about an innocent man saved from execution at the last moment. It's all lumped together under the title *The Mother and the Law*. A ridiculous hodgepodge. Were it not for me, a total flop.

"Has anyone at Fine Arts talked to you?"

"No," I said.

"They're afraid of Griffith. He's a god because *Birth* made so much money. You need me, Harrison. The two of us can hurt him."

"Why should you help?"

"The bugger's going to fire me! I may be deported. He doesn't like my dressing up and . . . but calling yourself Shakespeare and fifty-seven kinds is all right. Here." A hand went under the seat and he gave me a set of keys. "A bungalow off Sunset near Coronado. Stay there. Keys to the kingdom."

I took them.

"Harrison, there's a party tonight in a house where things are done that shouldn't be seen, and things seen that shouldn't be done. Photographs are taken. Secrets revealed. I'll show you Griffith. I'll show you Gish. With what I show and you publish, we can ruin him."

"Griffith will be there?"

"Everyone will be there."

"Then Edith and . . . He's meeting Griffith at a party tonight."

"Well," said Jesus. "That's two men you hate."

2

The sun stood higher and the road was filling with Babylonians. Tourists—a word coined here by boosters to make visitors feel they were on the grand tour rather than a dusty trip west—stopped and stared. Locals tried to be casual but they stared too—at the great set, at us, at each other. Carpenters and workmen passed by in a station wagon. They laughed and waved at Jesus. Babylonians came by taxi, jitney, buggy, even in a chariot. Beyond Coronado Livery and its electric sign (this was California: the new and old spring up together, horses and electric signs, gods in Fords, Babylon at the corner of Hollywood and Sunset), we came up behind a sunburned athlete driving a chariot. He had a real beard, a thick black wig, and oozed a self-absorbed confidence—Look, I'm good, watch me—as he touched the horses with a long whip for show and then whipped them with the reins. He reminded me of Murphy, who put on a show of friendship while . . .

"Get the hell out of the way!" I shouted, as we skirted the chariot and sped toward Babylon in a cloud of dust and pebbles.

～

"It wasn't always like this," I said. "I wasn't pathetic and Edith wasn't a liar. How could she have fallen for that preening little fool?" I slammed my fist on the dash.

"Whom women will clock is the mystery of the universe," said Jesus.

"She once charmed Henry James," I said.

"Henry James?"

We went slowly through the morning sun. I wanted to tell a story. I wanted to be Henry Harrison. Even for five minutes.

"It was in Sussex. I was eager to make an impression. I was planning a baseball novel. We own the Rochester Hustlers. The Eastern League."

"Baseball? In England, girls play a game like it."

"Edith had read everything James had written. She's an intelligent woman."

"The worst kind," interjected Jesus.

"We mapped out the evening. It was fun. We could take on anyone." Who can Michael X. Murphy take on?

"You have a thing about great men, Harrison. Did you want to ruin Henry James?"

"No. I wanted him to like me."

We rolled between steep green hillsides, passing fig and pepper trees, whose berries splattered red on the dusty pavement, and an occasional peeling eucalyptus, brought from Australia to provide shade for this city edging into a desert.

"The evening was hideously tedious until Edith, in the eager, innocent way James liked to portray American women, made a pronouncement."

It felt good to talk. To charm. Gossip. Narrate. Not think about charioteers and Louisville Sluggers.

"James liked them innocent," said Jesus. "He couldn't

bear the idea women get clocked.'"

"Edith announced that *Nostromo* was better than *Lord Jim*, and a thing called *Heart of Darkness*, the best yet from Mr. Conrad. James said, 'Why?'

"'Mrs. Gould,' she told him. 'Conrad's best woman.'

"James replied, 'Are books to be judged by their women?'

"I said, 'Men frequently are,' worried my wife had taken on the old lion. Edith was undaunted and said, 'Your books don't suffer from such a lack,' and James pulled himself up to that conversational height that dominated everyone and declared, 'I wasn't aware Mr. Conrad's books suffered from anything.'

"'Mr. Conrad's books run dangerously close to being about language, not life,' Edith said.

"Your wife *is* clever," said Jesus.

"James fired back, 'The way to overcome this peril is the incorporation of women?' and Edith told him, 'Mr. Conrad's stories, in the last analysis, are about the telling of stories.'"

"I expected chilling disapproval, but James bowed ever so slightly and said, 'And what of *Heart of Darkness*? *Darkness* has no women to speak of.'

"'Our Henry,'—Edith never defers to me, but she knew I wanted to impress James—'says *Darkness* is about the human heart at a level where there is no male or female.'"

"Marvelous," said Jesus.

It was.

"I hadn't read *Heart of Darkness*. Later I told James this and the spell was complete. He liked us both. Edith said afterward he admired her nerve and my physique."

"You're a good-looking man," said Jesus. "And James would have been sure to notice."

"We were made for the evening, and I thought I was made as a writer. I wrote the novel, but James didn't like the subject, and our correspondence became gossip about H. G. Wells, American cooks, and Mrs. Joseph Conrad.

"As we left, James said, 'Be careful. An intelligent wife is a luxury few can afford.'"

3

"How long ago was that, Harrison?"

"Nine years," I said, quietly.

"You need cheering up. 'Gells' will do it. That's what Griffith calls girls. He likes 'em young. It'll be his undoing. Maybe tonight."

"That's blackmail."

"Harrison, please. Americans respond to scandal, not moral appeals about Negroes."

We slowed to three miles per hour. Jesus pulled out a mirror from under the front cushion and inspected his visage. "Maybe we can find a church fair. They attract 'gells.'"

"A church?"

"When was the last time you saw Jesus in church?"

"You might cause a riot."

"Not a riot, Harrison. Theater. I could walk among the crowd. That's acting! That's what the Master doesn't understand. The world is a stage. Onstage you act, they react. They look! You look! You have the brilliant solitary isolation of performance, the communion of audience and player. Write this in your book. Motion picture acting is making love with your eyes closed. But let's avoid Mexicans. They expect miracles and are more impressed with the car."

We were in a parade going west. The great set rose in the distance, the balloon swayed, the road was crowded with vehicles and costumes spanning forty-two centuries. One of Belshazzar's guards cursed a stalled Studebaker. Six priests of Ishtar in an open carriage pointed to their horse, a dozen carpenters crowded into a seven-passenger King Eight laughed heartily. Gaggles of tourists looked from Griffith's parade to the horizon, where Babylon and balloon seemed tethered to the sky. I saw Ishtar, a momentary vision behind scaffolds and Fine Arts' walls. Jesus, combing his hair with a large-toothed pearl comb, nodded and said, "Biggest breasts in Hollywood." We were passed by two station wagons of women whose costumes seemed to dissolve in the sun, then by more trucks of sweaty extras holding wool beards in their hands.

"Suppose they take Harry?" I blurted out.

"Harry?"

"Our six-year-old. Suppose they disappear?"

"They won't disappear until after the party," said Jesus. "I suppose."

"Look at this," Jesus gestured at the crowded boulevard and the distant set. "Leave it to Griffith to create a spectacle where Jesus Christ is a minor character!"

"Babylon the great is fallen," I said coldly.

~

We came up behind a jitney carrying a dozen Virgins of the Sacred Fire. They held up bare arms and made profiles like figures in Egyptian painting. "There's eternity in desire, Harrison. It's brief, but immortal." Plump, supple arms made right angles, and tasseled breasts were thrust at us. The Virgins laughed. Bracelets rattled, breasts bobbed, and bejeweled halters shook like armor plate in the morning brilliance. It wasn't eternity to me.

Murphy sat at my table and I didn't see what happened in front of my face. I have that for eternity.

We went faster, almost bumping the jitney.

"Bloody hell!" yelled Jesus.

An enormous blue Fiat touring car suddenly appeared behind us. The top was down. D. W. Griffith, in a perfectly tailored suit, whiter than mine, whiter than Jesus, and a yellow Chinese coolie hat, sat in back next to Lillian Gish. He was holding a lion cub. Even in motion, Griffith had a violently memorable profile. He was tall with a nose like an eagle and piercing blue eyes. Here was the man who made a fortune selling hate. D. W. Griffith, an American king, who could lust after any woman, ride in any car, exhibit any pet, wear any hat—driven by a thin-lipped German thug, on his way to Babylon, where thousands would follow his orders as he attempted to influence men's minds in the moral swindle called the motion picture.

"D. W. looks like a Jew," said Jesus.

Griffith looked like a white vision. The lion snarled. The Virgins waved. Lillian Gish, a flash of green beauty, barely noticed us. The spectators were silent, fascinated by flicker king and flicker goddess. An Orthodox Jew shook his head, a little girl with a red bow in her hair and one on each wrist pointed, women's mouths opened, a Mexican waved a sombrero.

Jesus was upstaged.

The Fiat roared by. Griffith looked right at me. His eye was cold. Miss Gish raised her perfect chin as chestnut hair and emerald cloak flew in the wind. As in the motion pictures, Lillian Gish was Lillian Gish. Rarest of the rare. Little girl and ripe as a tomato. Familiar. Remote. Here and not here. Passing. Gone.

The crowd cheered in their wake and yelled, "Movies! Movies!" Local idiom for those who work in motion pictures.

II

A Walk toward the Millennium with Lillian Gish

April 2, 1916
9:00 a.m.

1

I stood three-quarters of a mile away from Babylon at the end of railroad tracks beside the hundred-forty-foot tube-steel tower, mounted on two flatbed railroad cars, from which Griffith and Bitzer would attempt to photograph the set. Like Lot's wife, I looked back. Babylon was red, yellow, white, green, blue—or maybe that was the sky. I saw why assistant director Joseph Henabery led me here. It wasn't necessary. He couldn't imagine how insignificant I felt.

I'd shaved at a filling station—a cuckold should look his best—and cut myself under the chin. It had stopped bleeding, but a small, red, quarter-inch curve slid up my jaw. I wondered if Henabery noticed. Griffith certainly would. They say he reads people keenly and I wondered how long I could hold my own. I decided on three questions, which if pursued, no matter how I looked or felt, would get what I needed: What did Griffith think of the reaction to *Birth of a Nation*? What had he learned? What was he conjuring now? These had to be my sword and shield.

Questions or no questions, it was difficult not to be intimidated by Babylon. I didn't know if the set was really a quarter-mile long, but it could well have been three hundred feet high. Hundreds of priests, soldiers, slaves, dancers, merchants, and princes swayed to music from an orchestra hidden behind the set; while carpenters, plasterers, and shirt-sleeved workmen in overalls—some swaying, some not—carried hammers, coiled wire, and tested the scaffolds and braces of the towers. Painters applied last-minute strokes to arches, columns, lions. Standing at the north end of the tracks, I looked from one end of time to the other, and at the scaffold for the illusion. I could see Babylon and see through Babylon.

A man in a red vest checked the tracks with a level to gauge the smoothness of the ride for the Shot. Assistant directors in neckties and wide-brimmed hats walked about barking orders, carrying megaphones, and a man named Blue sported a brace of pistols.

Between the columns and elephants were red and yellow carpeted steps where a hundred women raised bare arms—their bangles and bracelets flashing in the sun as they reached, danced, and prayed to Bitzer's black, beaten Pathé camera: the god in the tower, the god for tomorrow. One wouldn't think there were so many pretty women in the world. I thought of their boyfriends, husbands, lovers—their secrets, betrayals, guilt. I could hardly look.

The steps were flanked by ascending rows of wide-jawed lions couchants, which in turn were flanked by chariots, horses, and more women at tables covered with brocaded cloth, piled with fruit, brimming goblets, and jugs of wine. Urns held trees. Peacocks perched on thronelike chairs. A priest in a gold crown preceded an ark carried by four women through the dancers, but all were dwarfed by the huge frescoed bases of pillars decorated with jackal-headed gods and the story of Gilgamesh, first Semitic hero, who first lost a person he loved, then the world's chance for immortality, and finally his life.

The pillars, thick, fluted, twice as tall as Ishtar, bulged to red and yellow capitals which held balconies of people, themselves under pedestals that supported trumpeting white elephants seated on hind legs, trunks curled like letters in an occult alphabet, front legs raised: fierce and mysterious. W. B. Yeats said whatever men's passions gather about becomes a symbol in the Great Memory, and he who has its secret is "a worker of wonders" and "caller up of devils or angels." What devils and angels were called at the corner of Hollywood and Sunset?

The big, elephant-topped columns marched to the red back wall, which went still higher—finishing the picture, topping the frame, stopping the eye—and were lined with men—Griffith put men everywhere: nothing was too big, too high, or too remote. The spectator never lost sight of the scale, the spectacle. Below, and back, deep in the field, were gigantic symmetrical openings—a different effect—a place that couldn't quite be glimpsed: more statues, other gods, deeper walls, curtains at once hiding and suggesting some ultimate mystery. Over these openings, behind the elephants, high on a scarlet entablature bordered in leaping gold circles (applied by L.A. painters in sheets called Dutch metal) was a winged god holding a bowl that protruded from the fresco—a god in three dimensions—and two gold Trees of Life.

The columns, elephants, Trees of Life stood over a

courtyard of thousands, who surrounded an embroidered purple canopy for Belshazzar, king of Babylon, and his voluptuous Princess Beloved—a Swede, actually—who were to be wed tomorrow and today celebrated victory over the Persians. King and princess were fanned, fed, and feasted on love. Beloved had the whitest skin, the biggest eyes, the fullest breasts; Belshazzar the blackest beard, the tallest crown, the gentlest nature. We know all this beauty and sensuality will be cut down. Priests of Bel, war god and rival of Ishtar, will open the Imgur-Bel Gate for the Persians. Before nightfall, peace will be shattered, love raped, freedom slaughtered.

All lost.

2

"Mr. Harrison, let's go to the library," said Joseph Henabery. He played Lincoln in *Birth* and carried himself with Lincolnesque dignity. If the latter-day Lincoln noticed the cut running up my jaw, he didn't let on. Henabery steered me away from a group of assistant directors. They stopped looking at a twentieth-century factotum applying a level to the tracks and eyed me like the Klan might a Negro. We moved away and Henabery said, "Stay with me."

"You mean keep out of sight?"

"Stroheim can be a bit direct and Monty Blue might shoot you." This was said with an ironic twinkle. "You're the

Easterner who writes such damning things. But everyone is entitled to his opinion."

We turned our backs on Babylon and walked by low, jumbled buildings that looked modern and bungalowesque after the Babylonian pageant. We went by warehouses for props and scenery, dressing rooms, buildings for "projection," as Henabery called the place where Griffith and his henchmen watched the day's shooting, windowless buildings where "special effects" were created—reality fabricated and tricked—and the laboratory where film was developed.

"Is there a telephone I might use?" I said. "I want to call the woman looking after my son." Was Harry with Maria or Edith? With Edith and . . . ?

"Of course," said Henabery. "In the library."

The library was the first floor of what had once been an ordinary house at the corner of what had once been ordinary streets, Hollywood and Sunset. The house was now as tenuously anchored to reality as the balloon: lost in a jungle of roofs, telephone poles, Southern California Edison lines, open-air stages, laboratories, rehearsal halls. This was where research was collected and business done—the meeting of the real world and this one, and where, I was told, Griffith slept.

I was shown into a room full of books. A telephone stood incongruously on a long table in the midst of open books: encyclopedias, Tissot's illustrated Bible, magazines, and scrapbooks—mountains of them, full of clippings cannibalized from the encyclopedias, sliced articles by archeological scholars like Sayce and Gastrow, and pictures culled from everywhere about the historical periods dealt with in the photoplay. "We're not relying on memories of memories, Mr. Harrison." That was a line from "The Man Who Gave *Birth*," which indicted Griffith's re-creation of the Civil War and Reconstruction as a lurid embroidery of recollections and vicious scapegoating of the black race for starting the war, while demonstrating that armed, sheeted Southerners could whip somebody; in this case, misled, naïve Negroes, who were actually second-rate white actors in blackface.

"There's never been anything like this motion picture, Mr. Harrison," said Henabery. "It will make people forget *Birth*. Mr. Griffith will be with you shortly. Please feel free to use the telephone." He left with a small bow.

I called the house on Bunker Hill and Maria, the Mexican woman who cooked and cleaned, answered.

"Is Mrs. Harrison there?" I tried to keep my voice from shaking.

"She is gone for the day, Señor Harrison. Señora Harrison will be back late tonight."

"May I speak to Harry, please?"

She put him on. "How are you, Father?"

"I'm fine. How are you?"

"I'm very well," the child said seriously. "Are we going boating tomorrow?"

"Nothing in the world could keep us from it."

"You won't forget?"

"No," I said, biting my lip.

"Maria's going to take me for a walk, may I go?"

"Yes. Enjoy yourself. I love you."

"Yes, sir," he said, and hung up.

I was relieved the child was with Maria, but what was going through his mind? Did he know his world was falling apart? He'd heard us argue. Did Edith tell him not to worry, that everything was fine? Did she lie to him too? I wished I were with him, instead of waiting for Griffith. I tried not to think about Edith, tried to save those feelings for the bitter promise of a party in the Hills. It was good Harry hung up because if I'd heard his voice again, so tentative and small on the telephone—children sound so young and vulnerable over the wires—I would have cried.

I was alone with the piles, tomes, cuttings, pictures. If *Birth of a Nation* was a vicious manipulation of American history, this project looked like the history of civilization. What did Griffith want with a world so old that it was new? He had turned to the past, the deep past—the roots of memory: the Fore-World, the Germans call it—to create moving images, the future's language. What was he writing in that language?

Tissot's illustrated Bible was open to Jeremiah 34:2 and 3, which had been marked in red: "Behold, I will give this city into the hand of the king of Babylon," and,

"Thou shalt not escape out of his hand, but shalt surely be taken, and delivered into his hand; and thine eyes shall behold the eyes of the king of Babylon, and he shall speak with thee mouth to mouth."

I took off my white coat. It was warm in the library, close in those piles of the past, and I tried to prepare myself. The gauntlet thrown down in *The Atlantic* had been picked up in Los Angeles. I would see Griffith's eyes and speak to him, "mouth to mouth." That I was "delivered into his hand" the day my life became a farce was hideously unfair.

So were the last three years.

So was everything.

After reading Jeremiah, I decided to take Harry to Boston and write my book. His mother might live as an adulteress in Rochester, Paris, hell. But not with my son.

I had a plan. I felt better.

I tried to concentrate among piles of cannibalized history, but instead of practicing questions and subsequent questions, I thought about Edith. After a quick burst of anger, my throat tightened and the room got blurry. What hurt so much, what hit so hard, wasn't that Edith had fallen in love with someone else, but knowing the person who lied and slept with Murphy wasn't a person I knew. I could hate her. I could take Harry, but I couldn't have her back because the woman I knew no longer existed.

3

My head was on my arms when an angel walked through the door.

The most subtly beautiful woman, all dressed in green and yellow, stood in the door catching the light, which turned her auburn hair gold: gold like I had never seen—hair like I had never seen. The head tilted slightly as though she were a disapproving sprite. Timid yet radiant, mouth a skeptical bow, cheeks full, complexion perfect, hair up, swirling, falling, going every way yet perfectly neat. She was ethereal, wise, diffident, as beautiful and serene as the most poised woman, as frightened and ready to evaporate as a spectral child. A being totally aware of the illusion she cast, yet aware that it was an illusion—at once apologizing for the spell and aware of both your and her need for it.

It was, of course, Lillian Gish. And she had, of course, been sent to soften me up.

4

"Mr. Harrison," said Miss Gish. She hesitated. "Mr. Griffith asked me to invite you to ride on the tower."

I rose to my feet. "How do you do?" I said, embarrassed at being seen so unhappy and irritated at being sent the puppet, no matter how beautiful, instead of the puppeteer.

Miss Gish curtsied, looked up, and in a quiet but firm voice said, "I was going to tell you, you are a horrible man, but you look too sad to be horrible. You write horrible things anyway. You said that in the *Birth* I 'fluttered like an insane butterfly at the dreaded thought of miscegenation, and then rode on a Klansman's horse proudly like a trophy in a race war, decked out in white glory.' That hurt."

I extended my hand, which she took gently and then sat down. "Where's Griffith? Why isn't he here?"

"What's wrong?" Lillian said softly. Her face lit with care and trepidation. "You've cut yourself."

"It's nothing." I sat down and we looked at each other across books with pages cut, dangling, torn, stuck back in place, and the bulging scrapbooks of Griffith's auto-da-fé: books sacrificed for moving pictures. "Doesn't the 'Master' want to face me until you've, how shall I put it, worked me over?"

"Mr. Griffith will see you later," said Lillian, putting a slender finger to her lower lip and raising that perfect chin.

"What are *we* supposed to talk about?" I wanted Griffith and he sent a child. Or worse, a woman who acts like a child, who lets herself be manipulated. "You have much to answer for, Miss Gish. Much indeed. What's going on in this new photoplay? Why so much violence? So much carnality? Are you in it? Forgive me for being blunt." I was immediately sorry. It wasn't appropriate to be severe with Lillian Gish. I tried to be tough because she'd seen me be unmanly.

"Would you like me to recite Tennyson's *Ulysses*?"
"What?"

Without waiting for an answer, she began to recite. Starting with "It little profits that an idle king," Miss Gish spoke in a voice full of the lyrical mystery she projects in photoplays. The sun was in her hair and she tilted her head. The recitation was impressive, but I wasn't going to be disarmed by an actress reciting a poem. Not everyone can be seduced. Miss Gish continued, projecting a subdued, careful intelligence, but I kept thinking of Elsie Stoneman in *Birth* tied to a bedpost or riding with the Ku Klux Klan.

Skipping the middle, she ended with a resounding:
"'We are not now that strength which in old days
Moved earth and heaven, that which we are, we are—
One equal temper of heroic hearts,
Made weak by time and fate, but strong in will
To strive, to seek, to find, and not to yield.'"

∾

"Mr. Griffith says when overcome by emotion, one should recite," said Lillian. "Use poets' words when our own fail."

"That sounds like advice for a child."

"We all feel like children sometimes."

"Some of us try to grow up," I said, and smiled.

Miss Gish ignored the remark and with a toss of the head said, "Mr. Griffith can speak the whole of *Song of Myself.*"

"Macaulay could recite *Paradise Lost* in its entirety when he was twelve," I said. "Backward."

Lillian Gish laughed. When she laughed, she looked even more like a vulnerable child. Lillian shook her head again, letting her golden hair catch the midmorning light Griffith favors. "That was clever."

"Do you know what Dr. Johnson said of *Paradise Lost*?"

"What?" Lillian asked, as if truly interested. As if no one had ever said anything so interesting. As if I were, for a moment, the schooling and the college she never had, supporting her mother and sister on the stage and in motion pictures.

"'No man would wish it longer.'"

This time Lillian burst out laughing in an uncontrollable, girlish way. I think for a few seconds she actually lost control, and simultaneously gave the impression that losing control was the most delicious luxury.

"That's wicked," she said. "Wicked."

5

W hy are you so unhappy?" said Miss Gish.

"I'm not," I said.

"Aren't you?"

"I am not!"

I sat and looked at Tissot's Bible, the sliced books, and Lillian Gish. She let me look. Miss Gish was used to being looked at and had apparently learned that if you're quiet, your adversary may disarm himself.

"Miss Gish, this is charming, but I really must see Griffith."

"I am in the new photoplay," she said, glancing at my

chin. "I rock a cradle with the Three Fates in the background. I think it will be used to connect the different stories."

"That's all?"

"Yes."

"You flutter and scream and ride with the Klan in one photoplay, and in the next, you merely rock a cradle?"

"Yes."

"What is this photoplay?" I said, exasperated because despite my firmest resolve, I was beginning to like her. "What violence rising? What hatred?"

"None," Lillian said.

"What is it about?"

"I can't say."

"This is ridiculous! Where's the 'Master'?"

"Have patience, Mr. Harrison."

I got up and walked around the small room that looked like a rummage sale and auto-da-fé. Miss Gish watched me, but instead of another strategic silence said, "Why do you hate us so much?"

I turned away; her voice made me think of Harry.

∾

It was September. I was in the turret in our house where I write. The room has a marvelous view of Lake Ontario, especially when storms blow in and rain sweeps across the lake. I write and listen to the gramophone. Talk to myself. Walk around. Swing a bat. It's my private place. My fortress.

One afternoon I was dancing to the gramophone, talking, swinging. I'd just finished writing and must have looked like a madman. I looked up and Harry was in the door. He was five years old and he was smiling. He wasn't scared. He smiled. A five-year-old understands dancing and making faces because a child understands play, but I didn't understand. I didn't understand he was saying, "Can I play too?"

I yelled at him. I told him to never spy on me again and slammed the door. I punished the child when all he'd done was smile.

6

"Why do you hate us so much?" repeated Miss Gish, looking me in the eye.

"I hate *Birth of a Nation*." I said, thinking of Harry's face as I slammed the door. I didn't want Lillian Gish to know about Edith and Murphy. I didn't want Griffith to know his adversary had been cuckolded while writing his vitriolic analysis of *Birth*. I didn't want them to know while I wrote in a turret, proud of my ball club, my writing, and my wife, another man f***ed Edith. I didn't want anybody to know, but especially those two.

"I'll tell you why I wrote what I wrote," I said.

"Please," said Miss Gish. Her face lit up with a friendly but slightly skeptical curiosity. I reminded myself she was an actress, but it was easy to talk to a beautiful woman. Lillian

Gish could keep your mind off anything.

"My father was a Union soldier. He nearly died at Antietam in the cornfield. Much of my life has been spent wondering what that day was like and wondering what my father was like. There was too much he couldn't say."

"My father left when I was three," said Lillian, looking away and no longer skeptical.

"What was he like?" I said.

"I never talk about my father."

"Mine died when I was at boarding school."

Miss Gish nodded.

"My father didn't talk about the war until the last year of his life. He wanted me to know something. I'm not sure what it was. Once I said, 'I listen when you talk about Antietam, but I don't understand,' and he said, 'That's the problem, isn't it? If people understood, they might not do it again.' I don't understand. War is big and small. As big as thwarting the first Rebel drive north; small as the patch of dirt a man occupies in a field. Remember those lines of Whitman? 'Then with the knowledge of death as walking one side of me, And the thought of death close-walking the other side of me.' Wonderful words, but a man on his belly shot through the foot, legs, and back knows something beyond words. I have words. He had the cornfield. He was left for dead by two armies along with seven thousand corpses on the 'bloodiest day in American history.'"

"When you start talking, you sound like Mr. Griffith."

"I'm not like Griffith," I said. "I see no honor in a bad

cause and no art in a motion picture that deeply hurt people."

Lillian looked away again.

"For a year, to keep the foot wound from closing and getting infected—wounds must heal from the bottom and infection would mean amputation—he drew a piece of silk through his foot. Every day. He just did it. I wonder if he ever recovered. He was never without pain."

"You miss him terribly, don't you?" said Lillian.

"I wonder who he might have been without the war."

"I wonder about my father too." The sun was in her hair like fire.

"I used to confuse that quiet man and his wounds with Abe Lincoln."

"Men like to talk about their fathers," said Lillian.

7

All right," I said, "I'll tell you about seeing *Birth of a Nation*. I was in Boston visiting Tuck Kreuger, my friend at *The Atlantic*. He suggested I write about *Birth*. His wife had left him."

I was already in Tuck's position that night. Two in one flame, as Dante says.

Lillian sat back. Small hands in green lap.

"I wasn't ready for the crowd, especially the Negroes. A line of derbies stretched out the Tremont Theatre. The NAACP was trying to stop the showing. The lines segregated themselves, without help of police, who were everywhere.

"Blacks eyed the coppers. No underpaid, brogue-tongued cop was going to take out his anger on Tuck Kreuger, but a notoriously articulate Negro like Monroe Trotter was a bull's-eye. Many Negroes wore their Sunday best. Others had derbies pulled down over one eye as if taking aim at the white world. The white crowd was talky and curious.

"A lad hawking papers yelled, 'See it 'fore the govnah' closes it.' A kid in a scally cap yelled, 'Never happen. Walsh 'n' Curley need the niggah vote.'"

Lillian cringed at that word. Her repulsion was genuine.

"As Tuck and I walked by the ticket window, two black men asked for tickets—they were as well-dressed as college professors—and the window slammed shut. Less than a minute later, and this is the truth, two white men bought tickets. Monroe Trotter, who offended President Wilson by being too forward about segregation, came flying up to the window demanding to know why the theater was 'Sold out no longer.'

"I knew Monroe at Harvard. He was smart, quiet, and harbored deep concern about the treatment of his people. By himself, he was fine; if cornered or in front of people, he was ferocious. Monroe demanded to see the manager. Tuck and I went in.

"Noise brought us out. Trotter was yelling, 'Discrimination!' at the top of his lungs. Not so much at the clerk in

45

his cage, but for his constituents, who took up the cry. The police, brass-polished, pug-nosed, proud to be in uniform, proud to be in America, were ready. A captain told Monroe to quiet down, and Monroe shouted, 'This is discrimination, pure and simple!' Monroe had his bully pulpit and bully supporters. Trotter is good in front of supporters. It's made him a hero to his people and others skeptical of sending Negroes to Harvard.

"Monroe shouted, 'I demand to purchase a ticket!' The captain yelled, 'Quiet down or I'll arrest you,' and Monroe said, 'For what? Requesting to spend money?'

"'Incitin' to riot.' I remember the captain dropped the *g* and Monroe replied, 'Who's rioting?' distinctly enunciating the *g*.

"The captain took a billy club from the nearest officer, and Monroe said, 'We demand to be treated as citizens. I'm going in, with or without a ticket.' 'No, you're not.' Monroe took a step and got clubbed. His followers surrounded the captain, and the police charged, sticks up, beating and pushing anyone near the captain. The scuffle was brief. The coppers rounded up a dozen Negroes and whisked Monroe away. He left demanding badge numbers and names.

"Tuck said Trotter manufactured the incident for the newspapers."

"What else happened?" said Lillian. "Tell me everything."

The Tremont, I explained, is a high-ceilinged, cherub-dotted, gold and marble gilt palace. Lillian nodded.

She knew it. She knew them all—places the public goes to dream, enjoy music, savor gold leaf and well-dressed ladies, and be transported, as Emerson put it, "anywhere but here."

"The crowd mumbled, a few Negroes talked loudly about 'injustice,' then a black gentleman started to make a speech as a whole symphony orchestra trotted in with their instruments. Usherettes dressed as Civil War nurses tried to quiet the blacks. Too many ironies to fathom in that.

"The title flashed on the curtain and the lights went down. The audience, white and black, hissed. The curtain stayed down and the orchestra burst into sound—one huge, pure, awesome gush, a roar of sound. Indeed, Miss Gish, like Shakespeare, who knew how rude audiences are, so sailors howl and witches cackle, Griffith opened with noise. No protest can compete with a full orchestra, and that sound overwhelmed everything. 'BIRTH OF A NATION' blazed across the screen in the clearest letters I've ever seen.

"Before we saw a picture, Griffith announced we were in the presence of something new. Something harnessing sound, words, then vision."

"How did people react to the photoplay?" said Lillian.

"The slaves dancing after cotton-picking brought hissing. The crowd—and it wasn't only blacks, but whites, too—hissed in the easy solidarity of the dark. Rest assured those blacks were jigging around a bale of cotton, not a Harvard diploma. But the photoplay wasn't offensive. Yet. The crowd liked the families. One Northern and one Southern with sons and daughters for romantic intrigue, but they hissed the Northern senator. Please, Miss Gish, a pompous, limping liberal with a silver-headed cane and beautiful daughter?" Played by the woman two feet from me. "And a mulatto mistress? Everyone liked his sons and they liked the Southern family with its handsome Little Colonel and pretty daughters. Lots of boys and girls to fall in love. The flicker looked good."

"Don't use that word around Mr. Griffith," said Lillian. "He hates it."

"The scenes moved quickly. You saw something from one angle, and presto, you saw it from another, and then another, and another. Nothing wasted. No one bored. I'm afraid I wasn't interested in the girls and boys. I'm past the happy ending in my life, Miss Gish, past watching beautiful young people, ethereal, radiant . . ." I got a blush from the most ethereal and radiant of all.

"Then the war started, and Tuck, me, and audience were caught. I've never seen anything like it. The sweep of camera down the Confederate lines, bombs going off, shells exploding. I've never seen war but have imagined it since I was old enough to know my father was in one. I know the way war is recounted in books, and I know the halting, elliptical way my father picked his words. I didn't think I was seeing war, but war as dreamed by D. W. Griffith. It was new. It was a birth.

"Then the charge! The Little Colonel leads his men through the Valley of the Shadow and picks up the colors. Suddenly he fills the screen, which had been a panorama of war—war as God sees war: horses thundering overhead; men groveling in filthy trenches; the smoky line itself—a panorama no one has ever seen; even Tuck, who was at San Juan Hill.

"The Little Colonel swinging his saber filled the screen. I was caught like everyone else. It was a violent and wonderful moment, but I have thought too much, read too much, talked to too many soldiers, to think a man leading a charge can go over enemy lines, stuff a flag in a gun, not get killed, be cheered for bravery and succored by the enemy, who happens to be commanded by his best friend. Neither life, fate, nor friends are like that, Miss Gish, but Griffith made us feel. I knew there would be no stopping this photoplay."

"Mr. Griffith can do anything," said Lillian.

"The charge alone would have made *Birth* the best photoplay I'd ever seen, but Griffith was just warming up. The magnificent stills of the dead after battle. The one tinted red? 'War's peace'? After the best moving images of war, Griffith showed the best stills. He has mastered rhythm. After distant shots, close-ups. After action, stills. After life, death. After death, vision.

"But he wasn't finished, Miss Gish. The reenactment of the Lincoln assassination is without doubt the finest piece of moving image I have ever seen. Just when I thought the charge was the best photography I'd ever seen, we were in Ford's Theatre watching the saddest event in our history through the eyes of God. I wrote that in *The Atlantic,* Miss

Gish. Up to this point *Birth* is the finest photoplay I've ever seen. I sat in the Tremont Theatre in April in Boston in 1915, but I was in Ford's Theatre in Washington in April in 1865.

"Henabery, who played Lincoln, *is* Lincoln. There he is, right in front of us, in his simple profound dignity. The man who could bind the wounds. All wounds—North and South. Sanctify grief. Heal the nation. And there was Booth skulking like the angel of death. We'd see Lincoln. We'd see Booth moving as surely and fatefully as night. We'd see the audience. You laughed with your army brother, Miss Gish. Laughed like people outside history. So gay. So alive. So unaware death creeps like the serpent in the Garden.

"When Lincoln was shot, people screamed. They cried. For a moment Griffith had made us all—Yankees, soldiers, Negroes, the curious, bored, sad, lost, all who wanted to be 'anywhere but here'—into witnesses. Participants."

8

But it didn't end with Lincoln going to his fate and binding us in pain. We were not to be healed. Not by Griffith.

"I almost cried at the Little Colonel's homecoming, Miss Gish.

"The soldier returns. Home is in tatters but the family is intact, struggling, threadbare, almost starving. He walks to the door as changed inside as the place is outside. The Little Sister—God, Griffith's characters have awful names— puts raw cotton on her miserable dress, touches it with soot to make it resemble ermine, and bravely goes to meet her brother. The Little Colonel stands before the ancestral door taking in their suffering, which he sees has paralleled his, and Sis comes out, now practically a woman, and like him, a survivor."

How many times have I imagined coming home from war?

"The Little Colonel stands at the door, embraces his sister and a pair of arms—no doubt his mother, everybody's mother—reach out saying, 'You're home,' in wordless language. I stifled a sob. Griffith got to me. My mother died three years ago."

"I've been alone too," Lillian said.

"Then *Birth* changes, Miss Gish. The family idyll of war and honorable defeat turns to the hard matter of black and white. We go through Griffith's looking glass into the world of miscegenation-horror."

Lillian's eyes narrowed.

"Northern blacks come to town. Negroes can vote. Griffith parades an unending stream of shiftless, lazy, conniving, dangerous blacks across the screen.

"A really ugly Union soldier, made more grotesque by the fact he is a white actor in blackface, pursues the Little Sister. She runs to the top of a cliff. Whites yelled, 'Jump!' 'Don't let him touch ye!'

"Blacks yelled, 'Pathetic!' 'Disgraceful!' 'Untrue!'

"The Little Sister jumps. The intertitle says she chose death over dishonor. Really, Miss Gish!

"At this point, the whole damn photoplay jumps off a cliff.

"We see blacks rioting in the state legislature—drunk, shoes off, eating chicken. Loyal black servants are whipped by liberty-drunk ex-slaves. Whites are insulted on the streets, and then the crescendo! The miscegenation theme! You, Miss Gish, are at the brink of forced marriage with mulatto lieutenant governor Lynch. Griffith's crowning point! The daughter of the Northern senator is the prize for the mulatto! Lynch ties you up. You get untied, flutter, jump, dance around in hysterics at the thought that for white America is worse than death."

Lillian shook her head and pursed her lips.

"But we're not without hope. The Little Colonel has invented the Ku Klux Klan by watching children frighten Negroes with a bedsheet. People jeered. Tuck said, 'This is bad. Very bad.' The Klan begins to ride. The scenes switch back and forth: you whirling on the precipice of ravishment; your hypocritical father, at first delighted the mulatto intends to marry a white woman, collapses when informed the woman is his daughter.

"The Little Colonel's surviving sister, father, and mother are in a cabin besieged by Negroes. You are at the precipice. Crackerville is under the control of delirious blacks. It's all shown between shots of the Klan riding like the man who brought the good news from Aix to Ghent. To tell seems ludicrous. To see was amazing.

"The Klan rode and the audience yelled. Some for, some against, some having a good time. The orchestra was blaring *Ride of the Valkyries* and it *was* exciting. The attacker of the Little Sister had been caught by the Klan, who did what is customarily done in such cases, but that scene was cut, leaving it obscene in the Greek sense: offstage—though one could imagine what was removed from the photoplay and from the body dumped on the lieutenant governor's steps with 'KKK' pinned to the corpse. The masked figures dip a piece of the Little Sister's dress in a bowl of her blood, then dip a fiery cross in the blood, and swear revenge. There are double-circled crosses on each white robe. My God, Miss Gish, how can the cross be used by men who ride and castrate? How can anything touching Jesus be used in vengeance?"

Lillian's face flushed. Maybe anger, maybe shame.

"It's easy now to laugh at the charging Klan, cringing whites, rampaging Negroes, the hysteria. No one in the theater laughed. No one took his eyes off the screen. What's common decency against violence, screaming music, close-ups of *you* intercut with the galloping Klan? Tuck and I hissed, but as the Klan gathered, mounted, and rode, something mounted and gathered and rode in us. What is that anger, that fury? Is hating another race the primal depth of being human? Is it Negroes? Why does race hate galvanize every hurt, insult, humiliation? And boil over when white men ride to save parents and avenge women?

"I felt it. It was glorious. Horrifying. American."

9

Lillian frowned and shook her auburn head, but I said, "It wasn't over. *Birth* ends with an appearance of the Prince of Peace, but peace wasn't the mood of the cops. By the way, I'm glad Griffith dropped the sequence where America's race problem is solved by angels flying blacks back to Africa."

"Lincoln considered the same thing," said Lillian, "without angels."

"As we left, a young man, not much more than a boy, crouched by a stairway. He was crying, and we stopped. The crowd was murmuring, moving on. I heard a distinctly Negro voice say, 'Why? Why'd he do this to us? Why?' There wasn't any doubt who 'he' was, Miss Gish. The young man saw us, covered his face with bony, coal-black hands, and sobbed. It was the most pitiful sound I've ever heard.

"'Oh God, why? Why?'

"I felt his tears were my fault. I didn't know why."

Lillian looked like she might cry.

"Hands covering a face in the dark," I said. "This person had become a child. A child who couldn't be comforted. I resolved right there to write the most articulate, well-reasoned attack on Griffith I could."

Lillian hung her head.

"In the lobby Negroes were angry. They weren't a mob as the papers said, but we heard cries like 'Ban it!' 'Nothin' but filth!' 'What lieutenant governor of what state ever tried to force a white woman to marry him?' 'Trash, pure and simple.'

"The police were back. The same captain held a polished brown club, and a line of Boston cops, caps pulled tightly over military-cropped hair, stood with clubs out. They slapped their palms with the things as if keeping time to a march or counting.

"'We haven't done anything wrong,' said a tall Negro gentleman, and the captain said, 'Ya wanted to see the damn photoplay and now ya've seen it. Please be to get movin'.' Someone asked, 'Why should we move faster than other patrons?' and I knew there would be trouble.

"Somebody behind the coppers yelled, 'Look who's talkin' back to the police, will ye? Is it that Harvard coon?' and as if on cue, the police went for the Negroes. The blacks rose—fists up, hands covering faces, men shielding wives. They didn't, as the papers reported, attack. What they did was more like pulling yourself up to answer a question.

"Tuck tried to get between police and Negroes, but it was too late. Coppers flew across the lobby, sticks swinging. Black hands reached, grabbed, fended. Sticks swung, heads cracked, black and brown faces went red. Women screamed. White folks ran for the doors. It didn't take long. Men on their knees pleaded not to be hit. A Negro in a yellow suit almost got to the doors but was yanked back by the collar and thrown against a wall. Those who wouldn't go to their knees got pummeled.

"I didn't see this from Griffith's vantage. No camera sorted the flow of action, no sudden close-ups of faces, no glimpse of an upraised nightstick or satisfied Irish face. I saw clubs, blood, men on their knees. A woman pulled her hair and screamed. It only lasted a minute. There were, after all, white people present."

Lillian looked up with tears in her eyes and clutched my hands. "They don't understand *The Birth*. Bad whites led the blacks astray. Mr. Griffith doesn't dislike blacks. Neither do I."

"Neither does Tuck, but let me tell you what happened. We crossed Tremont Street and decided to go to the station to help those arrested. We hadn't gotten a block before a black man knocked into Tuck. It wasn't Tuck's fault but Tuck said, 'Excuse me.' It was curt, but not intimidating.

"The man said, 'No excuse for you,' and Tuck said, 'I beg your pardon,' in his Harvard best.

"'Damn show,' muttered the Negro.

"The man was in his twenties. I wanted to start a conversation and said, 'Were you at the photoplay?'

"'Damn white people,' he said.

"'Watch your tongue,' said Tuck.

"'Shut your face.' The man started to sneeze or had a nervous tic. He reached for his back pocket.

"Tuck hit him.

"Time froze. Someone could have hit me and I wouldn't have moved. The Negro's head flew back, blood flowing under an eye. The man staggered, unable to believe a man twenty years older, so well-dressed, could throw a right like Jack Johnson. The Negro raised his hand, which held a handkerchief. Not a razor or knife. He looked at us with disgust, and Tuck hit him again. Then again and again. Tuck was furious. Too furious. I yelled, 'Enough! Enough!' and the Negro stumbled away.

"Tuck looked at his right hand and said, 'I apologize. I'm a terrible host. A terrible person.'"

"That's what I saw, Miss Gish. And worse, what I felt. A scapegoat. Unthinking hate. All things I felt during *The Birth*.

"Why did Tuck explode? The photoplay? His wife? Because he could?"

10

Birth of a Nation hurt Negroes terribly, Miss Gish. I don't think you understand."

Lillian stood up, pulled back her lovely hair with both hands, and said, "Everything in *Birth* is historically accurate. Mr. Griffith saw to that. Corrupt white men led the blacks astray." She stood with her hands on the table, face flushed, imploring me not to misunderstand the *Birth*. "Mr. Griffith says disliking blacks is like disliking children."

I put on my coat. "Blacks aren't children. That's the point. The photoplay hurt people deeply."

"Only if they don't understand it," said Lillian hopelessly. "Blacks shouldn't follow bad leaders. Neither should whites. Look at the kaiser." She looked down at the books and pages strewn over the table. "Great art always has enemies."

"Suppose it hurts people who've already been hurt?" I said.

"The truth has enemies."

"I think you're saying what Griffith says. What do you say?"

Lillian touched the eviscerated Tissot. She shifted her weight back and forth, from one foot to the other, like a little girl.

"I don't want to argue. I just want you to think about what happened in Boston."

Lillian looked up with tears in her eyes. "I can't help what people think. I never mean to hurt anyone."

"Of course you don't," I said. "But it happens. I've hurt people I didn't mean to."

Lillian dabbed her face. "I won't cry. You'll think I'm a silly girl."

"You did things you didn't understand," I said.

"No! That's not fair! I knew what I was doing! Blame me if you want, but don't blame Mr. Griffith! I believe in the *Birth*. It's art."

"It might be," I said. "But it's cruel. We don't know

how cruel. We don't see it through their eyes."

I stood. Both of us rested our hands on the edge of the table, like statesmen debating.

We looked at each other. After a hard minute of looking at Lillian and looking away, and Lillian looking at me and looking away, she said, "Mr. Griffith is doing something different this time. I'm not supposed to tell, but it won't be misunderstood. It won't hurt anyone and could change the world."

"Suppose I don't believe you?"

"You can decide when you see Mr. Griffith. After we ride on the tower." Lillian brightened, and I can tell you, Lillian Gish brightens as no one I've ever seen brighten. She seemed to absorb the light and radiate it back in a golden aura around her sharp blue eyes, plump cheeks, perfect nose, all punctuated by that knowing, timeless, trademark look. I didn't believe her. I thought she was following a script, but her presence was exhilarating. Lillian Gish can instantly summon something utterly feminine; this is her gift. It was sexual and wasn't. It was spontaneous yet deliberate, and made her seem young and old, as if she'd always been both. I'd seen it on the screen and saw it across a table. Whatever it was, it was impossible to dislike.

"The light changes around you," I said.

"That's what Mr. Griffith said when we entered Biograph Studio the first time. In New York. My sister Dorothy announced, 'We are of the legitimate theater,' and Mr. Griffith laughed. He said I had a Pre-Raphaelite aura. Billy Bitzer agreed."

"You have extraordinary presence, Miss Gish, but you did flutter hysterically in *Birth*. You ran around with your nightgown flying, grabbing bedposts, black hands at your throat, whirling like a dervish. It was a show of maidenly fear at the prospect of a Negro. You did that for Griffith."

This time there were no tears, no pout, no retreat.

"I did that on my own," Lillian said. "It was my idea."

"What do you mean?"

"The way I moved my hands, shook my arms, jumped up and down, 'whirled and fluttered' as you put it. Do you remember what happens at that point in the photoplay? What do you see intercut with my hysterics?" Her voice changed. She was interrogating me. This was business.

"The Klan," I said. "The Klan was riding. That great, pounding, just-in-time ride to the rescue. Miss Gish, that was brilliant. No one's ever been rescued better. If you or Griffith never do anything else, that ride and rescue will be remembered forever. But why did you have to be rescued from the blacks? Why not from the Klan? From prejudice? That's the question the ages will ask! Just because you do something well, better than it may ever be done, you're still responsible for its content!"

"Even if I were responsible for its content, which I wasn't, it's historically accurate. We can argue that later. What I *was* responsible for was my acting. My art. I deliberately waved my arms. Yes, I was fluttering. I'm told I flutter, just like you cock your eyebrow when you ask a question, Mr. Harrison. We are all actors, aren't we? I was trying to imitate the horses galloping. I was trying to mimic their motion. To give continuity. To fit with the other part of the photoplay."

"You thought about that?"

"I thought about that," Lillian said. "I'm an actress."

11

We walked into the brilliant noon, I in belted English white and Lillian in an aura of golden green. She took my arm as we walked by low buildings and the laboratory.

"The Klan did violence because they'd been wronged by carpetbaggers and corrupt Yankees," she said.

"There's no excuse for lynchings and beatings," I said, but I wasn't thinking of the Ku Klux Klan. I was thinking of Michael X. Murphy, now taking in public what he enjoyed in secret. I gripped Lillian's arm tighter. She winced. I looked at Babylon and thought of the passage in Revelation about power given to the image of the beast so that the image of the beast should speak, because here was Griffith's beast, his empire, not the massive thing held up by scaffolds and wire, but the supple shadows on thousands of white screens in thousands of theaters. That's our Babylon. That's where Griffith has power over men and women—power over imagination. It's another dimension where the rules of time and space and truth are different and where, for now, Griffith is Belshazzar.

Lillian turned and looked at me. The sun lit her face, her lips, her small white hands. At noon she was a tiny, virginal creature. "Everyone will watch us. It will be like being in a parade. I will act as though I like you."

"I always walk in a Fourth of July parade before a Rochester Hustlers doubleheader."

"Then you're used to crowds," said Lillian.

∽

Every Fourth of July Edith and I used to lead the team into a full house. She didn't like crowds, so we went together, all in white, like figures on a wedding cake. I loved it, but Edith was tense. She did it for me.

Three years ago—the unlucky year 1913—I arranged for Murphy to march and give the speech. I love baseball, but there is a world elsewhere and that world was writing. My mother died that spring, and writing was full of longing for the days when she wore Grand Army of the Republic sashes and urged me to stay away from "baseball and fast women."

Last Fourth, Edith came into the turret wearing white lace and a huge vermilion hat. She looked as wonderful as she used to at League Park. "I don't want to face those people alone," she said. "Wear your whites. You look so good in them."

"I'm working," I said.

"What about your son? He wants to be in the parade with you. It's important."

"Not now."

"Please."

"Not this year. I don't feel like wearing white."

"Do it for him."

Harry came in wearing a Hustlers uniform Edith had specially made for him. He saw the look on my face and didn't say anything.

∾

Lillian and I walked into Babylon. Everyone watched. A group of assistant directors stopped talking and stared—the fellow with the brace of pistols, the intense little military Stroheim, and horse-faced Tod Browning, nephew of Pete Browning, the fine outfielder of the last century. They backed away and looked suspiciously at me, respectfully at Miss Gish. The great horde of actors, carpenters, and plasterers stopped and looked. All were struck by Lillian Gish. Karl Brown, the assistant cameraman, said, "She appears and everything stops."

With Babylon looming—twentieth-century factotums and ancient slaves, chariot drivers, soldiers, priests, and princes gaping—we walked to the tower mounted on six railroad cars at the end of the tracks. It was exhilarating to be watched by so many. It took me out of myself.

I looked at Babylon, the faces of Griffith's actors and crew, and at the woman beside me, who for them and America was an incarnation of beauty and mystery as strange and distant as rising, mighty Babylon, and I was surrounded by Griffith's creations—the set, the crew, Lillian Gish herself—all created to be photographed, all created to live in the dark, in this new language, this new world Griffith was discovering and exploiting like the conquistadors who subdued California four hundred years before.

Lillian turned to me as if I were the only person in the world, not someone being observed by hundreds, maybe thousands, because of her, and said, "This was all predicted in the Bible."

"That's a different Babylon," I said. "The one with the Great Whore."

Lillian looked shocked. "No Great what-you-just-said. I mean the language, the universal language. It was predicted that mankind would again have a universal language, and then the Millennium would come."

I looked at Babylon—elephants so high, walls so mighty, chariots, women swaying on the carpeted steps to the strains of an orchestra hidden behind the set. Griffith himself was somewhere in his city arranging details. For a moment, unhappy as I was, walking to a moving tower to be transported a hundred and forty feet in the air at the side of a child-woman whose face pleases us the way Mona Lisa pleases all—a sort of Millennium did come. Chiliastic predictions agree, when it comes, you won't notice anything else. For me, for a moment, all things converged and disappeared—losing Edith, meeting Griffith, finding Murphy. For a moment nothing mattered. It was as close as I was likely to get to Dante's point where all times are present. "Il punto a cui tutti li tempi son presenti."

Or was it Lillian Gish?

12

Henabery stood by the sixteen men who would push the tower the half mile to Babylon. They wore overalls and coarse shirts with the sleeves rolled up, and looked at Lillian with admiration and at me with a mixture of contempt, curiosity, and envy. The tower looked like a pyramid—sixty feet at the bottom, six on the top floor—resting on six flatbed railroad cars. Up close, it looked like a three-story tube-steel building—an unearthly pyramid, a pipefitter's dream of eternity. Four men on the first floor operated the elevator by rope. On the next floor young Brown, the talk-ative assistant, would crank a flexible shaft to drive Billy Bitzer's Pathé, so the cameraman, sitting with Griffith on the upper level, could concentrate on tilting and panning and keeping Babylon in focus. That would be Monday. Today was a dry run. No one would crank, and only Miss Gish and I would ride on top.

"Since you've taken such a lofty view of our produc-tions," said Henabery, "we thought we would give you the loftiest view of all."

Up close the apparatus was huge. I hadn't really looked at it when the choice had been between assistant director Dwan's contraption for photographing Babylon and Baby-lon itself—still hanging a mile away like a mirage in time. I hadn't imagined I might be riding in the tube-steel pyramid. A crowd formed for the dry run. I was introduced to Huck Wortman, the master builder, a short man with thick facial hair that made right angles at his nose. Wortman energetically chewed tobacco and spat. The former stage carpenter could build anything Griffith imagined. Beside Wortman was an apprehensive Englishman, Walter B. Hall, who looked every bit the bulldog—powerful chest, sandy hair, supercritical eye. He drew the pictures Wortman built. Hall designed Babylon, which Griffith dreamed, Wortman constructed, and Bitzer was going to photograph. I eyed the tower, beginning to realize I was going to pay for my opinions by being hoisted on a steel petard designed by a former engineer and assistant football coach at Notre Dame. Hall was the only man in the group who wasn't looking at Lillian Gish. He kept looking around. I'd heard he had a daughter he worried over like Polonius. I understood, but the eye never controlled a woman. Better Babylon.

Henabery, Wortman, whose spitting you could keep time by, and the distracted Hall were joined by Monty Blue with his shiny pistols and Johannes Charlemagne Epping, the bespectacled accountant and the man most rooted in the twentieth century. Epping went up to each man and said, "Who's paying for this? How much have you spent?" and then looked penitentially at a wad of yellow papers clutched tightly in his hand. More men arrived wearing comic Griffithesque hats. They were assistant directors. W. S. Van Dyke, Elmer Clifton, Dwan, and Eddie Dillon were laughing. Stroheim eyed me through a polished monocle; Browning, Christy Cabanne, and Henabery smiled. They chuckled about sending "the Harvard man up the shaft."

"I hope you're not afraid of heights," said Henabery. "If you panic, just signal and we'll lower you."

"The little girl's not afraid of anyting," said Stroheim, bullet head and monocle aimed at me. "Ve see if you dat good."

They laughed. I looked coolly at this tubular contraption that was taller than most buildings in Los Angeles. On another day I might have been terrified, but I felt a hollow numbness, and men were watching. I followed Lillian, who was helped over the steel wheels, went up an iron ladder to the cranking level, scurried up another ladder, and disappeared. I followed, not looking down. When I got to the top, huffing from the climb, I couldn't believe how small the platform was. I wanted to sit in the middle and close my eyes. Lillian sat in a folding chair a few feet from the edge. We were already two stories above ground, and she yelled, "Take her up!" louder than I thought her tender voice capable.

We went up. I heard laughter, but they couldn't see me. The hollowness met dumb fear.

"You're white as a sheet," said Lillian.

Two chairs, not attached to the deck, were just two feet from the edge.

"We can dangle our feet over if you like," said Lillian, with a devilish smile.

∾

The world was spectacular as we went up. We were on a moving, six-foot-square platform. It was open, and I felt sharp, blind panic—like thinking about Edith and Murphy.

I hate heights and had never been so high with so little between me and an edge. In this case, four edges. The steel tubes, which rose over our heads to complete the pyramid twenty feet up, were small barrier to the air. I thought I couldn't breathe, felt a dizzying panic, remembered Harry, and squeezed the legs of the chair.

"Look," said Lillian.

There was nothing to do but look. We saw the round, vast world. The ocean was off to the west. The desert was east. Los Angeles sat before us. The buildings were low and white and so spread out it was hard to imagine L.A. was a city at all, let alone one with three hundred thousand inhabitants. We could see the Hollywood Hills, all green, dotted with a few mansions, and Hollywood High School, civic Hollywood's last attempt to dominate a landscape where Griffith's rival, Thomas Ince, had a studio that was a sprawling photoplay ranch and Mack Sennett's Keystone Cops interrupt traffic, causing havoc until real cops show up, and it all gets in the photoplay. I saw Sennett's Keystone Studio on Glendale, which has a tower containing a bathtub from which Mack keeps an eye on his minions while bathing, and Carl Laemmle's aptly named Universal City, a place that fakes everywhere else. We saw Jesse Lasky's Feature Play Company at Sunset and Vine, and big, green Griffith Park.

"It's not named for D. W. Griffith," said Lillian, "but for Colonel Griffith J. Griffith, who donated the land, and later shot his wife. Mrs. Griffith survived, and the Colonel spent a year in prison."

"No man lacks a good reason for shooting his wife," I said. Lillian didn't laugh. I leaned toward her, away from the edge, remembering Eadweard Muybridge, pioneer of moving images, who helped win Leyland Stanford's $25,000 bet that a galloping horse completely leaves the ground. Muybridge killed his wife's lover and was acquitted, but that was frontier California, and the frontier is gone. Now there's Babylon.

We saw oil derricks all over the city and roads laid out in the dust going nowhere: an outline of where the city will go. Cars moved like dirt-hauling ants crawling to the horizon. Jesus' Model T was in the hills above Los Feliz.

In front of us: Babylon.

Fear was tempered with vision. From the subtle confidence of Lillian Gish to the vulgar majesty of Babylon, I'd never seen so much. We saw it all: The wires and hawsers behind the set. The balloon grazing from a tower. The pillars, elephants, the hidden orchestra providing rhythm for dancers swaying on seventeen carpeted steps, the Hanging Gardens, soldiers, priests, lions, nobles, merchants.

"Look," said Lillian, and there was Griffith himself, white coat and coolie hat off, shadowboxing in front of a crowd. "Mr. Griffith periodically breaks into song, boxes with the air, waltzes with one of us, or juggles Indian clubs, to break the tension of working seven days a week."

"It's not real," I said, finally able to speak over the awful, empty space and whistling wind. I was angry at being frightened, angry my life was no more solid than this enormous, ridiculous thing held up by wires and hawsers, and angry with Lillian Gish, who wasn't scared at all, and Griffith, who cooked up this trip through the air.

"It's not real!" I shouted. "None of it! That's not a city." I pointed at Babylon. "It's a set. A trick. Wires hold it up. Everyone in it is paid to be someone else. That's not a city either!" I pointed at Los Angeles. "It's a bunch of bungalows and oil rigs. A place where midwestern idiots think they can be somebody else. For God's sake, there's a fool dressed as Jesus Christ driving around in a Model T!"

Lillian laughed. "Getting used to the height?"

We were a quarter way down the tracks, being lowered slowly. Too slowly.

"You're not real either!" I shouted. "I don't know what you are. You're a face. A role. Something you created. Something Griffith created. Beautiful. Brilliant. But not real!"

I wanted Lillian to get angry. I wanted to rattle the eternal little girl–woman, so untouchable, so feminine. "Whatever you are!" I shouted over the wind. "It's better than Mary Pickford. America's Sweetheart makes me want to strangle her!"

Lillian smiled her Mona Lisa smile into the wind.

"I'm real!" I shouted.

Lillian looked at the enormous, bright landscape of Los Angeles and gleaming Babylon. "Does hating Mr. Griffith make you real?"

"I show my feelings! You're always acting!"

Lillian looked at the trumpeting elephants. "Does being nasty?"

"I'm real!" I yelled, choking with anger and fear of the height. "My wife just left me." I touched the cut on my jaw. "I have a six-year-old I have to take care of and I don't even know how to put him to bed." A tear flew off my cheek. "That fool dressed as Jesus knows this, and now you know and you'll tell Griffith, and all of you can have a good goddamn laugh!"

Lillian Gish did the unexpected. She took my hand. She held it as we rode through air, frighteningly high, to Babylon. The wind rose and fell, and Lillian said, "Do you love your wife?"

"I don't know who she is anymore," I said.

"Perhaps you didn't know her as well as you thought."

"How could Edith do this to Harry?" I yelled, hoarse with angry fear. "How could she do this to a child?"

"She didn't do it to the child," said Lillian, pursing her lips into a heart. "She did it to you." Lillian looked down. "I shouldn't have said that. I'm sorry."

"You seem so timid, but you speak your mind, don't you?"

Lillian looked at the elephants, Ishtar, then me. The enormous figure with the six-foot man at her breast loomed on the right. Lillian smiled.

"Do you know the theatrical expression 'A diamond will get you back to New York'?" I asked.

"If the show is canceled, or the manager runs off with

the cashbox, a diamond, presumably hidden on one's person, can be sold to get you back to Broadway. Mr. Harrison, I've been on the stage since I was four." Lillian spoke into the wind. "I've been looking for that diamond all my life."

"Well," I said. "I just lost it."

13

D on't look down, Mr. Harrison."

I didn't. I still could barely breathe over the awful, rising emptiness. I looked at Lillian.

"Can you forgive your wife?" she said.

"My friend Tuck says he's found Christ and has forgiven his wife. I don't believe him."

"You're not religious?"

"The only Jesus I found was driving a Model T."

Lillian laughed.

"Forgiveness is the last refuge of a scoundrel," I said, thinking that was a clever reprise of Dr. Johnson on patriotism. What I meant was the last refuge of the weak.

"Would you forgive for Harry?" Lillian looked at me as if she liked me.

"Harry needs to forgive me," I said.

"Will you hate Edith?"

I looked at Lillian Gish, who I could see was much more than the knowing sprite Griffith makes her. "I don't have the courage not to hate her."

"Because she hurt you?"

"Because I loved her."

"You're going to need courage, Mr. Harrison."

"Edith once said that," I said, not looking down, looking at Lillian, auburn hair twisted and blown over green shoulders. "Edith loved a man before me. It made me very jealous. Edith said we could belong to each other if we had courage, but only if we had courage."

"You had it once," said Lillian.

"I lost it. Like the diamond."

Lillian smiled that enigmatic, young-old, strange-familiar smile—a smile oblivious to men, heights, insults. I held her hand tightly and looked her in the eye to avoid the rush of world around us. It wasn't easy to look at Lillian Gish because I wasn't just looking at those soft blue eyes, full cheeks, hair worthy of Isolde the Fair, but at an image I'd seen on the screen. I saw a person but I also saw pictures created by Griffith, photographed by Bitzer, manipulated and processed and pasted into Griffith's flawless rhythm, and that image floated between me and the woman in the folding chair. Maybe it floats between Lillian and herself.

How could I think Lillian Gish liked me? How could I penetrate that smile, Griffith's instructions, her acting? I wanted Lillian to like me. I wanted to feel attractive the day my wife left me, but what was Lillian and what the shadow from the nickelodeon? I'd seen the shadow be many people. Make love. Be happy, miserable, almost raped in *Birth*. I knew the careful way the shadow regards the world and judges men, but how do you look at a person when an image has been fashioned onto your imagination? How do you look at someone made to be looked at? It's like being on a platform a hundred feet up in front of Babylon.

"I am real," Lillian said. "People think I'm not because I play all those stupid gaga-babies. Those sweet, stupid little girls. I'd rather be a vamp. It would be more fun. And easier too. Do you know how hard it is to flutter and be a fool, and try to make that fool intelligent?"

"Why do you do it?" I said, less afraid, though we were still startlingly high.

"Because Mr. Griffith makes art. I'm part of that art. It's new. Completely new. Can you imagine being part of something completely new, Mr. Harrison? There's never been anything as powerful. Look at the reaction to *Birth*. In the hands of a genius, it can do anything."

"The universal language," I said, looking up. We crept toward Babylon the way the centuries creep to the Millennium.

"This photoplay . . ." Lillian stopped. "It might . . . I can't tell . . . But you'll see. Everyone will see."

Between that face and cat-soft hand, up there with the four corners of the world, between beauty and terror, Hollywood and Sunset, I liked Lillian Gish, whatever she was. Was I being seduced? Was this the plan? Lillian, Babylon, then Griffith?

The teeming set, elephants, giant pillars, and extras

got bigger. Ishtar came at us.

"I'll tell you something, Mr. Harrison." Lillian looked serious—a look I didn't recognize from the lexicon of Gish-Griffith picture language.

"You told me why you feel real. I'll tell about myself. After my father left, Mother, Dorothy, and I went on the stage. By the time I was five, we would be split up. I would play one town and they would play another, maybe far away. We didn't have much. We lived in boardinghouses. Cold, mean places. I was taken care of by 'aunts,' older actresses. Mostly they were nice. I didn't have much. My possessions, and my clothes, fit in a suitcase. Do you remember the long, thin ones called 'telescopes'? All I had were a few child's things and a 'fur.' A little coat. That coat made me feel special. I felt such a little lady. One day, one January morning, one of those gray dawns when the world might be cold forever, we ran for a train. By 'we' I mean 'Aunt Alice' and me. I had packed myself, tightening the straps on the telescope bag, but as we ran over a bridge, the straps came undone. I hadn't tightened them sufficiently. My few possessions and my dear fur went in the river. We didn't stop. We didn't even look. We ran. We couldn't miss that train. My things didn't matter. It was a hard lesson, Mr. Harrison. But it was a lesson. I learned I belonged to the theater. I learned I belonged to work. I've belonged to work since I was five. I've been real a long time."

Babylon came up bigger than the horizon, bigger than the world.

14

"What do I belong to?" I said, as Babylon with its thousands was before us.

Lillian looked at me the way she looked at Henry B. Walthall at the end of *Birth,* after the white race has been saved, before the Prince of Peace appears on a white horse and subdues the Beast of War. It was a beautiful look, but I'd seen it on the screen and didn't trust it.

"You belong to your child," Lillian said.

"The way you belong to the stage? To this?" I pointed at Babylon.

"Yes."

We were closer to the ground. I could pick out faces and the décolletage of dancers.

Lillian let go of my hand and gently tapped it. "Let me tell you something." She sighed and tilted her head in that pensive, almost overwhelmed, girlish way.

"You may have lost your wife, but you have a child who will try to take care of you. I know that child. That's why I'm talking to you. I was that child. I tried to take care of Mother and Dorothy. I've never stopped trying. That child worries, Mr. Harrison. That child never stops worrying. He doesn't learn to play with other children and isn't comfortable with children his age. I never was. Maybe that's why I seem childlike now. Your child will be like that too. You mustn't hate Edith. You mustn't hate anybody. It's the only way to let Harry be a child. Don't let anger eat you up."

"I can't edit out what I don't like," I said. "I'm not Griffith."

"Being Mr. Griffith isn't easy. Look at what's been edited out of his life. He has no family. He has a wife but she doesn't have him." Lillian lowered her voice. "Mr. Griffith and I have work. We have each other. But there's a problem. He proposed today. In the car. Right before we saw you and Mr. Gaye."

"But Griffith's married," I said, truly surprised. Why would Lillian tell me? Was this part of a plan?

"That won't stop him. It's just another impossible thing, like the Shot. 'It's impossible so we'll do it.' That's his motto. We love each other the way we love work. If that changes, I'm afraid we'll lose everything, including work. Mr. Griffith's not domestic. He works sixteen hours a day. We're his family. This is his home. He's not comfortable in a house."

"Like you," I said.

"Like me," Lillian said.

We were almost at ground level, where Lillian would go back to being one of the deities of the Fine Arts' pantheon—the public person, made to look frail, ladylike, helpless, when in fact she could ride a hundred feet up on a six-foot platform without blinking. Stroheim said "the little girl" wasn't afraid of anything, but how would the little girl handle D. W. Griffith? How would she handle the master manipulator and autocrat? D. W. Griffith made her. Griffith was the diamond that kept the Gishes from dawn railroad stations and cheap hotels, and maybe Lillian Gish was the jewel he looked for during his lean years, lonely marriage, and all the hard photoplay work. Maybe Lillian Gish was D. W. Griffith's finest creation and he couldn't resist her. Maybe Griffith saw the shadow, not the actress. Maybe he'd just assigned her another role.

"What are you going to do?" I said.

"I'll try to find a way to say no."

"Why tell me? I'm the enemy."

"You've been honest with me," said Lillian, and squeezed my hand. "You're alone. So am I."

"I've never been so alone."

"Listen," Lillian said. "I am to tell you to meet Mr. Griffith at Edward Rogers' house tonight in the Hollywood Hills. There's a party. Everyone will be there. Everyone connected with *The Mother and the Law* and everyone connected with photoplays. I wasn't to invite you if you threw up, or were afraid, or I didn't like you. But I would have invited you if you'd thrown up, because you couldn't have helped that."

"I'll be there," I said, wondering what I'd touched beneath the shadow, or if I'd just been fooled by a woman again.

III

PARTY IN THE HOLLYWOOD HILLS

April 2, 1916
6:00 p.m. to midnight

1

Jesus picked me up at Fine Arts and insisted we eat, so we went to his bungalow above Sunset. The place was perched on a hill and surprisingly neat. We sat at the kitchen table and I said I was worried about Harry. Jesus suggested telephoning, so I called Maria and talked to Harry. He hadn't seen his mother. She was expected later. I told Jesus about Tuck and asked if I could call Boston. He said, "Fine, just pay for it, old boy." I telephoned, but Tuck wasn't home or didn't answer. I tried again. I hate the sound of a ringing telephone far away, but I wanted to talk to Tuck, even about Christianity.

"Of course Griffith didn't see you," said Jesus. "The Master sent his cat's-paw to win your heart. Griffith scared you with the tower and charmed you with Miss Geesh, as he calls her. You're in peril, Harrison."

"Liking Lillian Gish just made me dislike Griffith more. He uses her. He uses everyone."

"She's willing enough," said Jesus.

I barely ate but instead sat looking at three sets of white robes hanging in a built-in closet in the living room, thinking of men who find women through work, sharing effort, then desire. I would see two of them tonight.

∾

Edith and I had work. I thought we'd always have desire. We ran the Rochester Hustlers, made love by Lake Ontario, and dreamed of owning a big-league club. I turned to writing—worlds gone, old selves, new truth—but Edith still wanted a big-league club. She liked the planning and dealing. The competition. "Where's the Henry who would do anything to get a ball club? The Henry who bet on crooked games to get money to buy the Hustlers?" Edith wanted to get into the new Federal League. She asked. I didn't hear.

I suddenly realized Griffith is like Murphy. Another bastard who thinks he can have everything. I hated him for wanting Lillian. Could the actress who belonged to work resist the King of Babylon?

∽

Two candles and a bottle of scotch decorated the table along with cold meat and sliced tomatoes. "Mutton," said Jesus, between mouthfuls. He looked down at his sleeveless undershirt, concave chest, pale but hairy arms, and said, "Clothes make the man."

"I knew an Eddie Rogers at Harvard," I said. "But he would have to step in money to find it."

"This bloke stepped in oil at Long Beach. Now he wants to be a photoplay producer. Actually Rogers wants actresses. The wife has been sent east. There are peepholes on the third floor of Cibola. Cibola is what the chap calls his house. They make photoplays up there."

"And Griffith will compromise himself there?"

"Everyone compromises himself there."

"Is it time to go?" I said, getting up.

"Harrison, you're like a moth to a flame. The chance

82

to confront that man, see Gish, catch Griffith. You can't wait. Let me finish eating."

I walked through the bungalow while Jesus ate. Some moment of truth was coming. I didn't know what would happen with Edith or Murphy, but it would be final. What happened with Griffith would become the last chapter of my book. My lesson from the Master.

Suppose I just stand there? Suppose Murphy laughs?

Jesus belched and said, "A country that doesn't fancy mutton is uncivilized."

What do you say to a man who's f***ed your wife?

I stood by the three white robes trembling with anger. Jesus ate and belched again. It isn't the hurt, betrayal, or insult. It's the irreversibility. Look what we've done. You can't change it. You're irrelevant.

I squeezed a robe.

In a week Murphy will see how much he enjoys life with a woman who's lost her child.

I called Boston. No answer. I didn't let it ring long.

Jesus wiped his mouth. "Harrison, it's early, but if you can't sit still, let's drive."

"OK."

Jesus dressed and we went into a clear, early evening smelling of lemon trees and jacaranda.

～

"You look like you're going to meet your fate," Jesus said as we went west on Sunset, dust stirring in our wake, the hills a cold outline, and the light retreating, leaving behind a clear unreality. "What's the name of this man with your wife?"

"Murphy."

"What does Murphy do?"

"Business manager for our baseball club."

"How long has this affair gone on?"

"Three years."

"Let me guess. He's a competent, competitive ass your wife thinks will take care of her better than you with your writing and white suits?"

"How did you know?"

"I know." Jesus held up his hands. His robes flickered pale and dark through the shadows of pepper trees whose berries popped under our hard rubber tires. "I have dreams and an unhappy wife."

I nodded. I'll say nothing tonight and take Harry tomorrow.

"At our age, my dear fellow, women leave for a better deal. Not for adventure. Not for excitement. Not even sex. They leave to be taken care of. Am I wrong?"

"No."

Jesus gave me a marvelously omnipotent smile, shifted, spun the tires in second gear, and we started up a hill. "I'm going to keep an eye on you. Don't drink too much Innskillen." The bottle rolled on the tonneau mat on the floor of the backseat. "One moment you look like you're going to pieces, the next you'll kill someone. You'll do neither, but you will get through the night. You may meet Griffith. You may not. You may see Griffith compromise himself, saving my job and making your book, and you may not. Hopefully you will meet a woman, get clocked, and get on with it. The rest of your life, I mean. If not, I'll stay with you."

"Charity never faileth," I said, remembering Saint Paul.

"Harrison, you can only defeat the past with the present. There's no getting even. This isn't mathematics."

Jesus shifted into third. "I met a woman named Gerty this afternoon. One of those well-fed American women whose breasts are much larger than they look in a loose bodice. We went above Los Feliz and spent the afternoon jiggling this thing from fender to crank. Gerty kept saying, 'I got a movie. A movie. I never got one before.'"

"Is this supposed to make me feel better?"

"For God's sake, Harrison, do as I do *and* as I say. No one forgives. You can only forget, and there's only one bloody way to do it. Get clocked. Catch Griffith buggering a fourteen-year-old. You'll feel better."

We passed several horse-drawn wagons, a black Stutz Bearcat, a rooming house with a sign saying, "No Actors, Dogs or Jews," the new high school with its yellow dome sparkling in the last light. We turned some heads, but even on Saturday night, with Babylon rising out of the east, Hollywood was quiet and empty.

"You know what Gerty kept saying?" Jesus startled two pedestrians with the horn.

"That you're God?"

"You're too romantic."

"She wants to be in photoplays?"

"No, Harrison, the sort of woman who takes off with a man in a costume and ruts all afternoon in a Ford could only be satisfied by something that doesn't exist. She held me as if I were life itself and kept saying, 'If we could only make this last. Please make it last. Is there a way?'"

"There isn't," I said.

∾

We kept going west through the dusty and desolate Beverly Hills. Like most areas north of Los Angeles and out of the squat bungalow-ramble of Hollywood, Beverly Hills was just fields.

"Look at this," said Jesus. "Land is the pot of gold at the end of the American rainbow. All you do is wait and some fool will buy it. No doubt even Beverly Hills will be valuable some day. One day a Yank will sell the Pacific Ocean."

I decided to take Harry boating like I promised, then take him to Union Station. I had enough money for the train and could wire for more Monday.

"Harrison, what happens when there's no more California? No more West?" Jesus waved his white arm at the inky blue sky over a lemon grove. As night fell, he looked more like the Pale Rider than the Incarnation. "Motion pictures! An empire of light! Something for nothing! When you have no more America, make dreams! Sell light! What a country!"

"Whose dreams?" I said, looking at the hills.

"Dreams? Fantasies? The climate produces them. The first Californians, the aborigines, the Yuma Indians, thought their dreams more real than their lives. They lived to sleep, dream, then live by the dreams. Thought they were dreaming the past. Dreaming the future. Bloody idiots."

The pink Beverly Hills Hotel rose out of the dark like Bluebeard's castle, and Jesus said, "If Americans stay at a hotel where the only view is mustard fields, sooner or later they want to buy the mustard fields."

We turned off Sunset, literally in the middle of nowhere, and drove up the palm-lined driveway to the huge, pink, mission-style stucco hotel.

"Look at those walls and high windows, Harrison. It's like a prison, which is appropriate, as the Spanish rounded up those aboriginal dreamers, forced them into missions, put the men to work, gave the women syphilis and the children Catholic dogma. You think the hotel is vulgar, don't you?"

I nodded, wondering where Edith and Murphy would spend the night.

"No, Harrison. The hotel, the town, even Los Angeles, this flat excuse for a city, are more American than America."

"Why?" I said, wondering if I could really take Harry. Then I thought how happy Murphy was.

"Because they *are* vulgar! What is most American about America? Vulgarity! Fast money, flashy clothes, cheap women, huge houses, long automobiles! These are spiritual qualities! Vulgarity is an American emotion! It's transcendent! What you perceive as wretched excess is the future coming faster than we can assimilate it. Harrison, you see this as madness and shocking bad taste—but it's the future. There's freedom in vulgarity. Strength! Vigor. Bad taste, especially if it's really bad, is pure energy."

We returned to Hollywood so Jesus could show me "Glengary," an estate which combined the features of a Scottish manor, Nuremberg Castle, and Oxford University.

"A doctor built it. Upset the natives no end, and I don't mean the Yumas. The neighbors just didn't know what was coming. Look." On the other side of the street was an even bigger mansion—a crenellated thing with turrets, flags still flying in the dark, balconies, high windows, gardens.

"The doctor built it after Glengary. How can the good people of Hollywood object to actors, dogs, and Jews with Alfred Guido Randolph Schloesser in their midst?"

"D. W. Griffith must be the local gentry," I said bitterly.

"Harrison, cheer up. Sans Souci is dwarfed by the Japanese mountain palace of the Bernheimer brothers. Architecture run riot! Symmetry, balance, harmony, destroyed by excess! A whole civilization belittled by pagodas, reflecting pools, cherry trees. Trust a Yank to ruin anything! Adulterate taste with scale! Strangle satori! An American can make anything look like a restaurant!

"Where we're going makes this look civilized!"

2

Cibola was a three-story mansion coiled into a hilltop. Despite a string of big cars parked along the road where chauffeurs played cards and hid flasks as we went by, the house felt lonely, blazing against the dark hills.

"Stay behind me when we go in," said Jesus. "We'll stun them. I don't care who you are, or who you think you are, when Jesus Christ walks in, you shut up."

I looked back at the scattered lights of Los Angeles, then at the white stucco walls and red-tiled roofs, surrounded by gates, arches, courtyards, patios, pergolas, leaded windows all wedded together in that glorious California style: mismatch. Cibola had swimming pools, reflecting pools, waterfalls—the garish need to display water in the desert, like the Hanging Gardens. The walls were Tudor, Moorish, and Spanish, high and fortress thick, as if Montezuma himself were imprisoned—gazing at the Region of Mysteries, and wondering if Cortez were Quetzalcoatl returned to reestablish the order of the fifth sun, and why there wasn't enough gold in the world to buy freedom.

Jesus entered first. I was a few paces behind, and we were in a hall of mirrors—mirrors on the walls and ceiling, and a black floor so polished Jesus tried to look up the skirts of two ladies we passed. I looked wildly around but saw only myself—the white suit rumpled, a tired, apprehensive face— the cut on my chin. I was afraid Griffith wouldn't be here.

Then it seemed inevitable I would meet the master of images in a hall of mirrors.

We entered the ballroom, and Jesus got what he had predicted: absolute silence. Everyone stared. Everyone shut up. I recognized many who were somebody, others who thought they were somebody, and more who wanted to be, but I didn't see Edith or Murphy. I saw myself again in mirrored walls that went up to a blue balcony. A pale, domed ceiling rose over the second floor. An enormous silver ball, studded with clear lightbulbs, was suspended from the center of the dome. It was so bright a photoplay could have been shot here. The floor was black and white marble, like a chessboard.

The guests, some in Babylonian costume, were reflected in 360 degrees of angled mirrors. The images made women beautiful and gentlemen bigger than life. Time seemed to stop in the illusion of endless light endlessly reflected, so despite two hundred people and noonbright light, the ballroom felt like an ice palace made of the cold intimacy of mirrors. I imagined Edith and Murphy on the black and white floor reflected to infinity.

Looking and looking, I spotted dozens of photoplay people who ranged from what Jesus described as a "coven of Jews," to Griffith's actors in Babylonian costume ("The oil bloke is a big investor"), to young women in every sort of deshabille who looked ready for every sort of adventure. Hollywood is no country for old women. The motion picture people, talking in mirrors topped with Moorish arches, made an infinite circular progression that staggered my ability to see. I stayed close to the edge, to suffer reflection in only one mirror and avoid the scrutiny of eyes multiplied and magnified to powers I couldn't count, but finally found a stairway and retreated to the balcony. Jesus followed. Even he shied away from so much flesh, glaringly paraded in so much light.

Joe Henabery was on the balcony, and I said, "Have you seen Griffith?" and Henabery said, "No," so I found a room where liquor was served by Mexicans got up as characters from Griffith's new photoplay, *The Mother and the Law.* Brown, the shy but friendly assistant cameraman, smiled and slid by a gaggle of young women, who all said, "Hi, Karl." I went up to a hidalgo Pharisee, who struggled with his long beard and served saffron punch by a fireplace big enough to be the mouth of hell. An enormous, jagged scoop of sherbet that looked like the head of John the Baptist floated in the punch. I pointed at a row of gleaming silver cups, but the Pharisee said, "Señor, you need this," and produced a bottle of tequila. I had three shots which burned and steadied me. The fourth splashed on my shirtfront.

On the balcony a ten-piece orchestra in evening clothes prepared to play. I watched the crowd, holding the railing so my hands wouldn't shake. The ballroom contained ice sculptures of characters from *The Mother and the Law.* An ice Jesus sweated its own halo, droplets slid like tears down a melting Princess Beloved, a slippery Charles IX dissolved before our eyes, and a frozen Bobby Harron, the boy nearly executed in the modern story, got no reprieve from the heat of the crowd, which included Mr. Harron himself in spats, Mae Marsh, Miriam Cooper, and Dorothy Gish.

"Griffith's not here," I said to Jesus, who was admiring his reflection in a glass bookcase. "Neither is Edith."

"Griffith and Gish will make an entrance."

I had more tequila.

3

I watched and felt the hard, burning rush of tequila when Lillian Gish and D. W. Griffith walked out of the mirrors into the mirrors to the center of the ballroom. People dropped back. Griffith looked tall, blue eyes blazing in mirror after mirror in the blue ice of the ballroom, white planter suit exquisitely cut. I was jealous. Griffith radiated absolute success and absolute control. I watched and hated him. Griffith was the master of the evening, master of the photoplay, master of all his imagination surveyed. Who could stop him now? A cuckold who'd sliced his chin? D. W. Griffith had everything every man in that room, save me, wanted, and the power to make every woman, including Lillian Gish, into what she wanted.

The Master and La Gish walked into the center of the marble checkerboard. Griffith took her in his arms and they danced. The orchestra found a waltz, but they didn't need music—a hall of people stopped looking at themselves, talking business, seducing each other. They left the perfection of mirrors and the cold, glittery blue surface of ego and were transformed into guests at Cinderella's ball.

Jesus smiled and so did the photoplay people. Moneymen, stars, the sincere fellow from *Photoplay Magazine*, bit players and hangers-on, all watched and smiled. For a few minutes Griffith and Gish made them gawk like children watching the grown-ups—watching what they might be. Lillian wore an opulent, iridescent green silk gown, tiered with a pleated sash above the waist, that shimmered from emerald to bluish teal and made the air around her seem to shimmer, as if color could obliterate the boundary between person and air. Lillian wore black, elbow-length lace gloves and moved through mirrors and eyes and envy without looking at herself. Griffith was superb. He stole a glance at the mirrors with his keen professional eye—they were a moving image after all—but mostly he looked at her. How could he look at anything else?

They danced.

4

It's not that illusions aren't real—look at the motion picture—they just don't last. Soon other couples took the floor, including Mary Pickford and Fairbanks the acrobat, but not before a wonderful round of applause. Everyone in that bright room of greedy and famous faces knew what

Griffith meant to the business of making money out of light, fortunes from yearnings in the dark, everything out of nothing. They applauded vigorously, then paired up and took the floor themselves.

~

Then I saw them.

Standing by the far wall, in a crowd that included Bobby Harron and Dorothy Gish and her mother, were Edith and Murphy.

Edith was wearing a crimson crepe day dress with elbow-length sleeves of garnet d'Angleterre lace and square neckline. She wore a long strand of knotted pearls. Edith was slightly underdressed, as if she hadn't thought she was coming here, or hadn't given it a second thought—maybe the second thought was how easily it could come off. Murphy was wearing a gray pin-striped suit, no doubt his best, with a flawless white collar—not so easy to take off—and loud purple tie. They talked earnestly, or he talked and Edith listened. Murphy looked like a lawyer giving a summation.

I wanted to go down the stairs, push my way through stars and nobodies, and say, "You're going to be sorry. Sorrier than you can imagine," but that would have been stupid. Taking Harry had to be a surprise, a fait accompli—just like them. I wanted to feel strong, protected by my ruthless plan, but the crimson dress made me lonely. I watched Edith and realized I wouldn't see her take it off. I wouldn't be there when she unbuttoned it, asked for help, and neatly arranged the thing on the back of a chair. I imagined Murphy's nervous fingers seeking buttons in the garnet lace, his little, strong hands removing the pearls, the reddish mustache pressing against Edith's neck. I knew I'd fight.

They started to dance. Edith put one hand in Murphy's hand, and after straightening the white collar, the other on his pin-striped shoulder. He put his arm around her crimson waist. They were almost the same height. They kept a respectable distance, then Murphy leaned forward and kissed her. Edith smiled and kissed him back. The kiss wasn't clandestine or thrilling. It was familiar.

5

Jesus saw me watching them and said, "Handsome woman. He looks as awful as I thought. Dreadful tie." They stopped dancing and Murphy introduced Edith to Joe Henabery, who took them over to the Jews. I started for the stairs, walking through the orchestra, bumping the oboe player, seeing nothing left or right. Feeling nothing. I heard Jesus say, "I'll try to keep him out of jail," and kept moving— orchestra, balcony, Pharisee, oboe were unreal, unavoidable. I went to the mirrors. To Edith and Murphy. To the inevitable. Jesus rushed by me as we got to the ballroom. Murphy was shaking hands with Hollywood's colony of New Yorkers, who suddenly saw Jesus—robes supernaturally white, blue eyes impossible to look at, striding across the gleaming black and white floor—and stopped talking. Edith saw me and froze. Murphy saw me and flinched, then put his arm around Edith, as if protecting her. Edith mouthed the word "No," and pointed at the door as if we should talk.

Jesus stood in the middle of the checkerboard, palms out, and shouted, "Behold we go up to Jerusalem!"

Carl Laemmle, Jesse Lasky, Adolph Zukor, a man named Goldfish, Rabbi Myers, and his daughter Carmel looked warily at Jesus. The rabbi was the only one who noticed me and must have sensed something wrong. He quickly introduced me to Zukor, an intense man impeccably dressed in a gray morning suit. I shook hands but couldn't speak.

"He's appraising your clothes," said Jesus loudly. "He used to be in the business."

"English," said Murphy, who suddenly found his voice and wit.

"Mr. Harrison is a writer," said Rabbi Myers.

"Vat scripts you do?" asked Goldfish.

"He writes for *The Atlantic,*" said Murphy. Edith tried to pull him away; Murphy stood his ground.

"You write for an ocean?" said Goldfish.

"About Griffith," I said, no louder than a whisper.

"Griffitz is big like de ocean," said Goldfish.

"For now," said Zukor.

"Stars," said Carl Laemmle of Universal Studio, a short, heavy, balding man, who smiled at me as if we were old friends. "The public vants stars, maybe. Not just big sets."

"The future is in de stars," said Goldfish, and laughed hard.

"Of course, if this Griffitz project makes more money than God, excuse me, Rabbi," said Laemmle, "then ve build Babylon every time."

"People pay to see Pickford, not a costume," said Zukor. He pointed at Jesus, who stood with arms extended, lips slightly parted, white as Griffith's Klansmen, as if welcoming his flock.

"Don't point that finger at me," said Jesus. "I remember when there was a thimble on it."

"Stars," said Murphy, "are the key to this business." He was showing he could handle the situation. Handle me.

Edith walked away. I saw her in the mirrors. She was crying.

"Griffith makes so much money, he doesn't have to know business," said Lasky.

"More money than God," said Murphy, apparently unable to resist irony around men struggling with a new language and with Christians. I saw myself in mirrors. I saw Murphy. Alone now with the Jews, only Jesus' clowning kept us apart. Everyone looked up as Mack Sennett and Mabel Normand made their entrance. Mack and Mabel came in laughing. Sennett wore evening clothes with the finesse of a gorilla, but Miss Normand was stunning in pink chiffon. I've never seen a woman radiate such unselfconscious beauty, as if declaring beauty were fun and motion, not posed elegance. Mabel saluted Fatty Arbuckle, who tripped her and caught her before she hit the floor. People cheered. Mabel kissed Fatty. Murphy watched me.

"More money than God," said Goldfish.

"Not more money than God," said Rabbi Myers, "just more money than you."

I watched Murphy in the mirrors. Griffith and Gish watched Jesus.

"The Jews survived Babylon," said Zukor.

"Yeah," said Goldfish. "Vhy no Jews in Griffitz's Babylon? Mene, mene, tekel, upharsin."

"Eenie, meenie, minee, mo," said Carmel Myers.

Lasky laughed.

Murphy said, "Your daughter is assimilating." How charming.

"There iss no Jews in Babylon," said Zukor, mimicking Goldfish and looking at me, "becauss Griffitz hass not seen de handwriting on de vall."

"Could we get Gish from him?" said Lasky.

"That, I believe," said Murphy, "is a matter of the heart."

Murphy claiming knowledge of love infuriated me. I took a step but was bumped by the woman whose black-lined eyes, streaming raven hair, and voluptuous figure were as well known as Teddy Roosevelt's front teeth.

"Oy vay!"

Theda Bara patted the floor looking for the long-stemmed red rose she had carried in her teeth. Murphy picked it up and gave it to her with a suave bow, but sweat showed under his armpits just like it showed under mine. He smiled and received the Vamp stare. Nothing was real but mirrors and blue and light and I was moving—Griffith, Jesus, Lillian, lost in reflection—Edith about to be lost forever—I was gliding over marble, weightless, dancing, a ghost. I know what assassins want. Reverse time. Make it run back. Like film. I hit Murphy below the eye. His head jerked. I swung again and hit his shoulder.

Time didn't reverse.

Murphy stood and looked at me. Blood welled below his eye. He dropped his hands daring me to do it again. Little dark eyes full of pride. His courage. My ambush. He did the right thing; I the worst.

Murphy laughed.

"You son of a bitch!" I yelled, and tried to hit him again but someone hit me. Hard. From the side. I was on the marble bleeding from the mouth. I saw blurry lines. White. Black. Diagonal. Bloody. I tried to get up. I had to get up. Kill him. Nothing existed except killing Murphy. I forced myself to my knees. Blood ran down my face, shirt, trousers. Get up. Get up. Rip his throat. Finally, somehow, staggering, dizzy, I got to my feet and said, "Murphy!" spitting blood. I saw a vague gray shape and lunged, not with fists but with teeth, fingers out, and got hit in the side of the head. I doubled over on the floor, then somehow got to my knees, but couldn't get up. In Mexico I saw a bull refuse to die. Cheers rained down. Toro! Toro! I was on my face in my own blood. I slid. Crawled. When the bull went down, he kept his head up. The matador saluted. Murphy shouted, "Don't! Don't!" I went at the voice, sank my teeth into a trousered leg, and tried to bite through it. There was a terrible scream. A ferocious kick.

Men and women screamed. Ran.

The next thing I remember was Jesus dragging me away and Murphy saying, "Make sure he's all right."

6

I was in a small room on a small bed. A cobalt blue, tearshaped Tiffany lamp provided a low, easy light. My head and ribs hurt so much I thought they must be broken. My face had been wiped with a towel, now on the floor. Edith, all five feet seven inches of her, sat in a green Morris chair. Jesus leaned against the closed door. His robes were bloody.

"God," I said.

"Henry," said Edith. "The man you bit was Griffith's chauffeur."

"Max?"

"He hit you," said Edith. "If Michael hadn't grabbed him, he would have kicked you in the head. He might have killed you."

"That's why I kicked you," said Jesus.

"You kicked me?"

"I had to get you off him. You bit him quite badly."

"He hit me hard."

"Oh, Henry," said Edith, moving forward and throwing a shadow over a photograph of the house that showed its three stories winding into the hill. "You're a coward. You punched Michael when he wasn't expecting it. You bit someone. I'm ashamed of you. Your father, the soldier, would be ashamed."

"You, ashamed?" I said, sitting up, head hurting. "I gave Murphy as much warning as you gave me you were going to f*** him. Don't talk to me about courage. You're a liar. A cheat."

"Michael is braver than you," said Edith. "He laughed at you in front of everyone."

"I'm leaving," said Jesus.

"So am I," said Edith.

"Please, no," I said. My voice was suddenly as pathetic as a child's. God, I didn't want Edith to leave. The door opened and closed. Jesus and his bloody robes were gone. "Please, don't go."

Edith sat by the light. She looked so handsome, so able to say what she had to say. "We're finished."

"It's over," I said, but couldn't imagine not discussing the party, mirrors, Jews, gorgeous women, Griffith and Gish with her before going to bed. I couldn't imagine falling asleep or wind coming off Lake Ontario without her solid body. I couldn't imagine being alone.

"You gave me no choice," she said.

"You made your choice three years ago," I said. "Don't tell me it could have been different. It's too cruel."

"I don't know how it might have been," said Edith. "I've been unhappy a long time."

"You've been with Murphy a long time."

"I've been without you longer. You went away in your head years ago, Henry."

"Why didn't you tell me you were so unhappy?"

"I tried."

I looked at the heavy, closed curtains. They were red and yellow with Apache sun symbols, circles flanked by equal signs. Feathered serpents went up jagged pyramids. Aztec. "I can't imagine not being with you."

"Can you imagine being with me after Michael?"

The way she said his name sent a bolt of anger right through the pain in my head and ribs.

"I don't think you can," said Edith.

"I can. I can."

"But that isn't the point, is it?"

"I love you," I said.

"That," said Edith, "is the last refuge of a scoundrel."

I smiled at her use of Dr. Johnson. "We've known each other our whole lives, Edith. Do you remember standing in the hall at Miss Walker's Dancing School on Euclid Avenue because we giggled?"

"I remember," said Edith, "and it's not enough. You didn't take care of Harry and me. We needed you. Now you can't even take care of yourself. I pity you, Henry."

"I love you," I said quietly, touching my head.

"I love you too. In a way. And I always will. But loving you and living with you are different. I don't want to live with you." The light around Edith's head made her thick hair look so brown. I wanted to touch it. "I need more," she said. "I'm tired. I need someone to take care of me. Someone to take care of Harry."

"I can change," I said. "I can learn."

"You're not a giving person, Henry."

"Do you love Murphy?"

"I need Michael," said Edith. "You're a luxury I can no longer afford."

"After losing money in the Federal League? It was an expensive way to carry on an affair."

"I wanted a big-league club," she said. "Just like you did once. That's over now. I have to take care of Harry and myself."

I sat up. "I admire your nerve, Edith, but you gambled on the wrong league. Now you're gambling on the wrong man."

"It's over, Henry."

My side hurt but it was bearable. I touched my face. "You have it all planned?"

"There will be money when the Hustlers are sold. We'll pay our debts," said Edith, moving so she blocked the light. Her face was in the dark.

"Suppose I don't want to sell my half?"

"Do you have money to buy mine?" said Edith. "I have

to sell. I have debts."

I shook my head. I didn't have the money or want the club without her. "We could try," I said. "For Harry."

"Two are not one," said Edith. "People grow apart, Henry. It's a tragic fact."

"I could change."

"Henry, you're very charming. You're very handsome and you're wonderful company, but that doesn't make a marriage. Or a father."

"I love you." There was nothing else to say. I was out of words.

"You may love me, but you love yourself more, and that will get you through. No matter how awful you feel, you'll find a woman to take of you."

"Three years?" I could barely say it.

"I need someone who loves me now," said Edith. "Not someone who loves the past. You live backwards. The past is more important than your own son. And much more important than me."

"You are the past."

"I'm not, Henry. I'm something else. And sadly, so are you." Edith got up. She turned at the door, already a crimson ghost, and looked back.

"All right," I said. "I'm divorcing you." I didn't mention Harry. My plan was all I had left in the world.

Edith nodded and left. The door closed and I was alone in the small room with the Apache-Aztec curtains.

For the first time in my life, I truly wished I were dead.

7

I was alone in the saffron room with the blue lamp. Serpents and pyramids moved in a red and yellow swirl. The lamp pulsated and glowed furiously like something about to explode and turn the world blue. I was falling. Exploding. Except nothing was happening. I fell to my knees. I wanted to pray, but pray to what? I didn't believe. What would I say? Let me die? Give me another chance? With Edith? Harry? Griffith? I thought about crying or breaking the lamp or screaming and rolling on the floor but that would have been acting.

I slapped the floor over and over.

My head hurt.

My side hurt.

My head hurt.

My side hurt.

I did it until there was only a tremendous, rising numbness.

8

I couldn't stay in the small room. The humiliation of facing stars, Jews, nobodies, anybody, was better than remorse and Aztec curtains. Better hated than alone. Better an assassin than a cuckold. I pulled myself up. My ribs hurt but I was pretty sure they weren't broken. I drew back the curtain and looked at my face. It was bruised, cut, red, my mouth was sore. My tongue hurt.

I wanted to find Lillian, and if I couldn't, then Jesus or a stranger, a whore. Anyone until the sun came up.

I dragged myself out onto the balcony. The orchestra was playing. They ignored me. Other people moved away shaking heads. Bobby Harron and Dorothy Gish pointed from below. A ripple of recognition—something between a hush and a hiss—went round dancers, talkers, spectators; pointing fingers, tilting heads, nods and smirks flew across the mirrors. I stood on the balcony, hands apart, squeezing the railing so I wouldn't shake, and let them stare. I don't know how long I stood. The arrogance of shame was better than remorse, so I looked into the silver ball, blinded by white light, blue dome, smoke from dozens of cigars, mirrors. People stared and I soaked up murmuring disapproval. Thomas Ince pointed at me, then the door. Adolph Zukor sneered like his sneer could make me disappear. Theda Bara looked and looked away, full of public disdain, making sure everyone noticed. Mack Sennett shook a fist as if he wanted to come up and finish the job. Carl Laemmle wouldn't look, as if I'd hurt him. Fairbanks the acrobat, Little Mary, her mother and brother Jack were in a group that looked ready to lynch me. I saw Mabel Normand at the edge of the crowd looking away. Only Fatty Arbuckle smiled as if there might be another side to the story. I stood in eternity. No one would speak to me. No one could stare at anything else. Would Lillian talk to me?

"Throw the bounder out!"

"Disgraceful!"

"Coward!"

"Dog!"

Something white touched my shoulder. I thought it was Jesus, but it was D. W. Griffith.

"Biographer bites chauffeur. That's a problem Dr. Johnson didn't face."

Everyone below watched. Everyone on the balcony quieted. We had the attention of ballroom, balcony, and second floor. What a contrast! Griffith was radiant in his flawless white suit—as radiant as Jesus or a charging Klansmen. My face was starting to look like eggplant. My suit was splattered with blood and tequila. A pocket was torn, the armpits stained with sweat, and my shoes had dried blood on them. I'm sure I smelled.

"This is my interview?" I said, not extending my hand.

Lillian was behind Griffith. She smiled. Lillian was beside Julian Johnson, of *Photoplay,* and Adolph Zukor in a crowd that included Henabery, Mae Marsh, Bobby Harron, Dorothy Gish, Mrs. Gish, and Miriam Cooper. Griffith had an entourage: a reporter, beautiful women, the sharp eye of Zukor the producer, an assistant director, but no Max. He had people who count, and they were here for the kill. The public humiliation of Henry Harrison, Harvard man, photoplay critic, Yankee, in front of Hollywood.

"You're wearing white like the Klan," I said.

"You should be wearing a straitjacket, Harrison."

"Do you always bring a posse?"

"I might need one talking to you."

My back was to the railing now. I stood in intense light. The Master and entourage were to the right. The silver ball studded with impossibly bright bulbs must have been over my head like an explosion. The orchestra was at my left. Jesus appeared, white and bloody, as if on his way to the cross, and stretched his arms, blessing us, but no one looked. They wanted Griffith. I was trapped.

"You've returned the black race to psychological slavery." I spat the words out through an aching jaw. "The Negroes in *Birth* are a disgrace. An obscenity."

"Here's an expert on disgrace," said Griffith, loudly. The oboe player blew a disrespectful low note like a fart. People laughed.

Griffith stood tall. None of the men behind him was as tall. Behind him was an open door where more people listened, jostling for a better view. I saw the hidalgo, his saffron punch, and the hell-mouth fireplace. Light from the immense ball chandelier lit Griffith from head to toe without shadow. It lit me too—rumpled suit, blood, sweat.

"Your ignorance of Reconstruction is rivaled only by your ignorance of fighting." Griffith spoke like an actor on stage. "It belittles your magazine and your university."

The clarinet made a sound like barking.

"What university did *you* attend?" I shouted.

"The one where you are forced to learn the truth. The world."

I touched my face. It hurt. "What truth is there in making Negroes look like animals? You think because you make money, you know the truth?"

"Truth," said Griffith, turning to his crowd. "As Pilate said, 'What is truth?'"

The whole orchestra broke into a few bars of the Hallelujah Chorus. Jesus extended his arms as if being stretched on the cross.

"Why crucify the black race?" I yelled. Bloody spit flew. "Haven't they had enough?"

More Hallelujah.

"Harrison," Griffith gestured the orchestra quiet. "There are good blacks and bad blacks, just as there are good and bad whites. There are also susceptible blacks. Ignorant, uneducated, barely out of slavery, and not so long out of Africa. They are manipulated by unscrupulous whites. This happened in Reconstruction, and happens now in northern cities where machine politicians buy the Negro vote."

Griffith turned to the crowd with a slight bow. He was full of that cocksure Southern confidence that postures but can't think.

"You've done something wrong. Immoral. Bigoted," I said.

"Whereas you merely hit first and bite."

"I don't make money off it."

"No," said Griffith, "but you're willing to make money off me."

"I don't sell bigotry!"

The oboe made another farting sound.

"Harrison, if you can't see the difference between good and bad blacks, you're not likely to see the difference between good and bad photoplay directors."

"There are no good blacks in *Birth of a Nation!*" I shouted. My jaw hurt. "Only subservient house niggers or liberty-drunk villains with radical notions like serving in the state legislature, or marrying whomever they want. Don't you understand there might be some other kind of Negro?"

The place was silent. Even the oboe. Everyone listened. Jesus pointed at Griffith, indicating it was his turn.

"Not during Reconstruction, Harrison. The Negroes were under the spell of carpetbaggers."

"All of them? You can't possibly believe that."

The entire house was still. I was sure there were people who agreed with me but wouldn't confront Griffith.

"No one respects the blacks who deserve respect more than I!" said Griffith. "It's in *Birth*. The Loyal Servants mourn the Little Sister as much as any. The man is whipped for being loyal to the Camerons. Really, Harrison, must I explain the obvious?"

"The obvious is you accept blacks when they behave as servants and inferiors. Don't you understand, you can't accept some and not all?"

Jesus raised a finger, as if I'd made a good point.

"Tell me, Harrison," countered Griffith, "what Negroes do you accept?"

"I went to Harvard with Monroe Trotter."

"The famous Trotter? Who was rude to President Wilson?"

The orchestra struck up *Hail to the Chief*.

"Has the famous Trotter eaten in your house? At your club? Does he live next door? Is he your friend?"

"Monroe can eat at the Harvard Club."

"As an equal? Who are your other Negro friends?"

"I respect the group," I said, but Griffith was partially right. Negroes don't visit my house, my club, or live next door. The orchestra began *Ten Thousand Men of Harvard*.

Griffith quieted them. "Harrison, I've spent half my life in the North. I've seen the deal Negroes get above the Mason-Dixon Line. The so-called equality in restaurants, hotels, clubs, churches. Northerners talk equality but don't practice it. Your system is as hard as ours, with the exception of the vote, but the districts are drawn so blacks have no power. Harrison, the Negro has a hard lot North or South, but in the South we have rules, and when they're followed, we talk, live near each other, even like each other." Griffith spoke slowly. He was amazingly sure of himself.

The orchestra played *Dixie* but stopped after a look from Griffith.

"If you're so fond of blacks, why didn't you cast any in the Negro roles in *Birth* instead of white actors in blackface?"

Griffith looked out at the crowd; his white suit sparkled. He was like a pope on a balcony. "I needed my own actors."

"To make Negroes look like animals?"

"The *Birth* is history. I've offered ten thousand dollars to anyone who can prove it isn't historically accurate. No one has claimed the money!"

I caught Lillian's eye. She was next to Zukor and very unhappy. The ex-furrier said, "Enough. Throw him out!" There were cries of "I'll fight him!" "Cad!" "Tar and feather him!" "Bite him!" Fairbanks, Jack Pickford, and a cadre of husky men started for the stairs. The orchestra broke into *A Hot Time in the Old Town Tonight* and the image of John Wilkes Booth jumping off the balcony in *Birth of a Nation* flashed before my eyes.

Griffith looked out to the crowd and held up his hands. "At least the man says to my face what he said in print! Give him that! I'll talk to him in private!"

"What?" I said.

"Let's go," said Griffith, in a low voice.

I followed. The Klan-white, gleaming, self-possessed master of illusion, manipulator, and bigot led me away from the crowd. I looked at Lillian, who brightened. Zukor looked disappointed, Mae Marsh relieved; Miriam Cooper frowned. The music got louder. Griffith and I went by the Pharisee serving punch, and D. W. said, "Just keep moving. They'll forget you in a minute." We went into a stucco hall lined with doors, like a hotel. Griffith opened a door and we were in the saffron room with the Morris chair, cobalt blue lamp, and Apache-Aztec curtains. The bloody towel was still on the floor.

I sat on the bed. Griffith took the chair. He noticed the

lamp and said, "It looks like a parachute. I like a design from the last century which takes a shape from this one."

The Master studied me. His eye was sharp and blue. Not blue like the disappearing, diaphanous smoky light in the dome, or blue that would swallow the world, but blue that pierced, observed, judged. His immaculate suit, along with the light of the lamp, seemed to glow. The "Master" was too real and not real at all. He seemed to be onstage, and we seemed to be surrounded by props, even the bloody towel and my bruised face. It all seemed staged.

"Why did you help me?" I said. "I despise you."

"Sometimes a man needs help."

"Me?"

"Especially you."

"We're enemies," I said, rubbing my head.

"I dislike hypocrisy more than argument," said Griffith. "Someone needed to take charge, and you're writing a book about me."

"After biting your chauffeur? I'm a joke."

"Not if I help you. Max will live."

"Why in God's name would you do that?"

"I want you to change your mind about me. And publish it in *The Atlantic.*"

"I won't. You can't take back *Birth of a Nation* and I won't take back 'The Man Who Gave *Birth.*'"

"Harrison, you need to know me *and* the photoplay better. You also need something to do. Miss Geesh told me your life has become difficult."

"Is winning me over one more 'impossible thing,' like the Shot?"

"You and the Shot are indeed a challenge, but as I said, sometimes a man needs help. Besides, Miss Geesh likes you."

"You need help," I said, refusing to be deflected or seduced, even by kindness. "You should reconsider your treatment of the black race."

Griffith sat back. I detected the trace of a smile. "Harrison, you slugged one man and bit another. You go around with Howard Gaye, who dresses up like Jesus Christ and embarrasses Jews. We have some things to discuss."

"What?"

"Jews, Harrison. You didn't complain when Howard Gaye was embarrassing them. You laughed."

"I wasn't laughing at the Jews."

"But you feel superior to them. Admit it."

"I don't like anti-Semitism," I said.

"You don't like Jews either."

I shrugged.

"Are Jews all the same?" said Griffith. "Is Carl Laemmle like Sam Goldfish? Would you consider the possibility that prejudice wasn't invented in the South?"

I dropped a name instead of answering Griffith's question. "Henry James told me Jews are destroying American culture. He says New York is a 'Jerusalem disinfected.'"

"Destroying American culture?" said Griffith. "Who destroyed my culture with Reconstruction?"

"I've never made anyone look like an animal, Mr. Griffith. Never."

"You just feel superior to Jews?"

My face got red.

Griffith held up his hand. "I'm not attacking you, Harrison. I'm suggesting you judge a little quickly. I just want you to think about prejudice. Maybe we all have some. Just like we all have pain."

"Mr. Griffith, I saw a black man cry in Boston after seeing *Birth*. He put his hands over his face and kept saying, 'Why he do this to us?' I saw it. He just kept saying, 'Why? Why? Why he do this to us?' I've never seen anyone humiliated like that."

The director looked up. Each blue eye caught a point of lamplight. "What you just told me is terrible. Worse than punching a man who . . ." He didn't finish the sentence. Griffith leaned toward me. "I have hurt their feelings, Harrison. I know that. I didn't intend to."

"What?"

"I told the truth as I know it. As I was brought up to know it. Maybe this isn't the whole truth. I know I hurt them and I must not do it again."

I looked at Griffith carefully. Did he mean this? I hardly believed he'd said it, just as I could hardly believe he'd kept me from being thrown out of the house. I was sure Griffith wanted to convert a Yankee critic in a Yankee magazine in the heart of old abolitionist country. He would be protecting himself from a hostile book while showing the world he could handle a harsh critic. Was this really about Lillian? In the unreal room, with the bloody towel and Aztec curtains, the immaculate master bigot was changing shapes—showing me he could be reasonable. Kind. Capable of learning. Capable of growing. Generous.

Was it manipulation?

Griffith was right about my anti-Semitism. I've always taken comfort in feeling superior to Jews and anyone else who hasn't owned a ball club, written a book, wasn't the son of a wounded Union soldier, hadn't married a woman like Edith, but I am prejudiced. I felt safe behind prejudice and secure as a genteel anti-Semite. It hurt having it pointed out.

I looked up and saw myself in the window. I saw a man in a bloody shirt between pyramids and serpents—a man who'd hit, bitten, actually wanted to kill—rather than face the reasons his wife left him.

"All right," I said. "I do feel superior to ex-furriers and immigrants who butcher the language. I hid behind Henry James. I am anti-Semitic and it's wrong. But I'd never make Jews look bad in print. I'd never create a vicious caricature they couldn't live down."

Griffith nodded.

"Do you wish," I said, "to say what you said about blacks, through me? Publicly?"

"No." Those blue eyes were on me. "I can't apologize for what I am. I believed I told the truth and that is what I will say publicly. But I am a motion picture director and that is where I must make peace with what I've done."

"In the new photoplay?"

"Precisely."

"The new photoplay scares me," I said. "The destruction of Babylon. The massacre of the Huguenots. The killing of Jesus. Are you preparing America for the world war? For race war?"

"No, Harrison. Wait until you see it. This is love's story. Love's story through the ages. The terrible struggle of love through history."

"You're touching deep things, Mr. Griffith. Babylon has the mystery and danger of the ancient world, which hold the mystery and danger of the most ancient part of our minds. You're deep in our culture. Deep in our psyches. You may not understand what you're touching. The violence and cruelty. The hidden things people are made of. Look what happened with *Birth*."

"Harrison, I couldn't put it better myself. You see profoundly into motion pictures. That's why I want you on my side. You've taught me a few things."

"Do you acknowledge the hurtfulness of *Birth*?"

"Yes."

"Will you acknowledge it publicly?"

"No."

"It could change people's feelings. It might ease the hurt and help the way blacks and whites see each other."

"I stand by *The Birth,* it's who I am, or who I was, but I'm doing something different now. Something I hope will affect people just as powerfully, but differently. I want to use the power of the motion picture in a way that's never been done. Use it for good. Unambiguous, unqualified good."

"You're a complicated man," I said, "and an honest one, at least in private." He said all this so easily. Was I being disarmed? Seduced?

"Harrison," Griffith sat up, so marvelously white in the light of the Tiffany lamp. "Tonight I asked Miss Geesh to marry me and she refused. This is a hard night. A long night. Talk a little. Indulge me."

"What?" I said, genuinely surprised.

"A hard night."

"A hard night," I repeated. This was the other flank—first he admitted prejudice, now pain. Was the Master getting another performance from another actor? "Miss Gish loves you," I said, deciding, like Griffith, to be honest in private. "But she needs you more than she loves you. She needs a different kind of love. A friend. A father."

"I know," said Griffith.

"To try to make it otherwise would be wrong."

Griffith looked up with hurt in those amazing blue eyes.

"She wants to be herself more than a wife," I said. "She wants her career. Her art."

"Couldn't she have both?"

"Can you?"

Griffith was quiet. He looked at me carefully. "Harrison, let the scene with your wife play how it will." He accentuated each word.

"Edith and I are finished."

"For now," said Griffith. "But you don't know what will happen. You don't know how she'll feel when you're gone and she's only got him. Maybe Edith will stay with him. Maybe she won't."

"She says I didn't take care of her," I said. I was supposed to interview Griffith, and Griffith was interviewing me.

"Did you?"

"I thought friendship and being faithful was taking care of her."

"It's a start."

I stared at the teardrop-parachute lamp and said, "It's too late."

Griffith didn't take his eyes off me.

"When my son Harry was born, I waited all night at the hospital, hoping, praying, thinking of things to say. I offered God anything I could think of for their safety. In the morning a nurse said go in, and Edith was sitting up holding the baby. She was covered in sweat and the hospital gown was falling off one shoulder, but she was smiling. It was a smile I'd never seen before. She was exhausted but triumphant. God upheld his end of the bargain.

"I was afraid to hold the baby, but did, and Edith lay back and closed her eyes. I told her she never looked more beautiful and gave the baby to a nurse. I passed out cigars and complimented the doctors and was joined by friends for champagne. I thought that's all there was to it."

"You have to forgive," said Griffith, looking at me sharply.

"Would you forgive a woman who . . . ?" I looked at that stern angular face.

"You have to forgive yourself for letting this happen."

My head hurt. My tongue hurt. The curtains moved, trees rustled, wind whispered at the window.

Griffith listened. "You hate yourself more than you hate me."

I listened. I wanted to catch him and he caught me.

"There's nothing as poetic as wind in trees." After a minute of mysterious sound he said, "What did you lose, besides Edith, that you'll never get back?"

"Self-respect."

"Forever?"

"Pride. I lost the person I thought I was."

Griffith sat up. "What you lost, Harrison, was inno-cence."

"Edith lost that."

"No, Harrison, you did. You learned the world is dif-ferent than you thought. You learned your magic isn't as powerful as you think. You learned the world has other men in it. All of us think we are alone in Eden with our women, but we aren't. Even Adam wasn't."

The red and yellow curtains covered an entire wall. The wind stirred them into a shimmering maze of shapes, lines moved through circles, pyramids oscillated into triangles, colors plumed on serpents, and serpents chased red and green tails up the jagged steps of pyramids. Tears were in my eyes. "I didn't uphold the bargain."

"You will next time," said Griffith. "It's not what happens, Harrison, it's what you do about it. Are you going to kill that man?"

"No," I said. "But I'll divorce Edith and take the child."

"That'll be hard on the child."

"It's all hard," I said, thinking, I want it to be hard for them too.

"It's less hard if you learn from it." Griffith reached over and touched my shoulder. "What happened to make Edith follow this man?" He looked at me, carefully, judging. "What were you doing?"

"Writing a book."

"You had a ball club to run, a wife and a child, but you wrote a book," said Griffith. "Were you bored?"

"I'd gone as far as I could in baseball so I started writing. I told the story of King Saturday, the Indian, who once played for Cleveland. Writing is wonderful. It got to be a drug."

"What did Edith think of the book?"

"She encouraged me. She took over my duties with the club. That was too much with the child, so we hired Murphy."

"Your wife did your work and you wrote?"

"Yes," I said bitterly. "She did everything and I pushed

her away. I was only happy to see her when I'd finished for the day."

"And the book? Was it about Edith?"

"She was in it."

"Who else?"

"A woman I loved once. And a man Edith loved once."

"So the book was about you?"

"It was about the past," I said.

"Your past."

"My past," I said angrily. "But I never did what Edith did. I was never dishonest."

"You didn't have to be," said Griffith. "You had what you wanted."

We didn't say anything and I listened to the wind in the trees. "Why didn't she tell me?" I said, not to Griffith, but to the pyramids, the house, the night. "Why didn't she tell me she was so lonely?"

"You had to figure that out for yourself."

That stung.

"Harrison," said Griffith. "When you devote yourself to a book, or a photoplay, you go away. You live in another place. There's a price for that."

"But you," I said, eyes burning, "can live in another place. You can make worlds. You can go away and have everything."

"Everything except Miss Geesh," Griffith said. His face was red like mine.

"Let her go," I said.

"I love her, Harrison."

"You love work," I said. "So does she."

Griffith nodded but didn't speak.

I stared at the lamp and listened to the trees.

Griffith looked at me with that blue critical eye—the eye that never stops looking. The voice had sympathy; the eye didn't. "How long will you hate yourself?"

I didn't say anything.

"Damn it!" said Griffith, sitting up. "What's most important right now?"

"My son."

"What about him?"

"Keeping him from being raised by Murphy."

"Forget Murphy. That'll go to court. What are you going to do about your son?"

"Be with him as much as possible." I wished I hadn't told Griffith about taking Harry. That was my secret.

"Good. What else are you going to do?"

"Try to make a living while the club is sold and debts paid."

"So you will finish this book?"

"I'll try."

"Harrison, you may not believe this, but you're lucky. You're lucky because you'll treat your son differently now, and you're lucky because you have the opportunity to write about the photoplay. I'm doing something nobody has put into words, and you might be the man to do it, if you stop licking your wounds. I have wounds. I can't imagine anyone kissing Miss Geesh. That's going to be hard. Very hard. But I have more than wounds. So do you."

"You want me to stop attacking you," I said.

"Hang me. Do it for yourself." Griffith looked at me hard. "Do you know the saying, 'Generals always fight the last war'?"

I nodded.

"Don't fight a war that's over."

"What war?"

"Edith doesn't matter now. What matters is you. I'm not saying it doesn't hurt. I'm saying don't waste time."

We were quiet awhile, then I said, "You fought a war that's over. You fought your father's war."

Griffith watched the curtains. "We all fight our fathers' wars, don't we? In our own ways. But you have another war, and it isn't the one you just fought."

I looked at the pyramids and serpents. The curtains were as remote as Babylon.

Griffith saw and said, "The Aztecs were strange people, Harrison. Strange people with pyramids where beating hearts were cut out and held up to the sun. We have the Eucharist. They had to have blood. We wait for Him, and they waited for a god to cross the sea and time and sacrifice their whole culture. They couldn't understand something new. The past was the future. The future couldn't be anything but the past. Cortez slaughtered them."

IV

MIDNIGHT

April 3, 1916
12:00 a.m. to 3:00 a.m.

1

Lord, I believe; help thou mine unbelief." Jesus stood in the door of the saffron room, his long, delicate face flushed with drink, robes wrinkled. He flashed a mad, inviting smile.

I looked up, touched the cut on my chin, and nodded. I was puzzled, almost dazed, by what I'd seen of D. W. Griffith. In less than two hours the Master had gone from gleaming-white racist apologist, to thoughtful self-critic, to almost a friend. I knew he was performing, but there was the possibility the man was trying to understand his mistakes, and urging me to do the same. Griffith challenged me to be more than a self-righteous critic and scorned husband. Whatever his motivation, he saw things clearly. Griffith had let me talk and I'd said what I had to. He'd listened and told me what he thought. I thought I had an enemy; now I wasn't sure. What had been the last chapter of my book was an offer for the first chapter of a different story.

"I talked to Griffith," I said.

"That's another way of being alone," said Jesus. His robes took on a bluish tint in the Tiffany light that had made Griffith's suit so white. "No matter what Griffith said, he's only talking about himself. D. W. watches people to study their movement. Everything goes in the next photoplay."

"What happens if I go downstairs?" I said. I wanted to think about Griffith, not listen to an Englishman's gospel of cynicism.

"Nothing. You're under D. W.'s protection. Strange

bird. Bite his chauffeur and he looks after you."

"Strange, indeed," I said, looking at a man dressed in bloody robes leaning against a red door. "Griffith admitted to me *Birth* had hurt blacks and said he wouldn't hurt their feelings again. He said he'd never admit that in public, then offered to help with my book."

"Harrison, did you think D. W.'d say he hates niggers and recruit you into the Klan? Damn right he'd never admit saying that. He'd deny ever talking to you. They don't call him Master for nothing."

"Griffith's a complicated man."

"Bollocks!" said Jesus. "Griffith wants to say, 'Look how this Harvard–*Atlantic Monthly* man changed his opinion of me.' When Adolph Zukor saw a line of suckers bent over Kinetoscopes in New York's Tenderloin, he said, 'A Jew could make a lot of money at this.' D. W. wants more. He wants to be respectable. Griffith wants the world to call him genius. He doesn't want northern intelligentsia—that's you, bite and all—saying he's returned the black race to psychological slavery, as you put it so succinctly in front of the ninnies of Hollywood."

"Who's the real D. W. Griffith?" I said.

"The question is, who's the real you?" said Jesus. "Are you the champion of the blacks, willing to stand up and take on the most powerful man in motion pictures? Or do you cut a deal to save your book after making a fool of yourself?"

"You just want dirt to keep Griffith from firing you!" I said, angrily.

"Of course. But regardless of what happens to me, you have your conscience to answer to." Jesus lifted his palms heavenward.

"Your concern for my conscience is touching."

"Yanks are all the same," said Jesus. "If you don't have a selfish reason for helping them, they distrust you."

"The Jews feel the same way about the first fellow dressed like that."

Jesus laughed. "Touché, Harrison. Now back to business. The immediate issue is getting even with your wife. You're not going to hit or bite anybody, are you?"

"No. I'm sorry I hit Murphy but I'm glad."

Jesus' arms were at his side. "You had to try to get even. For your self-respect."

"I thought you preached forgiveness?"

"It's easier to forgive after you've gotten even."

I laughed out loud.

"Laugh, Harrison, and you'll get through the night. It's good you hit that idiot, otherwise hell has no bottom. Let's forget about him and deal with Edith."

"How?"

"By getting another woman."

I wanted to see Lillian but she was probably gone and that made me terribly sad. I thought about Harry, and how tomorrow we would be on a train heading east and Edith would be frantic. Instead of unrestrained license after years of lying and planning, Edith would worry—worry herself sick. It was cruel, but if she thought I was so weak I'd do nothing, she was wrong.

"How will I get back to the bungalow?" I said.

"I'll take you and whoever before I go to Gerty."

"Are you leaving?"

"Not before saving your soul. Let's start with a live show."

"Upstairs?"

"Who told you?"

The wind was down and the pyramids and serpents were still. I didn't want to spy on Griffith. Whatever he was, he'd been fair. Lillian had been more than fair.

"They're up there." Jesus' voice was particularly British and mean.

"Who?"

"All of them."

"Edith?"

"What shall a man give in exchange for his soul?"

"Let's go," I said.

"Do you think you can see something and it will change your life? That's Griffith. What can you see that you don't already know?"

I knew I shouldn't. But I had to. I couldn't stay away from the show.

2

Jesus led me up stairs so narrow we had to turn to keep our shoulders from rubbing the stone walls. We were somewhere in the back of the monstrous house. I had to see Edith and Murphy—I had to see the end—even if I couldn't bear it. I moved in a trance.

"The rear of the place was copied after a Norman chateau," said Jesus. "Lacking the Norman countryside, the bloke built passageways to view his own rooms."

We emerged into a wider, smoother stone passageway, lit by dim electric lights in shaded sconces, turned a corner, and found ourselves on a walkway with rough walls of granite block on one side and high arches and wrought-iron screens on the other. It functioned as an observation deck for the semicircle of rooms adjacent to the ballroom. We could see and listen into these rooms without being seen. I don't like heights but aggressively looked down. Suddenly Jesus pointed and we stopped.

It wasn't Edith. That was a relief.

"The Master," said Jesus.

In an alcove behind a row of potted African ferns, D. W. Griffith and Lillian Gish sat on a Carrara marble bench. They were lit by electric candles in silver sconces on a wall covered with palm fronds. Lillian looked very beautiful and very serious by the wavering electric light. Her gown was a mirage of iridescent greens, set off by neat black lace gloves and her preternaturally white skin. She sat next to Griffith, who looked very handsome in his impeccable white suit. They were like figures in a glass Easter egg.

"I love you," said Griffith, in a weary voice.

"I love you too," said Lillian. Her voice was fresh and

clear. Her eyes showed fatigue and a trace of pity.

"Please marry me."

"I'm an actress, not a wife."

"I know," said Griffith.

I started to move away.

"Don't you want to see the real D. W. Griffith?" said Jesus. "Will he threaten? Beg? Hit?"

I hesitated.

The Master rose. He stood tall and neatly creased, like an officer reviewing troops. "Marry me," he said. "It would look very fine."

"Let's not talk about this," said Lillian. "Let's talk about the Shot. Can Billy keep it in focus?"

"I don't want to watch," I said, moving away. "This isn't my business."

Jesus lingered, hands on the screen. "She wants to know if the Shot is too expensive to try again. He says it is. He says if it works it will expand the universal language. Bollocks!"

Jesus followed me, robes swinging like a demented angel.

3

We went again by arches and screens along the dim stone passageway. It was like walking through a dungeon. The stone was cold, the light bad—punishment waited. I stumbled and scraped my knuckles on the wall. Jesus glided along the rough, curving corridor until he stopped abruptly, we collided, and he pointed down.

In an alcove lit by flickering brass sconces, Edith and Murphy sat on a long, black velveteen couch.

"Voilà," said Jesus.

I saw them clearly. Murphy massaged his cheek. Edith looked kindly at him in the unstable light. Her hat was on a pastel carpet where pastel shepherds and maidens frolicked. Behind them, in a gold-leaf frame was an enormous oil of a scantily clad couple.

"They're not doing anything," I whispered.

"Do you think I'd let you look if they were?" said Jesus. "On the other hand, it could happen. I'll leave you to Eden," he enunciated the words quietly but carefully, "scene of our first betrayal." Jesus stepped back. "You want to see your wife destroy herself? Think it will stop the photoplay running in your head? It won't. Find a woman."

I said nothing and Jesus moved away. His robes danced down the dim passageway.

Edith's dress rustled. I heard it perfectly.

Murphy sat up. "I didn't think Mr. Effectual would hit me. He surprised me."

They had a name for me? Edith and Murphy had a name for me?

"You were wonderful," said Edith.

Her voice was comforting, admiring. It was awful.

"Henry kept coming after that man hit him," said

Murphy. "He's crazy. If he'd bitten me, he would have bitten through my leg."

"You saved him," said Edith, in the same soothing, admiring tone.

"Somebody always does," said Murphy. His voice was sharp, hard.

"Not this time," said Edith. "Henry's on his own. The last time was in Cleveland. Long ago."

"When he bet on crooked baseball games," said Murphy.

I stood, breathless, hands flat on an iron screen. Numb.

"Long ago," said Edith again, looking up at the screen. I wanted to shout, "You loved me! You did!" but it would have come out a whisper.

"That was a long time ago, Edith," said Murphy. "You were young and taken in."

"Yes," said Edith, "and it was wonderful."

"Edith, we're not young anymore. We don't need memories. You and I don't live in the past. We live now. We take care of people." Murphy touched his mustache. An awful little thing. It's remarkable how many short men have mustaches.

"Henry's very angry," said Edith, as if she hadn't been listening to Murphy. As if she'd been thinking about Cleveland and the past and the long time we shared.

I couldn't breathe. My palms pressed against cold metal. I heard steps and turned, but no one was there. Not Jesus or Griffith or Lillian. No one at all.

"Henry's always angry, Edith. He's a child. Spoiled by you and everyone else. Harvard man? He did nothing there but drink. Owner of a ball club? Purchased with money made betting on crooked games. What has Henry ever worked for? You did the work and he provided entertainment. What kind of life was that?"

"He worked to get me."

"Did he bite you?"

They laughed. Edith was back in the present. Mr. Effectual was gone.

I stared at her. The garnet crepe dress and lace were a deep, unsteady red, like flame at a distance. I couldn't watch and couldn't not watch. The alcove seemed to expand and contract—couch, sconces, shepherds, maidens, all shimmered. Time stopped, dilated, swallowed them and swallowed me. Could I watch them f***? Is that what I wanted? Pure hate? It was a photoplay—not real but too real, except I could hear. Edith unknowingly stared at me. I wanted to yell, "I'm here! Here!" and jump through the screen and make them see me, but I was gone. Mr. Effectual was gone.

Murphy got up and walked back and forth. His heels silently turned on the carpet.

"Someone always takes care of Henry," he said. "You needn't worry. A friend lets him write for *The Atlantic* and then arranges a book contract. Someone always helps Henry. He gets by, Edith. Henry always gets by. You and I take care of ourselves. You ran the Hustlers. I worked for everything I've got." Murphy touched his chest with his thumb. I don't know whether this was a courtroom gesture, or something picked up from his father, a trolley conductor.

"It was fine until Harry was born," said Edith. "Then it got too hard."

"You didn't need two infants," said Murphy.

"No, I didn't."

I saw clearly. I heard myself breathe. Edith thought I was something to be taken care of. Pitied maybe. But not a partner—not for raising Harry, or getting old, or even love in the afternoon. I belonged to Cleveland, to the world before Harry, a world she didn't need. I was gone.

"We'll make the money back," said Murphy. "We're a team. We can't be stopped."

"There'll be a divorce. Do you want a divorced woman? Henry may try to take Harry in court."

My mouth and tongue were dry. Mr. Effectual will take Harry. Mr. Effectual will make you very unhappy.

"I want you any way I can have you," said Murphy. "And we'll see about Harry. Henry may be mentally incompetent."

"And I'm an adulteress."

"Can he prove it? In California?"

"I'm tired of lying," said Edith.

"I'll get a good lawyer. The best. Henry will do himself in. Tonight he committed two felonies in front of hundreds of witnesses. He's irrational. Not fit to be a father. Mr. Effectual won't handle a divorce any better than he handled marriage."

I heard steps again. I looked but no one was there. No one.

"Henry has a right to be angry," said Edith.

Murphy paced in a circle over half-naked shepherds and maidens. He talked about my anger and said anger was all I had. He said I posed as a gentleman of ruined family and talked so much about Antietam you'd think I'd been there, and he wondered if anyone ever got so much out of being distantly related to two bad presidents. He doubted we were related at all. Murphy looked earnestly at Edith and said, "You have me. I can take care of you. I love you," and I watched Edith's hands because I couldn't bear to watch her eyes if she said she loved him. Murphy got angry and said what right did I have to be angry? Because no one read my book? Was I bored with baseball? Bored with her? He wasn't bored. He could never be bored because he loved her. Murphy paced. He touched his chest with his thumb again, then Edith reached up and pulled him to her. Her delicate fingers patted his reddish hair and she kissed the top of his head. It was a kindly kiss—sweet, almost mocking. Protective. "I don't think he'll ever forgive me," she said.

For an instant I wondered if Murphy were so different from me. He wanted to be loved and loved best. He needed her. I felt like running away.

"Forgive *you*?" Murphy shouted, pulling away and stomping on the carpet. "Have you forgiven *him*? Have you forgiven him for leaving you alone while he wrote in a tower! Have you forgiven him for yelling at little Harry

137

when he'd go in the tower? Remember five years ago when you couldn't sleep? Where was Mr. Effectual then? Did he stay up? Was he sympathetic? No. Henry needed his sleep. To write. To write what? A book about himself so filthy it had to be changed by editors! You started coming to work at five in the morning because you couldn't sleep. I was there for work. Then I was there for you. Remember those mornings? Remember when I burned my finger lighting the gas and you kissed it? We loved running that club. We're so alike. Edith, he abandoned you! He loves a girl who wore yellow in the 1890s. I love the woman. Edith, you're the perfect person."

"There are parts of Henry I will miss." Edith looked up. She looked at me without knowing it. She said goodbye without knowing it.

"Miss?" Murphy shouted. "Henry, who can talk for thirty minutes and start every sentence with 'I'? Henry's wonderful past? Henry's ideas? Henry's book? He's a little boy. He hit without warning and bit like a child in a school yard."

"All I said," said Edith, "was I'll miss some things about him."

Murphy turned his head so he was looking right at me. "Do you think he'll be thinking about *you* when he makes love to someone *else*?"

Edith jerked her head right, then back. She does that when angry.

Murphy started to say something but didn't. Edith was

silent. Why did the fool say that? It was the kind of thing I'd say. He said the worst thing he could because he was angry.

Murphy looked down at Edith's large hand resting over the black fringe hanging from the arm of the couch. I thought he would reach out and touch her, but he didn't. He had violated her privacy. "I'm sorry," he said. "I shouldn't have said that. I love you so much. It hurt when you said you'd miss him."

"You're right," said Edith, "he didn't think about me when we made love. And you're right, you shouldn't have said it."

"I'll never mention it again." Murphy kissed the top of her head.

"And you're right," said Edith, "I'm tired of taking care of Henry. One child is enough."

He loved her. I saw it. He loved her enough to say something hurtful, admit he was wrong, then comfort her. I turned away. I couldn't watch.

"We'll win in court," said Murphy. "It will be good for the boy. He needs a stronger hand. Do you want to raise a man women take care of?"

4

I found Jesus looking through the wrought-iron screen at Griffith and Gish and said, "Let's go."

"Give me half an hour, Harrison." He kept looking

down. "Damn it! All they do is talk. Lillian's not human."

"She's incorruptible."

"Give her time."

"There has to be something a person won't do," I said.

"Well, I wish she'd hurry up and do it."

∿

Jesus led me up stone steps through a white door into a hall barely lit by a solitary electric lamp with a purple shade. He pointed at a dim row of doors. "You can see into bedrooms, Henry. Chaplin. Arbuckle. Mack Sennett."

"I've seen enough."

Jesus bounded down the hall, going from door to door, which must have had peepholes. He looked, laughed, chuckled, pointed, and dashed to the next door, like a bee pollinating flowers.

I thought about looking, but watching strangers have sex seemed unbearably sad. Unbearably lonely.

The lamp sputtered and I was in the dark. For a minute, the white squiggles you see when you close your eyes competed with the afterimage of Jesus' robes disappearing down the hall. I was alone in the dark. A day of Babylon, a night of mirrors, Edith and Murphy, Jesus, the magic of Gish, the hauteur of Griffith, gave way to darkness. If, as I kept hearing, Griffith didn't want to make people think, or feel, or change, but *see*, I reached the Griffonian moment in reverse. I couldn't see and it was a relief. I was invisible and remembered Henry James nodding when I said I'd write in the first person, and the Master—the one without press agents—saying, "Don't be crucified by the first person," which I took to be the clever remark of an infinitely clever man, but in the dark, seeing shapes, lines, the blurry infinity of blackness, I knew what James meant. For a moment, when I literally couldn't see, I saw myself, hung, like meat, on the one-letter pronoun with its brutally single point of view.

I saw a paunchy, stained, middle-aged man hanging on a hook and looking down—limp, white, dead. He hadn't loved his wife or his child, and they went away.

V

LILLIAN

April 3, 1916
3:00 a.m. to dawn

1

The evening was in full swing at three o'clock. Dancers spun on the checkered parquet to the whirling rags of the orchestra, who gyrated on the balcony, jackets off and flung on the railing. Clarinets screeched at the ceiling, trumpets wagged, and the saxophone growled between the saxophone player's legs as the musicians cut loose. The dancers leapt, made a line which snaked around the ballroom, and threw their hands rhythmically in the air. Youth had taken over Eddie Rogers' house of mirrors, which at two in the morning was as bright as noon. There was jumping, cakewalking, laughing. No one paid attention to me. It was a midnight ramble and it was theirs.

I touched my jacket and remembered I had a letter from Tuck. I thought about going upstairs to read it but hesitated because Tuck's letters were full of pain and attempts to forgive his wife. I didn't think Tuck could or would forgive Starr, with or without the help of Jesus Christ—the real one. I wished him luck and I wanted to talk to him. I wished we weren't in California, where Murphy and Edith and I were just sinners in God's hand, cut away from friends.

I watched unchaperoned bit-players make a ragged, wild line and hop around the room—hands on wide satin hips, gloves on padded shoulders, coats shed and tossed at mirrors, braces undone—hardly a well-known face among them. They were free, playing for themselves, not the camera or the men who owned the cameras. Their energy made me feel better. I watched and wondered who would be famous? Who would drive a Stutz? Who would get rich? Who would survive?

Karl Brown bounced behind a pretty woman—a girl, really—who turned and smiled at him. Where were her parents? Who took care of that yellow hair and toothy grin? Brown touched the girl's cheek and she kissed him. Where were the parents of these gorgeous children throwing themselves at the night? Were mom and dad asleep in another time zone, grabbing a last wink before getting up to milk the cows in Maine, or awake in a Louisiana dawn pondering another day of chores just like all the other days? Maybe dad was sleeping off a drunk in Chicago or hadn't been heard from for years in Utica. Did a suspicious step-mom in Abilene or hard step-father in Cincinnati make life too difficult even for a pretty girl? Who knows why people leave small towns and grimy cities chasing what they tell us are dreams.

I stood on the balcony watching whipping hems and flying cuffs streak across parquet and mirrors, and saw Jesus and Jack Pickford talking to a sharp-eyed woman in a brown hat. Men approached her and were directed to a bevy of well-dressed but not flashy women, each in yellow with collars buttoned to the chin, who stood by mirrors. I came down the stairs and crossed the floor. Jesus filled the mirrors like a white bloody giant. A risen ghost.

Jack Pickford pointed at me and the woman shook her head, as if thanking him.

I walked over and the woman's hands went to her hips.

The madame was young but hard, competent, and looking her in the eye felt like pleading, even though I didn't want anything. The woman looked like she knew the price of everything, and something awful was in that precision.

"You're Harrison, right?" she said smartly.

"And you're who?" I said. "Mary Magdalene?"

"Sorry," she said. "No writers, biters or three-way men."

"There's nothing you have I want," I said.

"Don't be hasty," said Jesus.

In the mirrors I looked like a funhouse bum—dried blood on a rumpled suit and an ugly bruise on a cheek beginning to sprout salt and pepper stubble. "I want to go home," I said, which was as close to poetry as I could manage at three a.m. This disciplinarian *cum* accountant looked at me sternly. I think she wanted to turn me down in front of her girls to show them her discretion.

"My girls don't go with crazies," said the woman.

"Nymph in thy orisons, be all my sins remembered," I said, with loud disdain. "I write for *The Atlantic Monthly.*"

"Don't worry about the monthlies, mister," she said, looking over her shoulder at two burly men who looked like off-duty coppers, and pursing her lips and raising her head, gestured at me.

I put my arms out like Christ on the cross and saw myself again—a wrinkled, stained, crucified bum. Jesus put his arms out and grimaced, presenting the full force of beard, blue eyes, beautiful hands, head tilted in agony. The actor seemed to levitate. The woman threw out her arms—the put-upon, crucified procuress—and three fools looked at each other in mirror after mirror. A pimp, a cuckold, an actor—a cheap, conspiring mockery. The burly men circled, hands in pockets, eyes on me.

"Let's go," said Jesus, pulling me away.

We crossed the parquet to the door, and he said, "Sheriff's department. Leave it be."

"Awful woman," I said.

"Why criticize?" said Jesus. "You could learn a lot from her."

We stepped outside in the cold night. I didn't care about the woman. I wanted to sleep and plan for tomorrow. For some reason I thought of Edith and her smiles—the dare-to-touch-me-dare-to-show-yourself smile at Miss Walker's, the dare-to-love smile on our honeymoon in Maine, the incomparable smile after giving birth to Harry. I wished I'd learned from them. I wished I'd learned before now.

We passed a swimming pool where someone had thrown roses, which drifted toward chalky walls. The water made a small lapping sound. A big man, maybe Roscoe Arbuckle, had passed out near the diving board, a bottle in the grass by his hand—someone else deep in the night with no one to love—and we came to an azalea-bordered edge of lawn overlooking the city. A cold wind blew over the Los Angeles basin. Patches of light and great swatches of dark-ness stretched from the Hollywood Hills, across the speckled basin, to the black Baldwin Hills. I stared into a cold wind. Nowhere in America can one look over a city, as one can from these hills and see Los Angeles, which has trapped smoke and fog since the time of the Indians, and now snares population as America finishes its western trip, and comes to this valley, with its little girl-women, speculators, maverick religions, losers, and Englishmen dressed as Jesus Christ.

"Look," said Jesus.

Either a woman or spirit was standing by a eucalyptus tree looking at Los Angeles. The spirit wore a black dress with a white collar and white trim at the wrists and looked ready to disappear on the wind and be part of the night. Jesus whispered, "Lillian Gish."

I don't know how he knew. I didn't, but moving like a sleepwalker, gliding, unsteady, to the eucalyptus, said, "I thought you left?" hardly believing this was real. The green and black-gloved woman who fox-trotted with Griffith was gone. Here was a tiny person, black and white, face now pale silver as a sliver of moon suddenly appearing over the basin. No rouge, no green, no lace, no dainty perfect feet but something luminous, silver, white, black, that belonged, and could only belong, to the night.

"Without seeing you?" The spirit moved.

"After what I did? I'm just a bum now."

"Are you all right?" said Lillian.

"No."

Jesus went back to the house, floating like a ghost over

the dark lawn, by the luminous pool with its drowned roses and snoring Fatty Arbuckle.

Lillian gazed at the sprinkling of lights spread like a thin galaxy through the basin. "You need someone to talk to. So do I."

"What happened with Griffith?" I said.

"Weren't you watching?" she said.

"How did you know?"

"The house of secrets has few secrets. I'm used to being watched."

"I'm cheap and disgusting," I said.

"If I were you, I would have looked."

"There's no low behavior I haven't engaged in tonight," I said.

"Yes, there is," said Lillian and laughed mischievously.

"What did you tell Griffith when I wasn't looking?"

"I said no," said Lillian.

"When I looked, he seemed to accept it."

"Mr. Griffith won't stop."

"We spoke," I said. "Griffith was kind. He said he loves you."

"What did you say?"

"I said you have your life and your art. Just like him."

Lillian kissed me. It was so quick, so warm, so marvelous. "Come with me."

"Where?"

"I have a car and a driver."

"You should be home. Where's your mother?"

"Mr. Griffith took me home. Mother is busy chaperoning Dorothy and Bobby Harron. I came back. They don't know."

"Why did you come?" I said.

"To show you I'm real."

"I only said that out of self-pity. I'm intimidated by you. And attracted."

"You're hurt, so you see things clearly," said Lillian. "Maybe just for a little while. Maybe the rest of your life. But right now, you're different from anybody I know or can talk to. I only see men who are acting. You aren't acting."

"You're kind, Lillian," I said, "and you are real. Beautiful and real. Very real."

"Only until dawn."

"Like a fairy tale," I said.

Lillian kissed me again. Her breath was sweet.

I stank.

2

Lillian went directly to a Studebaker Limousine parked a little ways down the hill. Jesus was outside Cibola in front of a clump of palm trees. He had been watching.

"God, Harrison, you're going to spend the rest of the night with the Virgin Lillian? What a bloody waste. She'll be a virgin when the night's over. You're on your own now. I'll see you tomorrow."

"Thanks," I said, "for not wanting me to be alone."

"No one's alone who believes in Jesus." He spread his arms again, throwing an enormous shadow against the palm trees.

I continued down the hill past two big cars with sleeping drivers to the Studebaker, a six-cylinder, seven-passenger black monster with crowned fenders and three doors. A driver, wearing black from shoe to cap, opened the rear door. Lillian was in back, which was upholstered in dark Bedford Blue Cord. There was a foot hassock, a vanity which folded out and offered a labyrinth of mirrors, and a glass partition separating us from the driver, who could be communicated with through a speaking tube. Lillian smiled, the driver closed the door, took his place behind the partition, and we drove into the hills. The man was old and had silver hair, cut very short, and sported one mangled ear, which made me think of Edith's family retainer, that old Scotsman with ears that looked like they had been aged underground like Roquefort cheese. I remembered Mackenzie as Lillian kissed me because I kissed Edith on a beautiful day in '98 when I thought Edith loved me but Edith loved someone else. That was the first time I thought Edith loved me when she loved someone else.

We came to know each other. We healed each other. I tried when it was easy. I stopped when it got to be work. When Harry came.

Lillian closed a velvet curtain. The driver couldn't see us even if he turned his head. "He doesn't know who I am," she whispered. I didn't believe that and kissed her, thinking of Maine when Edith and I surrendered to each other, admitted lies and mistakes, and thought we had given each other the rest of our lives.

The windows were up. Lillian and I were separated from the cold night by heavy doors, the solid body of the Studebaker, spotless glass, and chrome handles whose sparkle was hidden in the dark and gleamed only when Lillian briefly turned on two soft pearl lights to close the vanity, leaving us surrounded by fewer mirrors.

Lillian traced the outline of my face with a white finger, luminous after the light was gone, and touched the bruises, the cut by my eye, nose, sore mouth. Then I touched her face. Lillian let me touch that face which floats through movie houses and sets America dreaming. "You're real," I said, but I hardly knew whether anything was real. A beautiful woman in a car is ultra-real and not real—an adventure, a dare, a frontier—but I was, and she was, however briefly, delivered from the last twenty-four hours when everything and nothing seemed real. A lifetime can be lived between three a.m. and dawn.

Kissing was indescribably soft and warm. Lillian pulled me to her, the white trim at her wrists on my cheeks. My hands were on her slender shoulders, small back, dainty waist. Her tongue tried my tongue. The whole world became kissing and touching. Where was I? In a theater? In that place we go when we are alone with a woman? I was here, now, always. Kissing.

"Why do you let me touch you?" I said.

"Because you need it. I need it."

I touched her cheek, felt around her eyes, slid my fingers across her mouth.

"That's nice. Please do it again."

"What a wonderful mouth."

Lillian laughed. "Do you know why I always look so serious? So pensive?"

"Because you are."

Lillian giggled. "Because my mouth is too big. You're not photogenic if your mouth is wider than your eyes."

"You? Not photogenic?"

"It's true."

We laughed. Then she stopped. "You're real too, Mr. Harrison. I saw that in Mr. Griffith's tower."

"I'm old," I said. "Older than Griffith."

She touched my mouth. "You're the age my father would be."

"Is he dead?" I said.

"Yes."

"I'm sorry."

Lillian turned away but held my hands. Her warm shoulder was against my shoulder and she squeezed my hands. "I went to see Father before he died. He was in a sanitarium in Oklahoma. Father's brother, Uncle Grant, thought I should see him. I was fifteen. I hadn't seen Father for ten years. So I went. Alone. It was a white two-story building with a porch. A place for people no one wants, people who are too much trouble, who ought to die. I got to Shawnee after midnight and they gave me a room. I couldn't sleep and kept pacing, getting ready to see Father. Do you know what I was doing? I was rehearsing. I was acting and there was no audience. It scared me. There I was getting ready to see Father, who I might never see again, and I was acting. Practicing the part of daughter and no one was there. It wasn't real without an audience. I wasn't real." Lillian held me. "It frightened me, Mr. Harrison. I kept thinking, I'm an actress, a very good actress, but what else? I must be something else? Why do I need an audience? When you said I wasn't real, it struck me."

"But you are real and an actress," I said. "You learned that when you lost your fur."

"It scared me," Lillian said. "When I'm away from Mother and Dorothy, I act. I have to act. When do I stop?" Lillian began to cry. She hugged me. "I wanted to comfort Father and there was no one to comfort me."

I held her. "Does that help?"

"Yes." She put my hand on her wet cheek.

"I never saw him. They decided he was too ill or looked too awful. I spent the night rehearsing and never played the part. I never got an audience. I didn't exist."

"You're kind," I said, holding her delicate face. "You're so afraid of not doing the right thing. So afraid you'll disappoint. You don't always have to be perfect, Lillian."

"I don't want to be."

"Until dawn," I said.

We kissed again. A long kiss full of need. Two people in a seven-passenger Studebaker who needed to be told they weren't alone on an April night.

"I can't marry Mr. Griffith because I'd always have to be perfect. Mr. Griffith loves the little girl who tries to be perfect."

"Does Griffith ever stop playing Griffith?" I said. "Does he ever stop being the genius? The southern gentleman? The boss?"

"No," said Lillian. "He's worked too hard for it. He doesn't want anything else. Mr. Griffith wasn't a good actor. He was, please don't say I said this, a terrible poet. He wasn't good at anything until he discovered photoplays. Mr. Griffith discovered himself when he walked into Biograph. So did I. He thinks he invented the photoplay because that's where he invented himself. Mr. Griffith only wants one role. He can't be anything else."

"You're so much like him," I said.

"But I can't be all the time." Lillian held my face with both hands. "Mr. Harrison, because your wife left you and you hit that man and bit Max, you're vulnerable. You're not acting. Please tell me I don't have to act for a little while." Lillian wiped her beautiful face.

"Hold me," I said.

We drove by Babylon, so big and dark, all the cables, hawsers, elephants lost in the hugeness of the night. We went down Sunset by Coronado Livery's electric sign, still on in the cold blackness of Sunday morning. When I looked again we were by Mack Sennett's Keystone Studio, where the comedian watches his minions from a bathtub because he didn't get enough hot water as a shivering child in Canada. We circled Silver Lake and went through Echo Park, Griffith Park, then back to the dark, looming hills, winding up and down, turning, gliding by Cibola. We went through Burbank, Glendale, Pasadena. We smelled the Pacific.

The night was cold and the windows fogged. The black Studebaker—our sealed, moving darkness—took the discarded husband and the actress who didn't get to play for her father through the end of the night. Surrounded by glass, Bedford Blue Cord, handles which sparkled in occasional light, we were, after the long day and night, safe.

3

Dawn was near and Lillian asked where I was sleeping. I said Jesus had a bungalow and I had a key. She asked if he were home, I said no, and Lillian asked if we could go there. I wasn't sure what she wanted. We had been close to making love. We had talked and touched—given and received —and I didn't want more. I might have taken more but comforting Lillian, listening to her talk about her father, worry about Griffith, her mother, Dorothy and Bobby Harron, made me less alone. For the first time during this awful day, I wasn't lonely. That would come soon enough—with the strange Los Angeles dawn.

We got to the bungalow before five. The limousine parked and the mangled-eared driver pulled his cap over his eyes and went to sleep. The night was fresh and sharp as we walked up steep steps. Los Angeles was a few scattered lights off in the basin. The key worked and we went in the house where two white robes hung like ghosts in the living room built-in. I found the electric light and we walked, hand in hand, to the kitchen. It was almost day. Lillian squinted and I lit a kerosene lamp with matches on the table in the breakfast nook. Lillian turned off the electric light, and we were in a small white circle looking at posts, partitions and robes in the darkness of the bungalow. Lillian saw the wooden tub on the back porch and said, "Would you like to take a bath?"

"What about modesty?" I said, wondering how long the fantasy of us alone in the dark could last. Nakedness would bring a new trance. Or new loneliness.

"We could heat water," she said. "We'd hardly be able to see each other in the steam."

I found a kettle and two large pots, ran water, managed to light the stove—a little Battle Creek gas range—and put on the pots and kettle.

"Will you read the letter from your friend?" said Lillian.

"Would you like to hear it?"

"Yes."

We sat in the breakfast nook, at a narrow table wedged between built-in china cabinets. No partitions reached the ceiling, so the one-story bungalow felt like a cabin at a lake. I opened the back door and rinsed the tub with water from the kettle. White, moist air rose from the big wooden tub into the black, cold morning. I refilled the kettle and took out the letter. Lillian sat across from me. Her hair was down. In the dim radiance, her cheeks were the only color in the shadows of the bungalow with its nook, robes and tub.

"Are you sure you want to bathe?"

Lillian laughed a most delicate small laugh. "*You* don't have to."

She was so free. So young. So unaware of consequences. Or maybe she trusted me.

"What do you want?" I said.

"Have an adventure."

I checked the water on the stove, then removed a half dozen sheets from the envelope.

Lillian leaned over the narrow table and smiled. "I never get to be a vamp." She laughed.

"I'm a pretty safe person to vamp."

"We'll see."

She enjoyed this. When did Lillian Gish get to be a bad girl? Lillian liked laughing at me. Her eyes sparkled.

"Suppose Jesus comes back?"

"Just read the letter, please." Her voice was full of rebellious excitement.

I was glad I didn't have to read the letter alone. Each Boston message, in Tuck's cramped, neat handwriting, had a disturbing yet uncertain finality. Between quotes from the New Testament and news of his daughters was always an unasked, but persistent, "Now, what?" which I finally understood. My life was one big "Now, what?"

The envelope held blue stationery and wrinkled white paper, apparently from a notebook. The first page had only one line.

I read, "'Jesus didn't save me,'" and showed Lillian the sheet with its one line.

"This is bad," Lillian said. "Your friend had found religion." The sparkle was replaced by a look of concern. A beautiful look. The woman and child mixed.

"'I don't have much time,'" I read. "'I am a captain in the British Army. New rank. New country.'"

"You may not see your friend soon," said Lillian, echoing my thought. Her voice was soft, gently acknowledging the possibility. My heart sank. Tuck might never know we were in one flame, like Dante's Ulysses and Diomed.

"Tuck may never know I share his pain," I said. "He'll know different pain. I suppose that's why he's going."

Lillian squeezed my hand.

I returned to the letter:

"'What else could Jesus do but weep if He came to this world?'"

The kitchen, even Lillian, seemed dark and far away. The kettle whistled. I dumped it and two pots into the tub and refilled them. The sky was turning gray behind the hills. Dawn was marching by the minute. The enormously difficult day was already here.

"'I asked Jesus for help, but He didn't answer. He lets you answer, and I couldn't.'"

Lillian and I looked at the robes in the next room.

The next page:

"'I thought I could live with the failure of my marriage but I can't. If I stay, I fail the girls. I fail everyone.'"

I scanned the rest of the page. "He mentions Griffith. 'Henry, my British friends would like Griffith to make an anti-German photoplay. They believe the motion picture is the most powerful propaganda weapon on earth and want a *Birth of the Hun*. They think if you, who have been so critical, present an offer, Griffith will be flattered. Helping our cause might undo some of the damage the cracker Svengali has done. You could write about this in your book. Personally, I doubt Griffith has passion for the struggle. There aren't many niggers in France, but I must tell you, anything that could shorten this war would be a Godsend. The fighting is worse than reported. Worse than Antietam or Gettysburg. Men are killed at a rate the public could not believe nor long tolerate.

"'The British offer full cooperation. The director can meet aristocrats. He can go to the front. Get financing. You would be well compensated too. Forgive me, but I thought you might need money. Yours, Tuck.'"

"No," said Lillian. "That's all wrong. Mr. Griffith hates war. Mr. Griffith says war is the enemy, not people. Mr. Griffith wouldn't work for a foreign power."

4

Lillian leaned back and watched me. The kettle whistled and I dumped more water in the tub, refilled pots and kettle, and checked the graying sky.

I read the letter:

"'I came to the flame and can't walk through it.'"

"That's Dante," I said. "*The Purgatorio.* After the Pilgrim climbs the Mountain of Purgatory, he has to go through flame to enter the Garden of Eden and find Beatrice. I told Tuck he'd come to the flame and had to go through to get to the rest of his life."

"Instead he goes to war," said Lillian.

I patted my wrinkled jacket and pulled out a cigar. "Do you mind?" Lillian shook her head no. "I only smoke when very happy or unhappy." I lit the cigar and blew smoke away from Lillian and the lamp, into the dark. "The poet Mallarmé said he liked to put smoke between himself and the world. I disagree. The world is too much like smoke as it is."

"I love the way you know literature," said Lillian. "I want to know it that way. Sometimes I think books are all that's real."

"What about photoplays?"

"They're not real at all. They're editing and tricks and then they go to movie houses. They're not yours at all."

I read again:

"'Henry, Dante is right. Hell is self-chosen. Remember how we used to laugh at the Catholic idea if you repent, even at the last second, you go to Purgatory instead of Hell? It's true. Hell is our choice and I don't have the strength to stay out. You told me I could be in Hell or Purgatory. Circles or steps. I wasn't strong enough. It was my choice.'"

"He's right," said Lillian.

I looked at the pages. Some were light blue—Starr's stationery, her name was at the top, crossed out in a hard slash of black ink. I showed this to Lillian. She looked and shook her head. Her hair touched my cheek. "I shouldn't have left him," I said. "Tuck said he was all right. He said he wasn't alone."

"Now you're both alone," said Lillian, and leaned over and kissed me on the cheek, then the mouth.

"And soon you'll be gone," I said. It was gray outside.

"I'll stay a little," Lillian said.

"Cordelia, Cordelia."

She didn't answer, and I read:

"'I walk up Beacon Hill when I can't sleep. I walk down the Hill when I can't work. I can't sleep or work often now. Have I not chosen you twelve and one of you is a devil?'"

"He's quoting John," said Lillian.

"'I carry my father's knife. The Bowie he had at Gettysburg. Why am I carrying a knife?

"'They're always in public, Henry. They ride around the Public Garden in his carriage, trot through the Common, go up and down Marlboro. Whosoever committeth sin is the servant of sin. She tells everyone, "He takes care of me. He's kind. He doesn't betray." This is her litany, a kind of liturgy. This is her way of punishing me. It's her way of killing me. Why doesn't she say he's rich? Why doesn't she say she controls him?

"'One thing I know, whereas I was blind, now I see.'"

I emptied and refilled the kettle and pots.

"'I followed them on a March evening. It was twilight, light snow was falling, and the street lights glowed as if Boston were the safest, most trusting place. Boston is a desert place.

"'The kingdom of heaven is at hand.'"

"Do you think?" said Lillian. "Do you . . .?" Her voice trailed off.

"I don't know what to think," I said. Dawn was breaking transparent, thin, white. The hills had foggy angels. I didn't want to think what Tuck might have done.

"'My father took a bullet out of his leg with this knife. The bread that I give is my flesh.

"'They went east on Beacon. The horse twitched, the driver dozed, they passed through the gray city as evening fell on the rich and no-so-rich, on those in-love and those not-so-in-love, on those with knives and those without knives. They got out on Arlington Street. Starr, then Daniel. The driver waited, dozing again. The Public Garden was empty except for snow drifting in the fading, cold light. Night was coming and they walked hand in hand as if no one saw. Daniel's heavy leather glove was in Starr's red mitten. Their hips touched as they walked. The wind was up enough to dust away my footprints.

"'Verily I say unto you one of you shall betray me.'"

Lillian looked up. There was enough light now to show color in her eyes, which were transparent, like the sky. Like the dawn. "This hate. His hate. It's like you, isn't it?"

I answered only with Tuck's words:

"'They stopped by "Maid of the Mist," the fountain near the Washington statue, but they didn't see me. They weren't looking. Daniel kissed her ear. He bit and tickled and Starr giggled. They kissed.

"'And Judas which also betrayed.'"

"Stop, if you want," said Lillian.

"I can't stop."

Tuck:

"'I stood. They shall look on him whom they pierced. Let the dead bury their dead.

"'I followed among the statues like the demoniac raving between the stones, but I was silent, we weren't in a graveyard, and no one was dead. When Daniel saw me, he froze. O ye hypocrites, ye can discern the face of the sky; but can ye not discern the signs of the times.

"'And now it was night. And when the night was come, he was there alone. Starr saw. My lips moved but she couldn't hear. An evil and adulterous generation seeketh after a sign, and there shall no sign be given.

"'Starr trembled. How long could they ride on Marlboro and Beacon? How long, O Lord?

"'I whispered, "The enemy that sowed them is the

devil; the harvest is the end of the world; and the reapers are the angels." I whispered again and again.

"'Starr tried to run. Daniel held her. Daniel held her like nothing on earth or Boston could scare him. Starr struggled, then stopped. Her strength failed. Now it was real. Whosoever will save his life shall lose it.

"'The kingdom of heaven is at hand.'"

The cigar burned out in the saucer I used as an ashtray. The red glow brightened, then stopped.

"'Who then can be saved? There should no flesh be saved.

"'They knew. God, they knew. It took this long, but they learned night comes. Night. The only democracy.

"'Know that it is near, even at the doors.'"

I stopped. The last cigar smoke rose in a thin, then nonexistent trail into the room of gray light, gray eyes, and the glow of the lamp, all less gentle, less visible, less important in the dawn.

Water boiled on the stove. Mist in the dawn.

I touched Lillian's cheek. It was wet.

"'I could have done it, Henry. My name *is* Legion: for we are many. I ran my thumb over the blade and they shook, too scared to run, too scared to scream. If Daniel hadn't held her, Starr would have gone to her knees. Then the awfulness of it got me, Henry. It wasn't the ease with which I could have killed them or even the wound the girls would have borne the rest of their lives. The awfulness was knowing Christ's words don't help. His words are just

166

words, and words are only words.

"'I go to France.'"

5

Lillian stood by the tub on the peeling, white porch under the graying sky, the hills behind her, and shed her clothes. The black dress with white trim fell on the deck, and a moving vision I could barely look at shook off the thin camisole I'd caressed in the car, and slid into gray-silver water topped by mist rising into cool air. I watched Lillian's hair, white skin, and incomparable gray eyes through rising moisture, took off my rumpled suit, socks and underwear and turned away from the tub, excited and afraid, knowing one spell was being exchanged for another in the raw dawn. I slipped into the pewter water and mist hid me too. Lillian ducked under, her foot and leg touched my leg and foot, and she came up pulling back rich, tangled hair, which looked dark over the silvery water that now caught a suggestion of the sky. She sat with water up to her neck.

Lillian's breasts came out of the water. They were indescribably white, exquisitely little, deliciously round. Dark, almost pebbled aureoles surrounded small, hard nipples. I was thrilled and sad. I saw what I'm sure no man had seen, and it was beautiful, but I also saw a very young woman who wasn't mine or Griffith's or anybody's—whose small, perfect breasts, large mouth, wide eyes and knowing looks were her creation, her secret, her mystery—a complicity between herself, fans, art—and I didn't think I should see it. I saw Lillian's breasts hover in cool air over warm water with the innocence of innocence ready to be lost, and wanted to say, "Stop. Stay who you are. You'll be hurt," but I just looked, mouth open, at the beauty of the beauty that entrances America. I saw her white shoulders and solid beautiful arms. The woman wasn't frail—little hands, yes, large mouth, eyes that are a child's one instant, a woman the next, a sprite, but not frail. The solid luster of her body shown in the dark water like the moon highlighting clouds.

I saw tears in her eyes. I was surprised. The wind dropped and the coyotes were quiet.

"Will you take Harry from his mother?"

"Did Griffith tell you that?"

Lillian nodded.

I held her hands under the water. "I can let Edith go; I can't let Harry go."

"Letting Harry stay with his mother isn't letting him go. He needs both of you. Even if you're apart."

"I know what happened was my fault," I said, sitting up, feeling the chill air on my chest. "I've been a bad father and selfish husband, but what Edith did was wrong too. She has to accept that."

"You've been forced to see things, Mr. Harrison, but you've got to see the right things. You've got to see who to love. That person is Harry."

Lillian splashed her face with a handful of water. She

cupped water in her hands and washed my face, carefully rinsing the bruises, and pouring water over my head, all the time gently nodding, perhaps unconsciously reprising her role as "The Woman Who Rocks the Cradle," the tiny part Griffith gave her in the new photoplay as a woman rocking a cradle while the Fates conspire in the background.

"Is taking him loving him?"

Lillian massaged my scalp, ears, neck, shoulders. "Let's clean the blood off you. We can make that go away." She touched the cut on my chin, massaged my hands and fingers, ran her hands over my forearms and biceps, and then went back to my shoulders and neck. Her side was next to my side. Her flesh was smooth and the water was warm.

"I've never told a man what to do. I never tell anyone what to do, except Dorothy, but I'm going to tell you because I know you." Lillian let her hands rest on my shoulders. Her wet face was in front of my face, the hills, the dawn.

"Look at us, for heaven's sake. When I woke up this morning, yesterday that is, I didn't think I'd be in a tub with a man I'd never met. Everything is so different. Mr. Griffith asked me to marry him and your wife left you. It hasn't been a typical day, so I'm going to tell you what to do."

"All right," I said. I loved Lillian at that moment. I loved her because she stepped out of the screen, out of the role she plays for Griffith and men and America, right into the dawn—and surprised me. There was something sad and lost in her mystery, but it fought back.

"Let Harry stay with his mother. You must. No matter how much it hurts. He needs his mother."

"I can't let them slap my face like that."

"Men," said Lillian, shaking me. Not so gently. "Nothing is more important than pride, is it? Nothing is more important than how you look to other men. I know. I see. Listen to me. I saw you attack that man. I saw you on your knees, blood all over your face. I saw your courage. Mr. Harrison, you had your moment of war. Now it's time for a different courage. Don't take Harry from his mother. It's too hard for a child. I know."

"It's too hard if I don't."

"You can only save yourself by saving the child."

I looked at Lillian's eyes over steaming water mixed with her shimmering reflection and snatches of the Sunday sky. Her hair was tangled and turning brown in the rising light. Angels of fog sat on the hills. Lillian spoke the truth. Lillian was the truth but I couldn't accept it.

"Hate will eat me up like it eats Tuck."

"If I let you make love to me, will you let Harry stay with his mother?"

"What?"

"I think you heard me."

"What?" I said again.

Lillian tilted her wet head and gave me that trademark old-young-wise-ethereal signature look she's given in so many photoplays—a look new and ancient, which perfectly fits each scene, and is only for you.

"Why does this matter so much?" I said.

"Because of the child."

"That's not good enough."

"Because of you."

"Not good enough."

"Because of me."

"Why?"

"I want to know love," said Lillian. "I'm not afraid of that either."

"I'm not the right person."

"You're close enough."

"Close isn't enough."

"You know me," she said, "as much as anyone knows me. More importantly, you don't love me."

"I do love you," I said. "I love the way you tilt your head and look at the world."

"You know I won't marry, or leave mother and Dorothy. You know I'm an actress and won't compromise, so after, we'll go back to our lives. I want to know love, Mr. Harrison. If only once. We'll be friends. We're friends anyway. You love your wife. You'll love her for a long time."

"You're mistaking me for someone else," I said. "Someone better. More profound. I love you."

Lillian looked at me in the thin light—everything was transparent, white, changing, becoming whatever Los Angeles is at five-thirty in the morning. She tilted her head. "Please don't see only what you want to see. See me instead. I don't belong to you or Mr. Griffith but I want to know

love." Lillian gave me a smile that can not be described—
worldly, mysterious, not altogether trustworthy. "It can't be
with anyone else. I don't have that freedom."

"What about Griffith?"

"Mr. Griffith wants a wife. A prize, a possession, and
he'd make a terrible husband, just like he'd make a terrible
propaganda film. Mr. Harrison, I have to protect my family
and you have to protect yours. My family is Dorothy and
mother, and maybe Mr. Griffith. Your family is Harry, and
Tuck, if you ever see him again. We have to protect the families we are given."

"This is charity," I said.

"Charity for me," said Lillian. "But you must agree
about the child and his mother." She held my hands in the
water. "Give me the luxury of once not having to be who
people think I am." Lillian leaned against me and I felt all
the electricity of her body against mine. The water was
warm, the air sharp.

6

I was hard in the Studebaker, I was hard in the tub, but I
was soft in the quickly made white bed in the room
where Jesus had thrown my briefcase. The more I touched
Lillian, the more I stroked her thighs, kissed the brilliant
high nipples, the mouth too "big" to be photogenic—the
more I wanted, needed, prayed, hoped this would make

everything right, even, new—the more I couldn't. I was paralyzed.

There were right reasons, wrong reasons, no reason. I couldn't. I just couldn't.

"It isn't your fault," I said. "You're very beautiful and very kind."

"It's better like this," Lillian said.

It was cold. The room was the color of water in a sink.

I held her. She shivered. I couldn't fight. Couldn't f***. Couldn't find the right words.

Lillian started to speak but I put my hand on her mouth and whispered, "There isn't anything to say."

∿

Lillian stayed, as she said, a little while. The moment was lost. What might have been—the wonder, her adventure, the small redemption—was gone. Lillian shivered. I lay there and saw myself lying there. I saw the middle-aged man, the slight paunch, bruises, limp dick, beside the disappointed vamp. Lillian's bargain, her charity and need to be special, found only a tired man with a hole in him.

"I'm sorry," I said.

"This is better," Lillian said.

This is death.

"Now you feel awful," she said. Lillian touched me. "I've always wanted to do that."

"The part that won't sin."

Lillian laughed.

Laughter isn't enough.

I lay there praying for what could have been. Me. Her. Once. A fairy tale and secret between friends. A private memory to be put away, sampled, and brought out when needed, but it wasn't. I couldn't.

∿

"Now you feel worse," said Lillian.

"Well, I probably won't tell anybody."

Lillian laughed.

"It's not the right time," I said. "I'm not the right person."

"You're nice. Too nice." She kissed my cheek.

"How can you even look at me?"

"Don't be silly. For heaven's sake."

"You're so very nice," I said, and touched the end of her nose with my finger.

Lillian smiled.

"It is funny," I said. "That's really all there is to say."

∿

I tried to be nice. I decided that's what I had to do and I tried hard. I was acting. Not lying, acting. Acting is—what a hell of a way to learn—doing what's necessary, when necessary, regardless of how you feel. It isn't real. It isn't false. It's like having manners.

"It isn't your fault," I said.

"Men," said Lillian. "It isn't fault. Can't there be other kinds of closeness? Other things that matter and matter deeply?" She kissed me on the forehead.

"I could tell you it's because I love Edith, or because I

know what love is and this isn't love, or because I can't take care of you, but that would all be lies. I want this more than anything. It would be once and forever and I can't."

"Hold me. I've never been this tender with anyone."

I held her.

"Don't you understand this is better?" Lillian said. "This is trust," but I was far away. Far from sealed darkness. Far from the dream of whom I could be, far from Lillian. Far from Harry.

I pulled the sheet over us as if we were corpses.

Love is for two and I was one.

For the first time in a day and night, I wanted to be alone.

～

How could I have thought one moment, even with Lillian Gish, could bring back the grace of being me? How could I have thought it would be so easy?

～

Lillian got up. It was light and the mysterious dawn was gone. "We're close now, you know," she said. "I'm glad you're the first man I touched." Lillian saw the briefcase, opened it, and found the notebook and pen. She scribbled what turned out to be a telephone number, kissed my forehead, and with the morning sun touching her smooth thighs, little breasts, and white shoulders as they disappeared into the black dress, said, "Please consider letting the child stay with his mother."

Lillian left.

I lay there. Hideously tired. Hideously disappointed. I touched my dick. It got hard.

VI

Harry

April 3, 1916
2:00 p.m. to 8:00 p.m.

HARRY

1

I woke up at two o'clock feeling better. The afternoon was bright. My head didn't hurt, and the aroma of eggs, bacon and coffee, along with light streaming into the pale room, made Jesus' rendezvous feel, momentarily, like home. Failure with Lillian was more ambiguous in the warm afternoon. It was humiliating, of course. The night was a bruise but also a relief. I looked at the high, infinitely blue sky and knew that, no matter how I felt, it was better to be embarrassed. What had seemed like a wonderful secret, a bit of perfect time in another country, was different with the sun on the green hills. The woman was half my age and trying to keep D. W. Griffith from changing her. Lillian didn't need her life to be more complicated. I felt awful about the male embarrassment—the secret that we had no secret was the worst secret of all—but looking at the hills and smelling breakfast in the afternoon, I was glad I hadn't taken something Lillian might want back. I had taken advantage of someone who felt recklessly sorry for me because I felt recklessly sorry for myself. Part of me wished we had—the part that wants proudly, sinfully—but I smelled bacon and coffee and knew getting drunk, fighting, and riding in a seven-passenger Studebaker with Lillian Gish were luxuries born and licensed in the shock of yesterday. Today I didn't have that excuse. Today was Harry and going east. That Lillian was braver and kinder than anyone could imagine hadn't, shouldn't, and finally didn't, cost her—

innocence wasn't the word—I looked at the deep azure sky
. . . privacy.

∾

I put on the stained, white trousers and my poor
excuse for a shirt and, feeling sheepish but better, went into
the kitchen where Jesus was filling the bungalow with the
marvelous smell of breakfast.

"Eat, dear fellow. Fugitives need to eat."

"Fugitives?"

Jesus bent over the stove. He was wearing a pleated yellow shirt with blue embroidered cacti and coarse, dark
trousers and was frying sourdough bread in a skillet with
bacon grease. His white robes were drying on a line strung
across the porch. With beard and hair pulled back and tied
with a white cord, Jesus looked like a Mexican holy man.

"Griffith and Max, a limping Max, came by this morning, Harrison, and it *wasn't* to rehire me. They were looking
for you and asked if I'd seen Miss Geesh, as the Master calls
her."

"What did you say?"

"I said no, of course, and told them you weren't here."

"Nothing happened with Miss Geesh," I said.

"Of course," said Jesus, with a dismissive wave. "A
night of whoring was called for. Now you have a problem."

"Problem?"

"Miss Gish came back to see you, didn't she? Her
mother didn't accompany her, right?"

"Right."

"You were with her in the early hours of Sunday morning, yes? Something no man, including presumably, the Master, has done? Griffith knows, or at least suspects, and you don't see the problem?"

"Believe me, there is no problem."

"Not for you, not for her, but for him! The Master's not supposed to be second."

"Believe me, I wasn't first."

"I believe, Harrison, but jealous men aren't reasonable. I have to tell *you* that?"

I shook my head. The idea I could be Griffith's nemesis, a sexual ghost, his Murphy, after such an abysmal flop made me laugh out loud. To fail and be blamed for success? The strangeness of April second continued—everything wrong, upside down, misunderstood. "How did Griffith find out?"

"You don't think your little angel told him?"

"Why should she?"

"Never presume to understand a woman, Harrison. Perhaps that rat Bobby Harron is diverting attention from his escapades." Jesus poured coffee into a dented metal mug that looked as though it had been to the Yukon and handed it to me. The coffee was hot and delicious. I don't usually take it black.

"Harrison, I can't explain it, but women like you. You're tall, and when not bleeding, almost handsome. You charmed Miss Gish. No small accomplishment. Especially in Griffith's eyes."

"Compliments with breakfast?"

"His pride is hurt, Harrison. Griffith's proprietary. He gets everything. Everything but Miss Gish, I should say, and here she is spending the night with you! His Yankee antagonist and biographer! The only man in Los Angeles, maybe America, who might threaten him. Certainly the only one to bite his chauffeur. And you, of all people, enchant Miss Gish."

I laughed. Jesus put three fried eggs and four thick strips of bacon on a ceramic plate embossed with an orange burro, and I ate. The meal smelled better than anything I ever smelled. It was funny, hilarious, ridiculous that D. W. Griffith would be jealous of an impotent cuckold. "I'll deny it."

"Of course you'll deny it, but who needs Griffith for an enemy? Not you. Not me. You and I go looking for dirt on Griffith, and you, God knows how, spend an unchaperoned night with his virgin queen in my house!"

"We talked," I said. "We're friends. Lillian's wonderful."

"The woman won't clock anyone, yet everyone loves her. Only in America." Jesus brought over the fried sourdough.

"You cook like a prospector," I said. "I've never had a better meal."

"It may be your last."

"In one day and night," I said, "I lose my wife, disgrace myself, injure Lillian Gish's reputation, and destroy my connection with Griffith. Murphy does what I'm accused of doing for three years, gets my wife, and no one cares."

Jesus shrugged.

"It's not fair," I said, suddenly feeling angry and sorry for myself. "I don't deserve it."

"Harrison, the only justice is poetic justice."

"I won't accept blame for something I didn't do."

"But you did do something." Jesus poured more coffee. "You were favored with the virgin's company at four in the morning. This is a scandal. You trespassed. Some people think Griffith's going to marry her."

"He's already married."

"The Master likes a challenge. Why else pursue Lillian Gish? He can have any other woman in Los Angeles."

"I'm not going to tell anyone, and if asked, I'll deny it," I said, finishing the eggs and wiping up the yolk with the thick bread.

"I'm mum as the grave," said Jesus, in the tones of a weary Englishman in an inhospitable colony. "But you'll have to deal with Griffith."

"Suppose I say the three of us were here?"

"Me? A character reference? Believe me, Harrison, Griffith won't spread the story. He won't hurt Miss Gish's reputation, but he may do something to you."

"Like?"

"Bar you from Fine Arts? Have Max shoot you? Tell the world you're insane? I don't know." Jesus brought over more bread and bacon. I couldn't believe how hungry I was. I finished the bacon and bread. "Being with Lillian had nothing to do with Griffith."

Jesus looked at me. The bright sun caught his blue eyes

and brown beard. His long hair was wet and neatly combed straight back. He sipped coffee, which he took black. "Maybe that's how what's-his-name felt about you."

"I knew what's-his-name," I said. "It was personal."

"Sometimes," said Jesus. "It's only about the woman."

I shook my head.

"Let's hope you enjoyed what you didn't do."

"I won't deny being with her," I said suddenly. "I won't deny it. I'm not going to lie. Edith and Murphy are liars. I'm a fool, I lost my wife, I bit someone and spent a night with Lillian Gish, but damn it, I'm not a liar."

"Good," said Jesus.

I felt better. "I may never own another mansion or ball club or remarry, but I'm not a liar. Let Griffith be angry. I *was* with Lillian Gish at four in the morning. She liked me. She compromised herself to be with me. I won't deny it." I ate and looked out at the green Hollywood Hills dotted with yellow and purple flowers. Jesus nodded and also studied the hills. He let me think and I looked at the hills and sky and thought about being afraid.

I was afraid if I didn't take Harry, I'd be weak.

I looked at Jesus, the hills, the infinite azure of the Los Angeles sky, and decided whatever came next started with not being afraid—and Harry.

I remembered what Lillian said about Harry staying with his mother, and that hurt. It hurt because I wanted to take Harry to hurt Edith. I didn't think I could take care of Harry better. It was because Edith hurt me. Taking Harry was the important decision. Not sleeping with another woman. Not fighting. Lillian knew it all along and was willing to sacrifice her virginity. A child helping another child. I looked at Jesus, the tub, the robes, and wasn't sure what I'd do. I had to see Harry. Talk to him. I looked at the high clouds in the deep sky and, strangely enough, didn't pity myself anymore. It was like putting down a stone.

"If Griffith wants to talk, I'll talk, but I'm taking my son boating. Then I have to figure out the divorce."

"Take my car. Just have it back by seven. I'm seeing Gerty."

"Breakfast was delicious," I said. "Feeding a man is the nicest gift in the world. Thank you."

"Harrison." Jesus smoothed his long hair with both hands. "Don't say I didn't warn you."

2

I didn't feel like driving Jesus' car but had no choice. Someone else's car is always trouble, but the Model T is as close to idiot-proof as possible, so, taking my briefcase with razor and telephone number, and under Jesus' careful gaze, with profuse instructions not to start the Ford in gear and fracture my arm ("You've got enough problems, Harrison"), I got it going and drove down to Sunset toward the city. The hills were green, and the lemon-scented April city didn't seem like houses on hills grafted onto a desert, but a soft collection of trees, purple flowers, steps up steep hills, roads that went off to the future, now only paved dust, and I bravely thought about Harry and our new life. I kept telling myself I could learn and change, as Griffith had said, but did that mean taking Harry? I failed Edith. I didn't want to fail Harry. I started a conversation in my head with Tuck, then remembered Tuck was going to France. I thought of Lillian, and separating Harry from his mother, and in the bright sun, proud I could shift and not stall, considered letting him stay with her, but also remembered how carefully Edith and Murphy had navigated their affair, how Murphy had taken my wife and reduced the mother of my child to a liar sneaking intimacy in the afternoons, and how Edith had needed or liked that, and I felt no charity. No charity at all.

I passed big families in open cars heading for the wide spaces of the Beverly Hills, or Venice and the beach, or maybe the mountains. Women carrying parasols strolled up Sunset with men in boaters. They might be going to Babylon or hoping to see Mack Sennett and the Kops disrupt the tranquil Hollywood Sunday with pranks and beauties while shooting an impromptu photoplay. Maybe they just wanted to be with each other. I kept noticing families and couples and all the open space that calls itself Los Angeles. Between Babylon, the big cars of motion picture people, the pranks, and moneymaking was empty space, lemon and orange trees, and sunny dust.

Closer to Bunker Hill, horse-drawn carriages trotted at

the elegant, time-defying pace of the last century. Horses and passengers held heads high as if their equipage, at least on a brilliant Sunday afternoon, had held back time, showing the noisy, sputtering twentieth century, which belonged to Mr. Ford and Mr. Griffith and the aeroplane, submarine, and world war, that style, patience, and a switching tail aimed above the horizon could bring life back to the elegant simplicity our parents and grandparents knew. For a few hours, proud families recaptured the rhythm and elegance of lost time, but as I waved at a little girl in a fine carriage, I realized the people in carriages didn't need lost time. They had now. Lost time is for those who don't learn. Don't forgive. Me. Griffith. The sight of a happy child gave me a sad courage about my new life. I felt less brave when a towheaded family went by and didn't wave—the boy and girl didn't smile, their handsome mother didn't look on approvingly, the proud father didn't regard the Ford with amused, competitive camaraderie. They saw me and looked away. When I got to Bunker Hill, I didn't feel brave at all.

The Los Angeles Times was beside me on the front seat, and I glanced at the war news while stopped at an intersection. The foreign slaughter was closer now because of Tuck. A headline declared "Verdun Climax Nears: French May Be Trapped." I sympathized with a besieged fortress. Another story, "Citizen of Los Angeles Is Prisoner of Bandits," told of an Angelino held for ransom in Sonora. I felt for him, too.

∽

When I reached the house, Harry ran out to see me. He was wearing a white sailor suit with a navy blue square collar and cuffs and must have been watching because he bounded out the front door. I swung open the car door, and Harry jumped on my lap and gave me a ferocious hug. "I'm so glad to see you, Father," he said, and I fought tears. Everything was falling apart and he loved me. I swore I wouldn't cry in front of the child, but seeing him so happy to see me was hard.

Harry rubbed my face and said, "A terrible beard," which was our joke. I once rubbed a day's growth against his small face and said, "A terrible beard," which became a game between us. "You better shave," Harry said, and led me into the large, turreted house. We heard the cars of the funicular railroad, Angels Flight, clang up and down, and Harry said, "I've been riding all day waiting for you. I was worried."

"I'm here," I said. "And we're going boating."

"Can we go to the cemetery? They have an island and a pond."

"Of course," I said. "We can go anywhere you want. Let's go boating first. I need to change my clothes."

"Father, Mummy's with Mr. Murphy," Harry said, looking down, as if he shouldn't, but had to, tell.

"It's all right," I said. "It'll all work out."

That wasn't how I felt.

∽

Harry watched me shave. The little Ever-Ready Safety Razor fascinated the child. He opened the small black box and examined the two metal blade holders, each stamped "Blades," and then held the short, knurled stem, while I lathered my face. Harry shook his head, exclaiming, "A terrible beard!" and sat on the edge of the tub to watch the male ritual of taking sharp blade to soft face, which my own father used to do with such cheerful dispatch.

I felt better after shaving, and Harry followed me into the dressing room off the high-ceilinged master bedroom, where I found a clean shirt, tweed trousers, a yellow knitted tie, and a tweed jacket. I also found $45, which was enough to get us on the train until I could wire for more tomorrow.

Edith's closet was open and I saw her clothes, the blouses, skirts, gowns, shirtwaists, and last night's crimson dress, hanging—clothes I knew so well; clothes I wouldn't see again—mute sentinels Edith wore to see Murphy and wore when she returned with her unimaginable secret. What had she felt? How did she walk right up to me? Look at Harry? These were costumes for roles I'd never imagined. I realized I'd never see Edith get ready for a brilliant evening, or undress after, replaying the wit and innuendoes of the company. A life hung in that closet. Those dresses clothed years, and I knew them all. My life would be mute without Edith. All that time to explain to another woman, or never mention at all. I touched the crimson dress. Edith loved shades of red. For a moment I would have lied, forgiven, accepted anything, to have her back. Harry was behind me, perhaps waiting to see if I would cry, and I stepped back, realizing I was just a dumb thing in Edith's closet, and had been for years. Leave her, I thought. It's what she wants. I saw her Book of Common Prayer on an oval table and felt like jelly.

Harry hugged me and said, "Just pretend it'll be all right."

Maria stood in the door watching us.

"We'll be back by seven," I said.

Maria nodded but looked at me like I was loco, and kept touching a silver cross between her heavy breasts while looking at Harry as if the child might not be safe with a man about to weep over a crimson dress.

"My father's back," said Harry, as if that temporary fact explained everything.

$\sim$

In the car, Harry sat in front with his crayons and paper resting on a yellow picnic basket. He opened it and told me Mummy packed the cheese sandwiches, oranges, olives, two bottles of root beer, Life Savers, pens, ink, pencils, chocolates, a deck of cards, even a hat and sweater in case we were late. Harry was never without his crayons and blue sketchbook, and Edith had made sure he had them now. She loved him. She loved him tremendously, and no matter what happened she would always love him. Edith had packed sandwiches for me. I wondered if I could really take Harry and hate Edith, and felt the weight of life without her in my throat.

I slumped over the steering wheel. It was only a moment, an instant, but Harry said, "Don't cry, Daddy. Mummy will be home when we get back."

This was too hard. The child was trying to take care of me, and that cut to the heart of what was happening—to him. How did he feel? Children seem so resilient, but what price do they pay? How did Harry feel when he saw me so unhappy? I didn't want to cry so I said, "I wish we could go back in time. That's all."

"Don't cry, Daddy. I'll draw a picture that goes back in time."

I let out the clutch and shifted into reverse. "You don't have to do that. I asked for a silly thing. No one can go back in time."

"I'll show you."

∿

Harry wanted to drive through the new Third Street tunnel. Its lights gleamed down the center of the dark arch like the vertebrae of a subterranean animal. When we emerged in the April afternoon, he was hunched over his pad, carefully selecting crayons, and intent on his drawing. Watching a child so completely immersed in a task is like watching the soul. How often do human beings find a place where there's no distinction between work and play, thought and feeling? Here was Harry, his family dissolving, traveling in another world, like Griffith: making, doing, escaping, comprehending. I couldn't see what he was drawing and it didn't matter. Harry was that other self, the angel children become when they enter their imaginations. I watched his light hair, his crayon, his concentration. This was the artist before the angel is strangled by school, hurt, lost. Even now,

Harry could go to the center of himself. It gave me courage.

We went west, rolling, bouncing, saluting other autos, past newly planted palms and eucalyptus, as Harry finished his picture. On a neat white page in his blue sketchbook was a black-crayon-paved road that went through a gate, and on the other side of the gate, the road was dirt-brown crayon.

"That's the gate in time," he said proudly. "See, you go through and the road changes."

3

Harry made me promise we'd go to Hollywood Ceme- tery, which someone at school said was "pretty" and had an "island," but I wanted to go boating first. I wanted to be alone with him on water, which was hard on a Sunday afternoon. The beaches were crowded, and Venice Lagoon featured young women playing "canoe football." Malibu was virtually under siege with locked gates and armed guards, as the late owner's widow tried to keep the public out. I chose Santa Monica.

We drove on Sunset as it winds toward Hollywood, between steep, vine-covered hills full of rocky crannies, and Harry said, "Canyon." We kept noticing steps that went into tangles of green, but no houses, no people. "That's where houses will be built," I said, and Harry said, "If people can afford them." We hadn't told him anything about money, but children know; they sense trouble in a household.

"There'll be enough money," I said, "we'll sell the Hustlers." Harry nodded with resignation. I pointed out two large hawks hanging high over us, hundreds of feet in the air. They swooped, then returned to a staggering motionless height, looking, scanning, watching. "They're hunting," said Harry, and I thought, everything lives by the eye here. The birds seemed bigger, the sky higher, and the light, from the mysterious dawn, to the perfection of ten a.m., to the high azure afternoon, wasn't quite real. Before America ends, it expands, dreams—different air, horizon, birds, steps going nowhere, a city filled with empty space, Babylon. Harry heard at school that General Otis, owner of *The Times* and implacable foe of labor, had a machine gun mounted on the hood of his car. We didn't see it.

∽

We found a shack, and a young man rented us a row-boat with two sturdy oars that squeaked in their locks. We took off our shoes, rolled up our trousers, and pushed the dinghy through the surf. Harry laughed about getting wet. This was an excursion without his mother and we decided we could get wet. As Harry got in the bow, spray from a breaking wave wet him and he laughed harder. I pushed us out, got soaked to the waist, and climbed in. It wasn't any harder than starting the Model T.

I didn't mind being wet and liked the exercise. I was glad to be away from the tents of happy bathers and the fam-ilies and sweethearts on Echo Park Lake. This end of the beach was almost empty. A few white houses faced the bay and immense ocean. I planned to stay close to the shore and row to the calmer water behind the breakwater a quarter mile away.

We were just a little way out—Harry liked being bounced by the waves—when I realized the ocean was stronger than it had looked from the beach. Beyond the breakers, which weren't large—several swimmers were a hundred yards to the right—working the oars was harder. I hadn't rowed in the Pacific but had been a fair oarsman on the Charles River. There was a current, and I labored just to keep us straight.

Harry said we were "Indians" and pretended to paddle but soon found he needed to hold on with both hands as the dinghy went up and down. I headed for the breakwater, but we were quickly farther out than I expected, and no closer to calm water. Harry thought it was fun until a swell dumped water in the boat and he gave a little shriek. We were a hundred yards off the beach, and I rowed harder. I puffed and pulled. The boat went up and down rather than straight, and the shore got farther away.

Rowing was hard work. Much too hard. Why didn't anything work? Why? I just wanted to take Harry boating, and here I was pulling as hard as I could to keep a dinghy from going out into the Pacific. I rowed harder and it got worse. The swells seemed bigger. It took all my energy to stay aimed at the breakwater. A man and a child lost in Santa Monica Bay? It wasn't a rough sea. It was a beautiful day.

Harry got very quiet. He knew I was struggling, and he

knew there wasn't anybody to help. It was cool, even cold. Water rolled over our shoes in the bottom of the boat, and we kept drifting out. I was tired; my legs were cold. I thought of signaling to the swimmers or two sailboats racing out in the bay, but they were far away and I didn't want to alarm Harry. Waves slapped the boat, which now felt tiny though we were only a couple hundred yards from the beach. I pulled and sweated. Choppy, persistent waves slapped us, and spray came over the bow and cooled my back. Suppose Harry fell overboard?

"Get in the stern!" I yelled.

"OK!" he yelled back and, clutching my neck as he nimbly swung by, sat down on the stern thwart.

"Tell me where we're going," I said.

Harry pointed. We seemed to be going straight out. Could I signal the boats?

A big swell took us up and brought us down. It would have been fun if I hadn't been so worried. The rising and falling was smoother out here.

I realized this was the first time I'd ever been solely responsible for what happened to the boy. Usually I complained to Edith or the nurse and made a fetish of being above what was happening because I couldn't control it. But here I was in a damn dinghy in Santa Monica Bay trying to figure out how to get to shore.

Harry looked at me to see if I was afraid. I saw worry in his face but also trust. I had an idea. I stopped rowing and let the boat drift to feel the current. It was against us. The rest felt good, my hands were beginning to blister, then I remembered tacking in sailboats.

"Let's turn," I said, and when a swell took us up, I used the down slope to bring the bow around so we were facing Malibu. By the time the next one took us up, we were pointing north, and I began to angle for the shore.

"Harry, pick a house up the beach and tell me if we keep going at it."

"I see one."

"OK."

"I'll point."

He did and I aimed where he pointed. Going back was hard, but we slowly angled in. Harry tried so hard. He kept his arm up and finger pointed—he must have gotten tired but held it up—and yelled when I got off course. The sun grew hot as I pulled, but I knew we were all right, and it seemed trivial and unheroic to have been so frightened, to have thought we might drift out to sea when all we had to do was use the current to get in. I worked hard, and we crawled to shore—pulling, coasting, resting, pushed out, pushed back—it was slow, like walking home in a blizzard, but it worked. In the surf we were splashed and bounced by breakers, soaked, and slammed into shallow water, but we were home.

We walked back to the shack, and I tipped the young man to retrieve the boat.

"We made it, Daddy," said Harry.

I'd never been so happy to get anywhere in my life.

4

We drove back slowly. Harry sat closer to me, taking my hand when I wasn't shifting. He kept smiling. So did I.

"We're OK," I said. "We're OK."

"OK!" said Harry.

"We made it, didn't we? We've got luck."

"Luck," said Harry.

"We've got luck," I said. "Together."

"Do your hands hurt?"

"They're a little sore," I said. "They'll be fine. Are your arms tired?"

"You saved us," he said.

"You helped. You had to point so I could steer."

"I helped," he said, and picked up his crayons and sketchbook and started to draw.

∾

The cemetery was down Santa Monica Boulevard, and we were happy to go through the gates and park. We both felt like walking and were glad to be on still, dry land. The hundred acres Van Nuys and Lankershim provided for a city of the dead were flat, grassy fields. It was as if the hills, as well as souls, came to rest here. The dead inhabited only a small corner of the ground set aside from citrus fields. We could see the towers of Babylon, the curve of Mount Lee in the clear distance, and walked toward a pond, which had a small island planted with sunflowers and shrubs.

Harry took my hand and said, "We're OK."

"We'll always be OK. You and me. No matter what happens."

"Does that mean I'm going to live with Mom and Mr. Murphy?"

"Would you rather live with me?"

Harry didn't answer, then, looking at his feet, said, "I'd miss Mummy."

Then I knew. I knew the child had to stay with his mother. It didn't matter how I felt. What mattered was how he felt. Edith loved him. It was me she didn't love, not Harry, and Harry needed her. I couldn't use him to punish her—not if I loved him. I had to let him go. That was the person I wanted to be. I decided then to stay in whatever city they lived in and behave like a gentleman. I smiled thinking of last night—all of last night—biting, bleeding, impotence. What else was there to do but smile? I failed a lot of people, but I wouldn't fail Harry.

We came to the small, glasslike pond and saw the back of a big, gray stone mausoleum. The place had the deep stillness the living want for the dead.

"Look at that, Harry. People who would only worship in a church get buried by a building that looks like a Greek temple."

"Is it really a temple?"

"No. It's a part of the cemetery."

Harry ran ahead letting out an occasional "Yip!"—something his teachers complained about, but as he ran between and over the stones, it sounded like life itself. I watched and was happy to be with him. Harry climbed on a stone marked Hart. He was skinny and small; his eyes had dark circles under them. I wondered how much sleep he got last night, and how much he would get tonight.

He joined me and we went to the pond. We lay down and enjoyed a little sunny, peaceful time after danger. Harry stretched out. We had the basket and a red blanket, and Harry looked at the sky and newly planted poplars, palms, and oaks, which will give the next generation a fuller sound of wind in trees. Harry closed his eyes. "Listen," I said, "it's like the earth breathing." Harry pretended to sleep. I remembered my father listening to wind in the aspens by Lake Erie. We'd drive out in a one-horse buggy to dunes beyond Cleveland and listen to wind in the trees. I waited for talk of war, and he would say, "Listen. Listen. You'll never hear anything better." I wanted to hear about the noise of Antietam, and he would say, "Listen."

The child crooked his small arm over his eyes and lay in the warm sun. Even after he thought I saved us, he said he'd miss his mother. He must have been thinking about it all day. I'd miss her too, but wouldn't say it. Harry wouldn't have to draw another picture.

I stroked the arm crooked over that small face. He would be raised by Murphy. At least a little. I hated that, but if I loved him, it would be all right. My father used to say, "There's no cheap grace."

5

We ate Edith's cheese sandwiches, drank the root beer, and devoured chocolates and Life Savers, a candy that is literally a flavored hole, crystallized sugar with no center. I said this was an odd model for a condiment, but Harry pointed out it provided a good place for the tongue. After resting by the pond, we crossed a little bridge, walked on the island, and then Harry wanted to explore gravestones.

"You'll stay with Mummy," I said, as we walked through rows of low stones. Many were smaller than in eastern cemeteries. Scattered at our feet were granite boxes the height of a bootblack's box, quarter scrolls on low pedestals, slanted markers no higher than a footlight, stones saying Father/Mother, which Harry didn't seem to notice, and a few completely round marble logs, fodder for celestial fire. Several bigger monuments had the mysterious, unfinished look St. Gaudens used in his memorial to Henry Adams's wife.

Harry took my hand. There's nothing like a child taking your hand. We weren't crossing a street, no perilous autos, no menacing strangers—just his parents' break-up—and he took my hand. His hand was all trust and warmth, vulnerable yet hopeful. It breaks your heart and keeps it from breaking.

"Do you want me to stay with you?" Harry said.

"I want you to be with Mummy," I said. I didn't hesitate. He trusted me to do the right thing, and I would. "But

I'll never be far. I'll live in the same city. I'm writing a book.
I can go wherever you go."

"I don't think I like Mr. Murphy."

I squeezed Harry's hand and smiled a that's-the-way-
it-is and I-don't-like-him-either smile. Some things are
better unspoken. Harry knew what I meant. "If Mummy
wants to be with him," I said—I was acting, as I had with Lillian—"you and I just have to help."

God, that isn't what I felt.

"Does Mummy love Mr. Murphy?"

This was hard. So hard. "I guess so."

"Does she love you?"

"In a different way."

"Do you love her?"

"Yes."

"In a different way?"

I wanted to say no, but I said, "People change."

"Did you change?"

I smiled. Words wouldn't do. "It isn't anybody's fault."

"Does Mummy love me in a different way?"

"No," I said, picking him up. He was so light. So little.
"Of course not. Look at what she packed for us."

"I'll get us back together. I'll draw a picture."

"Harry, Harry." I squeezed him. "There's no one like
you. Mummy and I just have to be apart now."

"Why?"

"It happens. Like when it rains. Like a big storm."

"Storms go away."

"Oh, Harry. Parents never change the way they love their children."

Harry hugged me a long time. When I put him down, he took my hand, swung it, and pulled me along, skipping from headstone to headstone. Last year we walked in the Old Burying Grounds in Concord. Harry was fascinated by the thin slate stones—Puritan slices of time, gray and chipped, standing as a reminder, yet durable as a good slate roof. Harry liked the Puritan tracery of death: bones, skulls, thin-lined angels, and their weird script: code from the Other Side—written by the living, spoken by the dead. Here the markers were smaller, plainer—odd that California headstones are simpler than Puritan. Our New England ancestors mocked life with the certainty of death. Death is more like an inconvenience in Los Angeles. A dip in the real estate market. The markers seem to crouch—no signposts in the hard soil of eternity. None of death's vengeful mystery. Mystery is elsewhere—the dawn, girls, Babylon.

"Look!" Harry dropped my hand and pointed down. We were almost standing on a small, flat headstone, sunk even with the grass.

Marion Howard
Dec. 27, 1905
Aug. 11, 1913

"Eight years old," said Harry.

"Seven, actually," I said, but Harry wasn't listening.

"It doesn't say how she died," he said.

"I've always wished they did," I said. "And told the

story of the person's life."

Harry let go of my hand and went from grave to grave, stopping at the grave of Sally Juanita Hart, who lived to be only seven. "What do you think she was like?" he asked. Another child only lived to three, and Harry wanted to know if I thought he missed his family. He ran ahead, then stopped in his tracks. I jogged up and saw:

Little Willie

and

Baby Harold

Died 1911

Harry shook his head and looked down. "I almost stepped on them." He kept looking. "Maybe they were twins," he said. We stood by the flat marker with embossed granite letters. Harry was sad. Not frightened. Not unhappy. He wasn't disappointed or frustrated like a child who didn't get the right present, or was angry at the unfairness and bad luck of fate—he was sad. He reached down and touched the stone.

The child looked at me and said, "What happens if I die? I know you go under the ground, what else?"

I hugged him. Harry was warm and squirmy in the sailor suit. He wasn't just asking the universal question. He was asking, "Can you take care of me?" "Do you know how?" "Do you care enough?" And it started with this question. I couldn't say, "I love you and Mummy loves you," because that wasn't the question, even though it's the answer. I couldn't say everything will be all right, because everything wasn't all right. Standing over Little Willie and Baby Harold, Harry was asking me to be his dad.

The warm afternoon, the wind in newly planted trees, the boat, the closeness, telling Harry he would stay with his mother—this was enough for me. This was already the best day I'd spent with him. But Harry needed more. I couldn't just say I loved him, I had to prove it.

"Jesus will take care of you," I said. I said it as though I believed it, and at that moment I did. As Tuck had written in a letter, a time comes when He and only He stands between you and the abyss. Or a child's question.

"How do you know?" said Harry.

I remembered when I was little, about Harry's age, my grandmother, my father's mother, told me Jesus loved little children more than anyone, and I said, "How do you know?" just as Harry had. Quick. Defiant. Prove you love me. Nanny said, "He asked for them. That's how we know." I remembered her voice, her hand. I hadn't thought of that moment for years.

"Because He asked for them. When His disciples tried to keep the children back because they were making too much noise, He said, 'Suffer the little children to come unto me.' He likes children better than grown-ups."

Harry considered this and smiled. "What about hell?" The smile became wicked.

"Well," I said, returning his wicked smile, "In Revelation, the last book of the Bible, there is a war between devils and angels, and the devil and all the dead who weren't good are thrown in a lake of fire."

Harry thought for a moment and said, "Why does God boil people?"

∾

We laughed about God boiling people for the rest of the afternoon. It was Harry's joke and it was funny. The dead, even the young dead, didn't seem so troubling. We found a vendor on Santa Monica and ate frankfurters and ice cream in a paper cup. As the sun went down, wandering into the Pacific, I was ready to take him home.

6

The house was empty. I asked Harry if he wanted to ride Angels Flight, but he wanted to draw, and I realized I had a key, so we went in. Evening shadows softened the pioneer parvenu taste. The stairs were dark. The house was empty in that way a house is empty when a woman is gone. Harry followed me into the living room. Even with the mismatched, layered clutter of Turkish tapestries, wagon-wheel chandelier, pink sofa, and mirror with smirking gilt angels, the room felt empty.

Harry sat on the floor with his sketchbook and crayons. I poured sherry. The stained-glass sunbursts and cacti in the big dining room windows were blood red and mustard yellow. I was afraid Edith would come back with Murphy and the sight of him, mustache and triumph, would destroy the person I had been this afternoon. Could that person survive seeing Murphy every time I picked up Harry? Everything I said to Harry was going to be tested, maybe within the hour, and as darkness filled this turreted mockery of a house, I felt less and less ready for it. I told myself Edith is Harry's mother. That's what's important. Living with Murphy won't be easy for him either.

"I've got to pack," I said.

"Let's go," said Harry.

The child followed me upstairs and sat in a pink fan-tail chair by an iron floor lamp in the dressing room. I rummaged in my closet, took down clothes, and stuffed them in the old leather suitcase that accompanied us on so many trips. I thought about trips Edith made with Murphy; 1913, 1914, and 1915 were a trick and a humiliation. I tried to take strength in knowing that was over and packed shirts, underwear, socks. Sixteen years of marriage tossed in a suitcase while Harry hunched over his drawing. I thought of Lillian, five years old, putting her world in her "telescope" and losing it. Children have so much courage. I had to have it too. The boy adjusted the large orange shade of the electric lamp and kept drawing.

"Harry, I'll come tomorrow. Where would you like to go?"

"Babylon! Can we go to Babylon?"

"I don't think so, but we could go to Venice."

"Venice would be fine." He tried to sound grown-up, but I heard worry in his voice. A desire to please. The afternoon had been so good, the night was so uncertain. I didn't want to leave him. I wished Edith would come. How long could I keep this up?

I went down the hall into the room I used as a study. For a wild moment, I thought Edith had taken the notes and first chapters of the Griffith book. Why not? I had considered taking Harry. It would take so little to hate each other.

She hadn't. They were in the drawer where I left them. I sat at the desk and tried to think. If Griffith hated me the way I hated Murphy, we would never speak, but I would write my book without him. I looked at books I brought from Rochester. There was Emerson, who felt the presence of other worlds, and Mark Twain, who was so extraordinarily connected to this one.

Emerson and Twain. One affected love for everything, the other scorn, yet both had it right. Both loved their wives. Thinking of Twain reminded me of Tuck, who hung Twain's portrait in his office. But Tuck was a soldier and I was packing a suitcase.

I picked up *Huckleberry Finn* and turned to the passage I read when unhappy. It's in the first chapter, where Huck is alone and unable to sleep; he's so alone—a demon for a father, no mother, no family, just two old women who want to "sivilize" him, and Tom Sawyer, who wants to play boys' games while Huck Finn feels a man's sadness.

"Then I set down in a chair by the window and tried to think of something cheerful, but it warn't no use. I felt so lonesome, I most wished I was dead. The stars was shining, and the leaves rustled in the woods ever so mournful; and I heard an owl, a way off, who-whooing about somebody that was dead, and a whippowill and a dog crying about somebody that was going to die; and the wind was trying to whisper something to me and I couldn't make out what it was, and so it made the cold shivers run over me. Then way out in the woods I heard that kind of sound that a ghost makes when it wants to tell something that's on its mind but can't make itself understood, and so can't rest easy in its grave and has to go about that way every night grieving."

I read it three times and thought about reading it to Harry, but he was drawing. That was his way. Words would have to save me. I thought about Twain writing about loneliness so well it makes a person less lonely. Of course he did it in a house booming with family. *Olivet* and *Sinai*, the cars of the funicular, banged their last run. Up in the hills coyotes barked, and I wondered if I'd always be pulled back to my river and ghosts. Would Cleveland, baseball, and King Saturday, the Indian ballplayer who once jumped a rising drawbridge over the Cuyahoga. Would they always whisper? How long would I grieve for Edith and Rochester? Can I only love what's lost?

～

Harry walked in. "Look," he said, and showed me a picture of a rowboat surrounded by monstrous waves.

"I guess we'll have to tell Mummy about it," I said. Edith would think it was my bad judgment. She might not trust me with the child again.

"We don't have to," Harry said.

"Scary, wasn't it?"

Harry nodded and gave me a half smile.

"Does it scare you now?"

"No, we escaped."

"I wouldn't do it again," I said.

"Do you have to go, Dad?"

I hugged him. "Yes, as soon as Mummy comes. Finish the picture."

We went back to the dressing room. I put the notes and manuscript in the suitcase. Harry sat on the floor by Edith's closet and drew. In a few moments Edith would be here, then I would go, and Harry would be in a house without mother and father. The rest of our lives had begun. I closed the suitcase and sat in the fantail chair. It was dark, and I had to get the car back and try to sleep. I was afraid of not sleeping and looked at Harry, who was shading the sea under the waves coming at the boat. I'd depend on him in the dark, but he couldn't know it. He could not think he had to take care of me. There were tears in my eyes. I got up so Harry wouldn't see.

In the study was the copy of *The Swiss Family Robinson* my grandmother used to read to me. Nanny always read it when we visited. One night I couldn't sleep, and she read what seemed like the whole book sitting at the end of my bed. I went and got it.

"I'll read this to you. You know the story. It's about a family marooned on an island."

"When I finish my picture."

"OK. Just remember, this is a wonderful book if you can't sleep."

"I couldn't sleep last night."

"Me either," I said, and hugged him. "You know, I'm going to get a copy of this book, and if I can't sleep, I'll read it and think about you. You keep this one."

"OK!" Harry said, as if we'd made a bet.

I sat in the chair by the oval table. Harry's picture made me think about dying. The thought of Harry dying was more than I could bear. It was unthinkable. Nanny lost two children before they were school-age. Children dying was so common then. How had she borne it? Had she worried all the time? Was that what made her love the ones who survived so fiercely? When Twain's favorite child died, he never lived in the house in Hartford that looked like a steamboat again.

What if Harry died?

I watched the child sit with his back to Edith's closet, bent over the sketchbook. It was intolerable. Grotesque. Incomprehensible. But it could happen. I picked up the Book of Common Prayer. Why had Edith been looking at it? What did the Episcopal Church have to say about the death of a child? What could it say? Offering words after a child's death is blasphemy.

I looked. I had to know.

I opened the small, red, gilt-edged book to the table of contents. After "The Solemnization of Matrimony," "The Thanksgiving of Women after Child-Birth," "The Communion of the Sick," and "The Order for the Burial of the Dead," was "At the Burial of a Child."

At the burial of a child?

The church acknowledged the burial of a child is different from the burial of the dead.

At the burial of a child?

The phrase so immediate. So desperate. I turned pages. Harry was working on a picture of what might have been his death, comfortably sitting on the floor—happy to be near me. What would I say if he died? What would Edith say?

I found the page. It said "Burial of a Child" at the top. Then lower, in larger letters, AT THE BURIAL OF A CHILD. There it was. "The minister, meeting the Body, and going before it, either into the Church or towards the Grave, shall say."

There it was—what to say when there are no words. Why did it say "the Body"? Why didn't it say "the child"?

Then there was something about the resurrection and the life, and I closed the book. I didn't want to hear about the resurrection and the life. I'd heard about the resurrection and the life.

I opened the book again. I don't know why.

"Jesus called them unto him and said, Suffer the little children to come unto me, and forbid them not: for of such is the kingdom of God."

There it was. The same words I told Harry. The same words my grandmother told me. I read them again and again and realized it's all connected. My grandmother, me, Harry, and some ability to take care of each other. Someone asks, you answer. That's love. That's God.

The words were there. They had been waiting for me.

I looked at Harry. He was still drawing—so intent, so alive, so much himself, but he could be taken. Anyone can be taken anytime and there are no words . . . Except . . . Except when I asked, Nanny answered. When Harry asked, I answered. We ask and He answers. Yesterday I didn't know what to do if Edith left. Today I answer.

Harry was looking at me.

7

I looked up and Edith was watching. She wore a loose-fit-ting, white lace dress held at the neck with a gold brooch of her mother's and tied at the waist with a green and gold cord. Edith looked summery and white and had a flat white hat, which had what I thought for an instant was a red cross but was actually a red ribbon. Harry and I were watched by a warm, white shadow, barely illuminated at the edge of the light from the single lamp that lit the child and his drawing, and me, holding the prayer book. For an instant, I thought everything was all right—that we'd woken from a horrible dream and everything was as it had been. All the strange-ness, violence, and anger had gone away and been replaced by this woman with a half smile in the shadows. It was us again in the small light, and everything was forgotten, unimportant. We would put Harry to bed, rub his back, and sleep. Sleep.

I imagined Edith's body, so solid under the white dress. She seemed to float in the dark, smiling, feeling what Harry and I felt. Couldn't we float? All of us? Rise? Gently fly and be away from all this?

Edith's expression changed. It got harder. Judging. She was ready to defend, accuse, bargain. "You managed to bring him back," she said, with a dismissive turn of the head.

"I brought him home," I said.

The tightening of her thin mouth, the turn of head, the control in her voice, dissolved my fantasy of beckoning, floating.

"Michael's outside," Edith said. "He'll come in when you leave."

I nodded. I imagined Murphy saying he needed to protect her and Edith saying she could protect herself—at least from me. I kept looking at her—solid body, wide shoulders, big hands, precise voice—and remembered the lilac smell by the lake and hot dreaming contact of love. Lost. A man waited outside.

"Look at my picture," said Harry. He ran to his mother, who hugged him. "Dad saved me."

Edith looked at the picture.

"We went boating," I said. "Once we went with the current, we were fine."

"It was fun," said Harry.

"You're all right?" said Edith.

"We're fine," said Harry.

"Say good night to your father, precious," said Edith, squeezing Harry and tousling his fine brown hair. "Then get ready for bed. Maria will help you. I'll come soon."

The child ran to me, hugged me, and said, "I love you, Daddy. Here." He gave me the picture.

"I love you too," I said, carefully taking the picture and hugging him. "I'll see you tomorrow. Now go. I have to talk to Mummy."

Harry kissed me on the cheek, said, "No terrible beard," and went to Maria, who was waiting in the bedroom.

"Well," said Edith, "you and he seem to have had quite a time."

We were both in the light. Edith's lively brown eyes looked hollow and were set off by lines that meant she hadn't slept. Her large hands were on her hips.

"I have to tell you something," I said. We were three feet apart—about the distance allowed with a woman you can't touch. "Harry has to stay with you. Live with you. It's what he needs."

"What?" Edith stepped back and stood straighter.

"He has to live with his mother. Even," I stopped, stumbling on the name, riding small courage, "if you're with Murphy."

"You won't try to take him?" said Edith.

"Harry needs to be with his mother."

Edith sat down in the fantail chair. "And how did you decide this?"

I turned. Edith took off the flat, white hat and held it in her lap, pulling at the ribbon. "I asked him."

"You asked him?" Edith looked at me as if she hadn't understood what I said.

"Harry's the important one now," I said. "You may have a divorce." My voice broke. "Forgive me. This isn't easy. You may have a divorce and marry whom you like. We'll sell the ball club. The ownership's pretty clear. We shouldn't have to fight about it. What I'd really like is to see Harry every day. I'll live in whatever city you choose to live in. We can be civil. We won't have to see each other much."

I saw a tear in Edith's eye. She turned away. Her eyes were lustrous, deep.

"But you're so angry," she said. "After what I've done. How can you say this?"

"I am angry," I said, "but I'm finished doing stupid things . . . Harry has to be happy. I . . ." I stumbled again. "I want to get to know him. He's going to need me."

"And you want me to be happy?"

"I'm not doing this for you."

"You're doing this for Harry?"

"I'm doing it for me."

We were quiet. The house was quiet. *Olivet* and *Sinai* had finished for the day, and it was dark except for the single light. Harry must have been saying his prayers with Maria. It was time to leave. Time to be alone.

"Harry couldn't sleep last night," said Edith.

"It doesn't look as if you did either."

"When he did sleep, he had a dream. Did he tell you?"

"No."

"He dreamed you were hanging from a window sill by your arms. The window was closed. He and I were on the ground. A bird flew you to the ground but not to us. Harry woke up after the dream and couldn't sleep. I'm worried about him, but maybe everything will be all right. If you mean what you say."

"I mean what I say," I said curtly, grabbing the suitcase, but even yanking the leather handle, I had one last wild hope Edith would say don't go, stop, please, and this would end, or hadn't happened, and the three of us would be in the small light, but Edith closed her eyes and nodded.

"Can I get Harry at two tomorrow?"

"Of course."

The suitcase was heavy. I put it down and looked at Edith. I had the strongest, saddest feeling I was doing the right thing and it was the only thing. The wild last hope was replaced by bitter, dumb peace. Later I would be devastated, but now I had to be my best. I stopped waiting for a miracle, or maybe the miracle was that when we got to the end, when hell had a bottom floor, when a man was outside, I didn't try to hurt her. I was Harry's father.

"I forgive you," I said. "Please don't say anything."

I didn't mean it, but suddenly I knew this was the only way to say good-bye. Anything else was unfinished business. This was good-bye.

"We won't be friends," I said, "we'll be Harry's parents."

"I . . . I . . ." Edith could barely talk. "Do you remember how we used to joke about being left on a desert island with someone else? Henry, you left me on that desert island . . . You were wonderful, Henry. Wonderful to talk to. Wonderful some of the time. But you never took care of me. You went off to a world you made. That was your home. You never gave me anything."

We had fought this fight many times. I was finished with it. I had a suitcase and a child's drawing. A man was outside.

"You were just being human, Edith. Who hasn't been? Go your way. Let's be good to Harry."

Edith rose and took my hands. We looked at each other and cried silently. This was my answer. Edith was gone. Harry mattered. Everything else hurt but didn't matter.

I was, if only for a few minutes, the person those people who weren't there wanted me to be.

VII

THE MASTER

April 4, 1916
Midnight to dawn

1

I found my way back to Jesus' bungalow in a kind of clear trance. As I drove through the Third Street tunnel, away from Bunker Hill, I knew I'd done the right thing, surprised myself by doing it, and felt a deep, melancholy peace. This sadness was deep as night but held a secret strength. I'd been Harry's dad for an afternoon and evening and could be again. I wished I could tell Edith about the cemetery and being Harry's dad, but Edith was gone. Edith wasn't my best friend. She wasn't my friend at all. I was numb without her, but I'd get used to it, just like I'd get used to not telling her every important thing. The Model T obliged and didn't stall, even at the traffic light on Sunset.

Sunset Boulevard was unreal in the dark. Hills, stairs to nowhere, Cibola winking over a ravine, Los Angeles back there, and my life stretching into the dark made the cool night alive and unreal in the way the place must have been for the Spaniards who first saw an endless azure day replaced by darkness and coyotes.

Jesus was pacing anxiously in the living room. He wore a yellow suit, which looked oddly right with the beard and hair tied in a ponytail. He looked uncomfortable, pacing in front of his robes.

"I'm sorry I'm late. I had to talk to Edith. I told her Harry must stay with her."

"Interesting," he said. "How are you?"

"I'm all right. I need sleep."

Jesus looked at me carefully, apparently deciding not to be angry. "You look better. Things went well with your son, didn't they?"

"Very well."

"Maybe you'll be all right. I left you some dinner but I really must go. Can't keep Gerty waiting. Harrison, you're looking at me oddly."

"I'm used to you in white."

"You and Gerty will have to love me for myself."

∽

Jesus left cold meat, bread, and wine. I ate, and after washing, and carefully putting Harry's drawing on a deal table by the bed, lay down with the wine and *The Los Angeles Times* in the room the color of water in a sink. I finished "Citizen of Los Angeles Is Prisoner of Bandits," flipped the light switch by the door, and fell asleep.

∽

Sometime after midnight the front door was kicked in. I jumped up and had time to slip into my trousers and grab the wine bottle by the neck as D. W. Griffith and Max pushed open the bedroom door. Max slapped the wall and found the light switch. I could barely see in the initial flash of the overhead bulb but smelled whiskey. Max had a bottle. Griffith pointed a pistol. He wore a suit so white a spotlight could have been trained on it. Griffith was immaculate—crisper and whiter than Jesus—in some ultimate planter fantasy.

"You are going to answer for Miss Geesh!" Griffith

shouted, his voice as Southern as his father's must have been. His face contorted with a ferocious attempt to control anger and furious condescension.

"Not to you, I'm not!" I shouted back, suddenly furious. Furious they could barge in with guns. Furious Griffith was so superior. Furious everything in my life could be violated. Furious I couldn't get away with something I couldn't do. "My life is none of your business!"

"My business is honor," said Griffith, and with great ceremony, handed his pistol to Max, who, dressed in black from shoes to chauffeur's cap, seemed to rise from the blue pine floor to the whitewashed ceiling like a gigantic shadow. Max strode toward me. I thought I was going to be shot, but he extended two enormous hands. A pistol rested in each palm.

"What the hell is this?" I said.

"Choose your weapon," said Griffith, coolly.

"What for?" I said. "To protect myself from lunatics?"

"I demand satisfaction," said Griffith, eagle nose tilted absurdly upward.

"You'll get none," I said, trying to sound equally controlled and haughty.

"Are you a coward as well as a bounder?"

I laughed out loud. "Lillian refused you, so you want to fight. That's Southern logic. Like punishing the Negroes after losing the war."

"Have you no honor?"

"Are you pretending to be your father?"

"Defend yourself or apologize," said Griffith.

"Apologize for what? Your failure? Your disappointment? I'm not trying to marry Miss Gish."

"Mention her name again and I'll have Max horsewhip you."

"Now Lillian's your property? Who the hell are you to talk like this?" I was livid. "Who the hell are you? You make money from hate and wear a white suit! A Klansman by other means. You want to fight, I'll fight!" I took one of the pistols from Max. It was a marvelously balanced, single-shot, silver-handled dueling pistol. "What do you think I have to lose?" I had everything to lose but was too angry to think. "You picked the wrong man! I've had enough!"

Griffith stepped back. It was a natural reaction. I had a bottle in one hand, a pistol in the other, and was furious.

"Honor?" I said. "Two against one? You *are* the Klan. You're a coward and you've always been one. That's why you make movies instead of being a soldier!"

Griffith visibly struggled to regain composure. His head went up, down, and shook, before the blue eyes steadied on me, and the enormous nose sniffed. I was watching an actor recover a line. "Then you accept my challenge?" he said, making a sweeping gesture with both hands.

"Yes!" I barely knew what I was saying, carried by the inviolable rhythm of words, always my only weapon, but as soon as I said yes, standing shirtless by a deal table, hot with anger in the room where I'd failed with Lillian, I knew exactly what I had to lose. Holding the pistol so it pointed at the ceiling (I'd seen this done on stage), I said, "Let's go."

"To Babylon," said Griffith. "No one will see or hear. Let Max hold the weapons."

I gave Max the pistol with a look of utter scorn and put on a shirt, the tweed jacket, and shoes. I folded Harry's drawing and put it in my pocket. Griffith stood with his arms across his chest, grand and impatient. He was back in control and playing a great role. Perhaps the Master expected me to beg and grovel. Perhaps I was supposed to be humiliated and frightened. Maybe he just wanted to scare me. Maybe he wanted to kill me. If he was surprised at my willingness to fight, he didn't show it.

We went out in silence. Griffith first, then Max, then me. It was cold outside but not completely dark. A slender moon provided enough light to see high clouds and the dim outline of the balloon and Great Hall off in the fields below the hills above Sunset. The Fiat looked like a dreadnought anchored at the bottom of the steps.

"It's a marvelous view," I said, as I stepped into the backseat, trying to sound brave. To my surprise, Griffith also got in back, though he sat four feet away. I was sitting in the same place Lillian sat when I saw them yesterday. The open car smelled of freshly cleaned leather, now dampened by night air. A lion cub was tethered to the brake pedal. Max released it and the cub bounded over the seat to Griffith, who picked it up, stroked its ears, and said, "Good girl, good girl." The cub was the size of a small dog and immediately began to purr. Other than agreeing to duel and seeing Griffith pet a lion, we might have been driving to a business meeting.

"Everything is a fine view, if you just look," Griffith said, as Max gunned the big motor. D. W. looked straight ahead. The eagle profile and keen eye searched the dark as if looking for things not there. Max drove carefully out of the hills. The chauffeur was in no hurry, and Griffith looked only at the lion or straight ahead. I might as well not have been there. The moment we stopped talking, I thought about Harry and got a lump in my throat. Why? Why after finding my son was I going to kill or be killed by this ridiculous son of a bitch and his awful chauffeur?

We turned onto Sunset. Griffith finally looked at me and said, "I saved you from a mob." The steady noise of the powerful engine and the distance between front and back seats kept his words private. "But I didn't save myself from you."

I looked up. His tone was different from the bullying Kentucky theatrics in the bungalow. There was uncomprehending hurt in his voice and inconsolable resignation in the piercing eyes. The cub purred—an insane juxtaposition to the anger and hurt playing over Griffith's dark, angular face. The Master didn't have to talk. He knew, or sensed with the perfect instinct of jealousy, that I had been offered what he was refused. I knew something he didn't, and it had made him a ghost. Irrelevant. Grieving. Lost.

"It had nothing to do with you," I said. "I was alone at

three in the morning. Miss Gish was upset about refusing your offer of marriage."

"It has everything to do with me."

"Did Lillian tell you?" I said suddenly.

Griffith started to answer, stopped, and I knew she had. I almost laughed. She wasn't perfect. She told to keep from marrying. That's why she was willing to lose her virginity.

"Harrison, you were going to write about me. Even after you attacked my chauffeur, I was going to help. We weren't friends, but we understood each other. I understood about your wife. You about Miss Geesh."

I almost said I was sorry. Griffith saw. I just shook my head.

"You put me in an intolerable situation," he said. "Because . . ." Griffith looked away. He looked at the dark off in those hills—so empty and unreal for me—for him, no doubt, dense with betrayal and secrets. "Because you knew how I felt about Miss Geesh, the insult is mortal."

Griffith didn't say anything, nor did I. We listened to the easy power of the big Fiat engine. The wind was cold. A coyote howled and another howled back. The Master held the cub. I couldn't tell him there was no insult. I couldn't tell him Lillian and I had nothing to do with him, because to him Lillian and I were everything. I understood. Edith and Murphy had nothing to do with me. Edith and Murphy had everything to with me.

I said nothing because there was nothing to say.

2

The enormous Fiat followed Sunset to where it bends north to meet Hollywood Boulevard and continues west. Max drove deliberately. The pistols rode on the front seat. Griffith didn't speak and the lion slept. Fine Arts finally came up on the left—low, bright buildings rising out of dark fields. Work was being done. The kingdom of photoplay respected the clock no more than the classical unities. Lights were on in the laboratory, the cutting and projection rooms, and the house where Lillian Gish brought the sun, when she was light and beauty, a day, and maybe a lifetime, ago. I didn't know her then, and surrounded by men and guns, knew her less. It didn't matter. This was between Griffith and me.

Fine Arts lit one side of Sunset; plywood walls lined the other. The steady motion and purr of the Fiat gave the ride an unreal, night inevitability. I couldn't imagine we would face each other with guns, shoot, die maybe, and couldn't imagine we wouldn't. We were rowing like Dante's Ulysses, who demanded to know what is beyond the sun, to experience every sin, and died for it. We moved slowly and I could have grabbed the pistols, jumped out, and run into Fine Arts yelling that a madman was trying to kill me, but then the madman would turn out to be D. W. Griffith, and I would be judged mad—gone from chauffeur biting to wild, gun-wielding, midnight accusations. Griffith could say it was a joke and I panicked and acted crazy again. It would be my final disgrace—the end of my book. People on the set still laughed about the time D. W. let an old, tame lion walk up on Fairbanks, the acrobat, and cocky Allan Dwan, which scared the hell out of them until the Master appeared and walked the beast back to its cage.

Griffith looked at me, and said, "She was pure."

"No one's pure," I said.

"She was the only one," he said, and looked away.

"You don't know her," I said. "Why did she tell you about me?"

His face got hard, and I knew what really happened was irrelevant. What really happened was farcical and humiliating, but for Griffith, whether he knew the truth or not, I was evil and Lillian sullied, though I hadn't been evil and she wasn't sullied. But Griffith couldn't understand, couldn't accept, couldn't see the humanity because it happened differently in his imagination.

I could accept Edith and Murphy because of Harry, but Griffith had no one. Pain will have pain.

Max drove ten miles per hour. We approached Babylon at funereal speed. Three men in a dirge of misunderstanding and revenge, waiting to see who would break, who would run, who would kill. Was it a joke? A bluff? A lesson? There was always the possibility Griffith meant what he said, and over a matter of honor, we would reenact our own Civil War.

The Fiat slipped through the intersection of Holly- wood and Sunset, rolled by Fine Arts, and paralleled Baby- lon. Would we really walk into the master's night city and face each other with guns? I thought about Harry. I thought about running. Griffith had made me see I was different from my father, and that made me angry. I wanted Griffith to play the role of coward. We were both trying to get a per-formance from an actor.

Where would I go? Back to Bunker Hill and ask Edith for help? Tell Harry his dad was a coward?

The Fiat crawled. I wondered if Griffith was insane, then asked myself if I would have shot Murphy last night. The answer frightened me. We moved in a trance of big car, steady engine, eagle profile, and lion, between the lights of Fine Arts and the mystery of Babylon. I rubbed my ankles, which were cold. I hadn't put on socks.

3

The Fiat stopped and I was alone with Griffith, guns, and growing fear. Griffith watched me, looking for fear, smelling it like a dog, waiting for me to run. This was my test and punishment. Open cowardice in the night city. Max tethered the lion to the brake pedal, stuck the pistols in his belt, and opened the rear door for Griffith. I opened my door myself. The wind gnawed at my ankles and whipped sand and gravel across Sunset. We were outside the walls, so we heard but couldn't see. Babylon sang in the dark. Tim-bers creaked and strained. Griffith looked at the high dark-ness and stood for an eerie moment listening to many noises—wood, steel, wind. Wind finding strange shapes, strange places, whistling around Ishtar and lashing gods created to live in eternity or infamy. Eternity if *The Mother and the Law* made money; infamy if we killed each other. We stood and listened. Griffith gave me the chance to run, but I just watched his white silhouette.

If we killed each other, people would say this photoplay was too big, too ambitious, too crazy, so Griffith took a critic to Babylon and they killed each other over a woman neither could have. It will be a Los Angeles legend.

Babylon spoke. The great set was no more silent than the old nickelodeons. It was a massive atonal harp playing God's music on scales stranger than any in Vienna. We could have been at the gates of Babel when God confounded the tongues of men. We heard voices, warnings in the wind, insane instruments, and I thought of the currents that buffet the lovers Paolo and Francesca in Hell, forever keeping them together and forever keeping them apart.

Griffith looked at the wall, seemed to count, and then in one motion hurled himself at a section of board that swung open with a small crack, as neatly as the door to Eddie Rogers' secret hall.

"My way in," Griffith said, and disappeared through the dark opening. Max followed and I was standing, with cold ankles, on Sunset. I could have run away, I could have walked, but something held me. Standing so cold in midnight, I couldn't stop listening. Babylon was talking. It was calling. Pulling me in. I didn't quite believe Griffith's challenge, but Something was here. The guns might be props, the challenge a game, the duel a fake—all calculated to scare and test, like Griffith telling Miriam Cooper her mother was dead to get the actress to cry real tears—but the wind, gods, voices, and gigantic place sang music I had to hear. We were actors now, the audience Ishtar and Gilgamesh—and I couldn't let go. I had to listen. Babylon called.

I didn't run.

"You join us," said Griffith.

I nodded. I could barely hear. Babylon spoke a high, thrilling language. The slender moon showed the long outline of the Great Hall. The balloon shook violently, visible, then not visible, as a cloud pushed across the moon. Babylon was big enough during the day—maybe not the quarter mile long and three-eighths of a mile deep press agents claimed, but at night it was big in a way nothing I've ever felt was big. I was drawn in. Pulled. Sucked. It was fear. It was the dancing balloon. It was Antietam. We stopped, and Griffith surveyed his city. He was tall, rigid, a ghostly white blade. Max watched me, pistols in belt, black from head to toe save for the gun handles, which glistened like Griffith's suit.

"You didn't run," Griffith said, but I barely heard him, overwhelmed by wind, elephants, hawsers, and the vast goddess-filled darkness that brooded over Hollywood and Sunset. High, crowded night hung over the area, which, before Griffith's walls, was an open plain where sheep grazed, farmers raised figs, and long ago, Secretary of War Jefferson Davis indulged his penchant for lunatic ideas by outfitting the United States Cavalry with camels to patrol the California desert. The beasts proved as intractable as Davis himself and ran away, wandering the canyons and creating the strangest sight in this land once inhabited by men who favored dreams over reality—until Griffith erected the hovering mystery, complete with balloon, that rose next to us.

"You're talking to yourself," said Griffith.

"Camels once roamed here," I said, angry at being overheard, like when Harry walked into my tower.

"Jefferson Davis," said Griffith.

"The first Southerner," I said, "to do something ridiculous in this place."

"And not the last."

"A man named Camel George herded them until he betrayed the bandit Vasquez for a reward."

"We're the outlaws now," said Griffith.

I hardly heard. Babylon called.

4

Griffith and I walked to the steps of the Great Hall. His suit was luminous in the moving light. My tweed trousers and jacket were dark. Griffith was the better target. Max stayed three paces behind.

We came to the carpeted stairs where tomorrow, if there was tomorrow, the Denishawn Dancers would dance for Tammuz, Ishtar's departed lover, to celebrate his return from the underworld. The wind was up and clouds raced in front of the moon so we could see, then couldn't, then could. Griffith stopped. I stopped. Belshazzar's canopy shuddered in the wind—no luxury for a doomed king now. Griffith looked into the whispering dark where canopies, tapestries and couchant lions hid trembling places for secret sins and nameless gods. Above us was Ishtar, white as flesh in scudding moonlight. Flanking us was solid darkness—the massive bases of columns, their frescoes Braille legends concealing Gilgamesh, who mastered everything but grief and conquered everything but death, and Bel-Marduk, jealous war god whose high priest opened the gates to Cyrus. Levitating a hundred feet above, over the singing wires of the Hanging Gardens, were the elephants, white like Ishtar—huge, magical, occult trunks saluting the night.

I stepped over the railroad tracks, which came at the Great Hall as if to bisect it and neatly separated Griffith from me. We faced each other, like friends or brothers, knowing that when we showed our backs, Max would bring the pistols and we would march, turn, fire. The pillars, wind, gods, and elephants talked at once.

I stood and listened, thinking: None of this is real! Not the guns! Not the duel! You can't be your fathers! He's playing!

The balloon groaned at its moorings, and I thought: Griffith has no family. He acts! He makes up stories and builds unreal cities!

"The pistols, man!" yelled Griffith.

Call his bluff, I thought. Face him down! He's dreamed his father so long he has to face a man with a gun even if it isn't real.

I looked at Ishtar, then the elephants, which seemed to be a thousand feet in the air, and thought: He's crazy! He believed in Lillian like you believed in Edith! He'll fight!

I staggered. Griffith saw. Said nothing.

You can't be your father! Be Harry's father!

"Does either of you have a pen?" I shouted.

Griffith waved at Max, who reached in his pocket, stepped gingerly over the dark tracks, and handed me a fountain pen. I took out Harry's drawing, and writing on my knee, scribbled in a shaky hand:

"Harry, I love you. Always remember our afternoon in the cemetery.

Love,

Dad."

"Give this to my son . . ."

5

Max put Harry's drawing in his coat, removed the pistols from his belt, and offered them for inspection. The moon appeared, glittering in the silver curve of the handles and serpentine "JWG" on the butts. I picked up one, then the other, touched the polished black barrels, avoided the dark muzzles, ran my thumb over each glistening brass hammer, and looked away. The elevator tower stood a half mile down the tracks. I could still run into the night, run at the walls and hills, run forever, but I held the guns, which were light as toys and balanced as my right hand.

"Are these real?" I said, handing them back to Max, trying to sound scornful. "They're not props?"

"They're my father's," said Griffith.

"Here," said Max, and handed me a pistol. With great ceremony, he walked around to Griffith and presented the other.

"Ten paces, turn and fire," said Griffith.

We were still facing each other. Babylon was over my shoulder. The wind was up, and the crazy babble of wire and god-noise was so high I had to shout, which was good because I was trembling. Why play this game? What jumble of father and madness was this? I hated Griffith. I hated his strange, insane city.

"I'm braver than you!" I shouted. "I have more to lose. I have a son!"

"If you're so brave," said Griffith, suit gleaming in a patch of racing moonlight, "why aren't you wearing white?"

"I didn't have time to dress for the evening."

"Do you wish to be excused on the grounds of fatherhood? I will consider that an apology."

"You want a way out, don't you?" Christ! What was I

trying to prove? Gods and elephants roared. The city was moving.

"I don't hide behind a six-year-old," yelled Griffith.

"No!" I shouted. "You run from a woman's rejection."

"For that, you shall fight. No apology accepted."

"None offered!"

"I'm braver than you!" shouted Griffith, throwing his head back as if saluting or mimicking the elephants. "I have everything to lose! Look around! I bring the future! I am the only man on earth who can! I am the Millennium!"

"You're insane!"

"You're a bounder loose in the world of decent people because his wife left him."

"Not before she had my child!"

"Big talk from a man who peeks in rooms! You owe, Harrison, I collect."

"You owe every decent person in America for *Birth of a Nation*! Bigot! Hate-monger!" I held my pistol straight up, as did Griffith. We were like images in a mirror or the top and bottom of a playing card. No one moved.

"Listen to me!" I yelled.

"A last request?"

"If you kill me or I kill you, you'll never make another motion picture. No more *Births*! No hate spectacles. I put an end to it. So be it! I pay the debt!"

"How could you understand?" yelled Griffith. "Your country wasn't occupied by enemy troops! Your home wasn't destroyed! You didn't lose a way of life! *The Birth* won't be judged for what it says of the past. It will be judged for what it contains of the future! I see another dimension. I mastered the universal language! I can stop the world war! But there is conduct I will not abide!"

"You're drunk!" I shouted.

"I am the Millennium!"

It was insane, two men holding guns, yelling into Babylon.

"I know how you'll be remembered! I've written it!" I hadn't. I was making it up.

"Talk, Harrison!"

"This stunt gives me an audience!"

"Talk!"

Clouds crossed the face of the moon. The elephants seemed to be waving their trunks, and the wind bellowed. Ishtar was closer. Clouds covered and re-covered the moon. The sound was awful. We *were* at the gates of a new and dreadful world.

"Talk or I'll shoot!" shouted Griffith.

"You're a great craftsman! A great pioneer! But not a great artist! No! Craft is not enough! Technique is not enough! A universal language is not enough! Art is content as well as form! Meaning as well as technique! You would never be as careless with a camera as you have been with history. You show the world a new language then say terrible things in it. You, more than any man, are caught in the schism between form and content! This is how you will be remembered whether I live or die!"

"Look around, fool!" yelled Griffith. "This is how I'll be remembered! For the greatest photoplay that was ever made! Or ever will be! Love's story through the ages! Only I can do it!"

"Not if you're dead!"

"My father didn't back down," said Griffith. "Neither will I." He turned, flashing his white back at me.

"One!" yelled Max.

Griffith cocked his pistol.

6

Two!"

I cocked my pistol and took a step.

"Three!"

I stumbled, got my balance. I was going to die.

"Four!"

I went into the darkness. Ishtar and elephants shimmered in the wind.

"Five!"

Harry.

"Six!"

Where was Jesus?

The wind grew stronger. Babylon was louder. Wires and voices screamed.

"Seven!"

I felt so light. Was I floating?

"Eight!"

Our Father who art.

"Nine!"

Harry, forgive me.

Ten!"

I turned, stood sideways, and aimed. I felt nothing. Griffith raised his arm. We looked at each other down barrels and over sights—weightless as angels who walk on the wind.

A gun shot roared into the wind. Something flew by my cheek. A crack and ricochet echoed through Babylon.

Griffith looked stunned.

I staggered. Was I alive? I had no idea what to do.

The Master stood sideways and perfectly still. A lean white blade. Cloud-broken moonlight raced over him.

"Cover," said Max in a loud, hoarse whisper. Griffith moved his pistol over his heart but every other white part of him was still.

"You must fire!" said Max.

"Now, Harrison!" yelled Griffith. He was absolutely pale in pale light.

My arm trembled. I aimed. Griffith's right eye was directly in my sight. He was twenty paces away, defenseless, and my arm wasn't shaking. I raised the pistol and fired into the air.

"Satisfaction," said Griffith, who strode over to Max and slapped his face.

7

Max vigorously shook his head yelling, "I didn't know! I didn't!" Griffith swung the pistol, his arm made a furious white arc and the butt slammed Max above the ear. The chauffeur bent over, holding his head. His cap with its little black brim flew off and pinwheeled along the ground as the wind picked up.

"Wait in the car!" ordered Griffith, pointing with the pistol. Max walked off holding his head where blood flowed from a scalp wound. The hat vanished.

"Harrison," said Griffith, looking at his pistol. "It wasn't supposed to be loaded."

"You son of a bitch!" I pointed my pistol at him.

"The duel wasn't real, the issue was."

"What issue!"

"How much you respect Miss Geesh."

"That's ridiculous!"

"You respect her enough to fight. I'm satisfied."

"You're crazy!"

"You didn't make love to her, did you?"

"I didn't say I didn't!" I shouted, amazed I could stand without trembling. The wind snaked around columns, whipped wires, punished my ankles. Babylon was almost black. Ishtar was a ghost; the elephants were lost in the night. The invisible city made insane music.

"It doesn't matter if you did or not, you were willing to fight. I like that."

"A bullet went by my head! You idiot!" I realized I felt wonderful. I was alive. No one was hurt. I was just mad as hell.

"That, unfortunately, was not part of the lesson."

"What goddamn lesson?" I was right in front of him, holding the pistol in his face.

"I staged a duel. It wasn't real any more than this is real." Griffith made a sweeping gesture with his gun at the groaning darkness. "To find out if you're an honorable man. If you'd run, I wouldn't bother with you."

"I don't care!"

"You have just witnessed a play, Harrison. It starred you. It also starred me. I found out that whatever you did with Miss Geesh, she meant enough to you to fight. You found out you aren't a coward. That may not mean anything to you, but it means a great deal to me. You, sir, are a man of honor."

"And you, sir," I shouted, "are a goddamn idiot!"

"I think not, Harrison. I put you in another world. You thought your life was in danger. You had to decide whether to fight or run. It's something you may have wondered about yourself. It's something I wonder about myself, and unexpectedly, thanks to your courage, I found out. Your decision was more difficult. You had an hour to think. I had only a few seconds. Harrison, you've also been in the position of that man Murphy, which on reflection will make you think differently about him and yourself."

"I did make love to her!" I yelled, furious that Griffith

had orchestrated the duel and had the nerve to draw a moral from it.

"You won't hate yourself so much," said Griffith.

"No, I hate you!"

"Men who shoot at each other sometimes become quite fond of one another."

"I did make love to her!"

"She says you didn't."

"I did!"

"You didn't."

"Then why the goddamn duel?"

"Do you believe everything women tell you, Harrison?"

"Of course not." I was beginning to enjoy this.

"I prefer to believe a man facing a gun."

"You dumb cracker!"

"Excuse me, Harrison, but you have just been allowed to live in your imagination. You have been given a dream, which you thought was real. Consequently, when you think, rather than shout, you may learn something. It's infinitely better than actually fighting or being alone and miserable."

"I didn't learn anything!"

"As it turned out, you fought a real duel. You defended a lady's honor. You defended your own. A Yankee with honor."

"I thought the duel might be fake! You're the master charlatan!"

"Yes, but you knew I was jealous, and you know what it

is to be jealous. You bit my chauffeur."

"Jesus Christ," I said. I was calming down. I felt wonderful.

"To be honest, it occurred to me Max might load the guns. He's a sneaky sort. But I've never been able to hit anything with those damn pistols, and I assumed you'd be safe, but after I fired, and heard the ricochet, it was real. You didn't shoot back. You were brave. I too was brave. I surprised myself."

I stepped back and lowered the gun, which I'd been waving like a prop, and started to laugh. I couldn't stop. I laughed into the wind, howled at singing wires, hooted with groaning hawsers, cackled at dark gods. It was ridiculous. It was hilarious.

Griffith began to laugh. He's never supposed to laugh. His closest associates say he never laughs, but the Master began to shake, then bounce, he even grabbed his sides. "Damn!" he kept saying. "Damn!"

"I did make love to her," I said, unable to stop cackling. Hooting. Giggling. Shaking my head. "I did!"

"You didn't!" Griffith hopped with laughter.

"I did!"

"You didn't!"

"I did!"

"It doesn't matter," said Griffith.

"It does!"

"It doesn't!"

I felt like we would never stop laughing.

Griffith managed to stop first. "If you had, when facing a gun, you would have denied it. You wouldn't have been shouting about my place in history!" He bent over, hands on his knees.

I shook my head and laughed harder. I was hopping from one foot to the other. It was like dancing.

"Harrison," said Griffith, trying to stop. "It doesn't matter if you did. You paid the debt of honor."

"I should have shot you!" I said, and we went through another round of doubled-over hilarity. I felt a delicious rush of confidence. Nothing mattered. Not Murphy. Not Edith. I won. Griffith won. I never felt better in my life.

"Come," said Griffith. "Let's sit."

We went up the carpeted steps. The moon was hidden and the night was absolutely black. Babylon whispered and groaned. I slipped, but Griffith steadied me. We sat under Belshazzar's canopy beside a sentinel lion perched mutely at attention. Behind were winged gods with the bodies of bulls and heads of men. Over us, a tasseled curtain flapped, and we looked out toward the tracks and elevator tower, lost in the dark.

"Lillian doesn't love me," I said, suddenly.

Griffith, in an utterly surprising gesture, put his arm around my shoulder. "She doesn't love me either."

"Lillian loves her art," I said. "Like you."

Griffith nodded. "Marriage wouldn't work."

We were quiet. Wind pushed clouds off the moon and elephants returned as the Hanging Gardens swung like gigantic birds. Lions and gods appeared out of the dark. Ishtar was lustrous in the full night.

"I'm sorry about your wife," said Griffith. "I saw her. We spoke. The woman has a fine, intelligent eye. A natural elegance. You must have made a fine pair."

"I love her," I said. "I'll always love her, but it's over. Yesterday I had to decide if Harry should live with her. It was harder than dueling. I had to do what's best for him, not me, so I told him he must live with his mother. That means living with Murphy, being raised by Murphy. The child offered to stay with me, but I said no. I told him we have to treat his mother well. That's what loving him means, Griffith. I lost my wife but found my son. It will be hard, but I'll live in the same city they do and see him every day. Last night, I told this to Edith."

"That's why you didn't shoot me, isn't it?"

"What?"

"You've made peace. You didn't need to kill anyone. Not even a man who shot at you. I envy you."

"It's been a remarkable day."

"Good God," said Griffith. He shivered. "I might have killed you. I didn't think those damn things could hit a barn." He stopped. "Did yours have a bullet or blanks?"

"I don't know."

"We'll never know," said Griffith.

"What will you do with Max?"

"Fire him . . . unless you want him arrested."

"I don't think so," I said. "It's over."

The wind died. The tasseled flapping stopped. The Hanging Gardens were still, and the balloon didn't bang. The wires, gods and secret places stopped their strange language.

"Harrison, before we fought, you said you'd pay the debt owed for *Birth*. You said there'd be no more hate spectacles. There won't be. I'm paying the debt. No one else can pay your debts. This photoplay, and the shot tomorrow, is payment. I can't wait until you see. I'm telling the greatest stories in the world in a way no one ever has."

"Babylon," I said.

"The fall of a city," said Griffith.

"Homer."

"The story of Jesus."

"The Bible," I said.

"The massacre of innocents on St. Bartholomew's Day."

"Hatred," I said.

"A modern story of love and injustice."

"Love triumphs?"

"Yes, Harrison. Love triumphs."

"Then an image Miss Geesh thinks might end the war?"

"Images will change the world," said Griffith. "It's the way I mix them. They'll hypnotize, then run at the audience. The ending will be the most intense ever seen. In anything. Literature. Painting. Music. Images will fly like thoughts. Perfectly timed. Perfectly delivered. No one who sees it will be the same."

"This is man's story," I said.

"Man's struggle," said Griffith.

"Man's struggle against . . ."

"Intolerance!" cried Griffith. "I'll call it *Intolerance!*"

8

What do you hear?" said Griffith, standing in front of Belshazzar's canopy and listening to the roar, the voices, the wired babble of Babylon. I looked over the steps, down the railroad tracks, at the tower elevator. Griffith's dark needle was a solitary spire in the shifting night.

"It's a shame photoplays don't have sound," I whispered into the wind. "I've never heard anything like this."

"Music is the only accompaniment for the photoplay," said Griffith. "Art deserves art."

"But the sound. It's not of this world."

"I think a cable has snapped behind the north wall. Huck better check tomorrow." Griffith descended a few steps and looked back at Babylon as if he could see in the dark. His white suit was a blur against the colossal darkness. The guns were in his belt. "What do you hear?"

"Voices," I said.

The wind rose and cut my ankles. It was cold. We were at the center of currents swirling around massive, strange shapes.

"What voices?" said Griffith.

"The dead."

The moon emerged with lions, pillars, Ishtar, so big in the night. We were surrounded by noise, shadows, and intermittent light like the raw chaos at the beginning of the world.

"The dead who loved me," I said. "The dead who loved someone else."

"They're here," said Griffith. "All is here."

The night was cold. The duel already seemed long ago.

"I hear men who died in the war," said Griffith. "There are many."

"They speak," I said, "but I don't understand. They're here, but I don't see."

"I see them," said Griffith.

I listened.

"They're in the wind," said Griffith. "People we loved. People who loved us. We don't know how to listen to the dead."

"Or the living."

Griffith was silent.

"We try to love them," I said, and spread my arms to encompass the night horizon of pillars, towers, lions, afraid soon I'd be alone in the harsh April night.

"It's lonely," said Griffith.

The wind blew harder. It swirled up the steps, flapped the canopy, swung the Hanging Gardens, and moaned in the timbers.

"Maybe we're not meant to hear," I said.

"'Bless the Lord,'" said Griffith, "who walketh upon the wings of the wind: Who maketh his angels spirits; his ministers a flaming fire.'"

"There's no fire."

"Or angels," said Griffith.

"Only voices."

"Antecedents," said Griffith, and then, his voice solemn in the wind, quoted Whitman:

"'With antecedents,

"'With my fathers and mothers and the accumulations of past ages,

"'With all which, had it not been, I would not now be here,

"'as I am,

"'With Egypt, India, Phoenicia, Greece and Rome.'"

He stopped. He listened. I don't know what spoke to Griffith in the hawsered, unstable night, but I heard Edith—her laughter at dancing school on Euclid Avenue, cheers for King Saturday and the strong, muffled slap of gloved hands at League Park, love's firm words against the ocean on the rocks in Maine, a clear voice directing servants, a tired voice up too much at night, an angry voice, a distant voice, a lying voice. I didn't want to hear more.

Griffith raised his arms:

"'We touch all laws and tally all antecedents,

"'We stand amid time beginningless and endless, we stand

"'amid evil and good,

"'All swings around us, there is as much darkness as light.'"

Griffith declaimed and I thought about the times I could have seen how lonely Edith was, how tired, how she needed help, but I went to a tower to write and play the gramophone. To dream. To go back—back to Cleveland, to a saloon woman whom I loved, to the Indian, to my father, to gaze at the Smith graduate who wore yellow. I was dreaming while Edith became someone else. We had a new generation in the house, but I was back there—making a book—writing, remembering, sustained by words, not hearing, not seeing, so now I'd come to the strangest place on earth, with a man who had guns in his belt, who saw dead men in a motion picture set.

"What do you hear, Harrison?"

"Edith's voice. Her laugh."

"Don't listen to the past. Listen to the future. Your life starts here."

We listened. Wires sang high in the invisible city.

"I do more than hold the mirror up to nature," said Griffith. "I am the mirror. Everything is new, Harrison. Including you."

I listened, and Griffith said he heard his kingdom—the kingdom where he makes war, Jesus, lovers seeking shelter: the prophet's "time and times and the dividing of time." He wanted to talk and I wanted to listen. Then I talked. I told Griffith to be careful. I told Griffith success could pass like a shadow, youth, a dream, Edith—even the money for *Birth*, all the freedom and power. Be careful. Careful. I spoke, but Griffith barely heard. He heard Babylon. I heard lost selves, dead friends, abandoned love. Griffith heard the future. I talked about the baseball rebellion and 1890, when players started their own league and were destroyed by the National League—a truly American last best hope—but Griffith talked Marconi. D. W. heard the wireless in the wires. He talked about transmitting images. He talked about communication moving at the speed of thought, as if some day people will send thoughts to each other. I warned him about men who rise to the top: Rockefeller, Spalding, who ruined the Players League, Adolph Zukor, what Murphy would like to be— the killers who know owning, organizing, controlling is the world. Griffith said he heard the future and the future was different.

"'And the form of the fourth is like the Son of God,' which is to say Imagination," he said.

"The book of Daniel," I said.

"Babylon," said Griffith. He talked about picture language and his unbridled power to make money, which, if done right, could set us free from the owning-controlling organizers, maybe from capitalism itself.

"Heady stuff," I said.

"The motion picture can do anything."

I nodded, but I think Griffith thought me thick-headed, deaf to the song in the towers, the wind in the harp.

"I can do it," he said, to the shadows of the fabulous,

ridiculous place. "All the Zukors and Inces and Laemmles, all the tailors and furriers in New York and Budapest, need the new language. They need us, Harrison. They'll need us more when this photoplay is done. Fine things, great things, will happen. And you will write about it."

"What if *Intolerance* loses money?"

"I hear worlds and voices," said Griffith, "but I don't hear that word."

Suddenly he burst into an aria from *Tannhäuser*.

9

We sat where Belshazzar and Seena Owen would sit when the sun was up. The canopy shook over our heads. The clouds were moving and Griffith stood up. The guns in his belt made him look like a Mississippi cardsharp.

"Let's go to the tower," said Griffith.

I looked down the carpeted steps to the tracks and the tower elevator off in the night. The wind was cold.

"Then home," said Griffith. "There's something I want you to see."

"The Alexandria Hotel?" It was well known the man who built Babylon lived in a hotel and the possessions he prized most were finely tailored suits and sheet music. Last year I wrote, "The man who makes worlds prefers room service to roots, music to speech, and a troupe of actors to a family." I didn't feel so smug now and would be happy to sit in his room, or under the famous Tiffany ceiling, and drink coffee until dawn.

"A hotel isn't a home, Harrison. Fine Arts. Where we work."

We went down the steps past where we dueled—where Griffith staged fear, which became courage—but as the wind tore at Babylon, I felt an immense loneliness rising in its roar.

Griffith walked on one side of the tracks and I on the other. The elevator tower rose in the dark, a slender modern gadget facing Ishtar and the elephants of Babylon. The looming place and single, ingenious needle for Billy Bitzer's battered black Pathé waited for Griffith's Shot. Everything in this weird place had been built for Bitzer's little box, which would sit in an elevator, in a tower, and be pushed a half mile by sixteen men so the Master could duel the impossible.

"What?" said Griffith.

"The impossible."

"You were talking to yourself, Harrison."

I smiled. "You have a fatal attraction for the impossible, Mr. Griffith."

"Not fatal!" he cried. "Personal."

I didn't know what he meant. I didn't ask.

"I told you the motion picture could do anything," said Griffith. "Make people laugh. Fight. See. Think. But whatever it does, it must always attempt the impossible. That's how it opens the doors of imagination."

"Impossible or merely spectacular?"

"I will show Babylon as people have never seen a city. As angels saw it. As God sees. Seeing is the universal language."

The moon was out and Colonel Griffith's initials glittered in the escutcheons on the butts of the pistols. The tower elevator looked black and immensely tall, rocketing into darkness.

"Someday motion pictures will have sound," said Griffith. "That's why we must use the universal language now."

"Do you want people to see or think?" I said, looking out for holes in the rough, sandy ground, remembering that rattlesnakes live just a little way off Sunset.

"Huck fills the holes," said Griffith, leaning into the wind, harsh profile cutting the night, as we walked away from the impossible language of Babylon. "Snakes are one of the few things I dislike."

"I hate heights."

"I know what you fear, Harrison."

I stopped. "Do you want people to see or think?"

"See, then think," said Griffith. "If people could see the war in Europe. If they could see the future. If they could see . . ."

"Love?" I said.

"People have to see love for themselves."

We walked toward the tower elevator, which soared high into invisibility.

"You've been made to see, Harrison."

"So have you."

"I know," said Griffith.

∾

We sat on the railroad-car platform, feet dangling over the wheels, looking back at Babylon and listening to the wind cut around the tower rising over our heads. I was cold and Griffith was quiet. I thought of Edith, but it was too late for Edith, who was someone else now, so I thought of Tuck, but it was too late for Tuck, who was gone, so I thought of Harry. Empty as the days would be without Edith, it wasn't too late for Harry, and that meant it wasn't too late for me. The moon was out, and I looked at Ishtar and wished I could say good-bye to Tuck, but there wasn't any good way to say good-bye to someone who wanted to die, just as there wasn't any good way to say good-bye to someone you love whom you weren't going to love anymore. Silence was better, and Tuck's letter was a kind of silence, just like my telling Edith, "I forgive you."

Tuck hates, so he will die.

I remembered the letter and its offer. This might be Tuck's last request, which meant honoring it was a way to say good-bye. I didn't like that, but decided to do it.

"I received a letter from Tuck Kreuger, my editor at *The Atlantic*. He has an offer from the British government."

Griffith turned. His profile was harsh against the darkness, his face tight with concentration. "Are you working for the British? Is that what this is about?"

"No. Tuck's wife left him last year, and he became

obsessed with the war and helping the British. He joined the British Army and is going to France. He wrote before leaving. His friends offer full support if you wish to make an anti-German motion picture."

"I've been approached before. The British understand the value of the motion picture." Griffith looked away. The harsh concentration softened.

"Tuck's my friend," I said. "I don't think I'll see him again."

"God help your friend."

"At first, Tuck got religion. Jesus was going to save him. Now he is going to France."

"This war is terrible," said D. W. "I would stop it if I could. Maybe my photoplay . . . I don't know. War is the enemy. Not people."

"Tuck won't come back."

We looked at Babylon as shadows crossed steps, courtyard, and pillars, like clouds covering a winter moon. Griffith said, "You have to work, Harrison. You have to write. Otherwise it's too lonely. Too sad and too hard. Too many people we didn't love."

The wind rose. I was cold.

Griffith looked at the elephant- and goddess-filled distance and spoke into the wind. "I saw Jesus once, Harrison. I was a child, walking home after an ice storm. We have ice storms in Kentucky. It was after my father died, and there was no one to provide. No one to protect. You didn't just lose a fight, there was no one to tell after. I was walking and saw a face in some ice-covered branches, so I stopped and looked. It was Christ's face. I'd never seen anything like it before and have never seen anything like it since. I introduced myself, but He didn't answer. I wondered why. I had properly introduced myself, but He didn't speak. Now I know why, and it was a damn big why. I was shown something words can't say. Something words can't do. That was the lesson. I had, without knowing it, been shown to see.

"I was shown another world, Harrison. Another man might have become religious, or devoted himself to God, but for me it was a door. A door to a world of light. Partly the old, eternal light, and partly a new light. The light that cuts the darkness to the screen."

10

I want you to see what can be done with crude and raw material," said Griffith.

I looked back at the elephants hovering over Ishtar and the gold Trees of Life highlighted by the moon.

"What I do with film, you can do with your life."

We left Babylon through Griffith's private, shoulder-operated door, leaving the wind singing in the hawsers and creaking timbers and gods, pillars, Gilgamesh. We left where we dueled and Griffith's tower gamble, and I felt lonely because I'd spent my life playing at owning ball clubs and writing books, and Babylon was Griffith's great place to play. It was a fantasy for a man in a white suit with guns in his belt—a trick and mystery—but soon the enigmatic night city would be the glorious woman-filled dream of the motion picture director. Out on Sunset Griffith stood straighter, his gait got longer, he almost strutted. The man was returning to his most fabulous creation: D. W. Griffith, general of a sun-drenched army of painted women, high priests, charioteers, fake beards, and thousands of extras crowded into a make-believe city. The once down-at-the-heel actor had built a city and filled it with stories and beautiful women. I felt lonely because I'd been evicted from make-believe, but when we stopped and looked back at the high, crowded darkness, Babylon was mine too.

Because of Lillian. Because Griffith made me do something imaginary and real.

In the middle of Sunset, the Master bowed to Babylon. He turned—guns in his belt, suit luminous, a dapper creature of the night—and bowed to me. I turned, shivering, sand whipping around my shoes, and bowed to Griffith, then Ishtar, and right there, right then, knew I could write about the motion picture. I knew. It didn't matter if *Intolerance* was a colossal failure, a world-rousing success, or a curious experiment, I could translate the new and impossible language. I would explain and catch Griffith's magic in a book. Standing on Sunset, hailing Griffith, I felt something shudder in the dark. The wind was up and the place was stark, hard, frightening, but not speaking. The voices were silent and the dead gone, so maybe I heard a ghost who slapped his wife or tried to make love without loving. The rest was night.

I stood on Sunset looking at the invisible. Griffith watched. He didn't ask what I was looking at and I couldn't have told him if he had, because too much had happened, too much that couldn't be taken back—much too much, except I had found Harry and knew I would write about the motion picture, so I gazed out at Babylon, which a minute ago held all the chaos and emptiness of the world.

∾

We climbed seven sand-whipped steps to a building with shuttered windows and a sloping roof. Griffith opened a door, and yellow light flooded the night. I stopped and listened, but the wind in the telephone wires was only wind, and straining cables only cables. We were, as Griffith put it, home.

"Who owns all this?" I said, suddenly wanting to say what a friend would say.

He stopped. "I do."

"Completely?"

"It's complicated, Henry."

I was surprised he used my first name. "It's vital. Everything will depend on it."

Griffith answered with Whitman. He sang out:

"The Past—the dark unfathom'd retrospect!

The teeming gulf—the sleepers and the shadows!

The past—the infinite greatness of the past!

"No more talk of money, Harrison." Griffith held the door, and I stepped into a low-ceilinged barrack that was a cross between an electrical plant and a chemical factory.

"This is where the real work is done. While actors sleep, we do magic."

I tried one last time. "Listen to me, Griffith, the motion picture industry is like baseball. It mixes talent and business. The owners need talent. Talent needs a place to perform. Right now you are talent and owner, but I tell you, it won't stay that way. Baseball didn't. You must have control."

Griffith smiled. He wasn't listening.

We were in a hall of closed doors. From behind the first door—DARKROOM KEEP CLOSED WHEN CLOSED—came a whirring sound, which D. W. proudly explained was film being "wound down," transferred from one spindle to another, cut at places where scenes or lighting changed, so test strips could be developed to see the quality of the photography.

"Money bows to magic," said Griffith.

"Money never bows."

"Watch this!"

Griffith turned out the light where we stood, quickly opened a door, which he closed as soon as we were in, and we were confronted by an evil-smelling room lit with low red light, where Count Dracula, or a ghoulish relative, was dipping a long strip of skin into a blood bath. The man, as bloodless as one of the count's victims, paid no attention except for a slight movement of a dark eyebrow.

The Master boomed out:

"'So with curious eyes and sick surmise

"'We watched him day by day,

"'And wondered if each one of us

"'Would end the self-same way,

"'For none can tell to what red Hell

"'His sightless soul may stray.'"

"Vilde," said the specter. "Oscar Vilde."

This magic was smelly. The room reeked not only of the chemical bath and strips of skin, actually film, but of the specter himself, who I assumed was one of Griffith's Russians, who worked hard and answered only to the Master. The specter wore a stained white blouse that looked like it hadn't been changed since Mother Russia. He continued to dip and examine strips of film. We watched awhile and left.

"Magic, Harrison," said Griffith, and I was shown the drums where film was developed. D. W. loftily pointed out one of his men, who invented the system that keeps film out of human hands and in drums. A little fat man, as full of life as the specter was devoid of it, went from drum to drum, inspecting the process with a red lantern. He smiled and said, "Good. Good." In other rooms film was processed on racks: wetted, moved, fixed, dried. I saw all the sorcery by which pictures were produced in such linear quantity they move in the dark. It was done on an assembly line like Henry Ford's automobiles.

"Ince sends film to New York," said Griffith. "We do it here."

I thought of asking if he had patents on the process, but we were in Griffith's kingdom, and that kingdom, Griffith seemed to think, was built on magic.

"In here," he said.

11

The heart of Fine Arts Studios wasn't rooms of women developing film, smelly Russians, or Karl Brown looping film, checking the aperture plate, or swabbing hidden recesses of the Pathé. The heart was the projection room, a smallish room with black walls and bare bulb hanging from the ceiling. A half dozen tired assistant directors, the Smiths, Jimmy and Rose, film cutters from New York City who'd joined Griffith at Biograph, sat in folding chairs. D. W. took his place on a sagging, cracked, leatherette lounge chair, reserved for him, and said, "Run it, Billy." Another Billy, not Bitzer, but a more anonymous cog in the Griffith machine, ran different versions of *The Woman Taken in Adultery*.

D. W. was the Master now and paid no attention to me or anyone else. Von Stroheim took the pistols with a knowing, monocled wink, and the bare bulb went off. The Master looked at version after version and nothing penetrated his concentration. I was lonely and a little hurt, sitting by myself, watching a man watch pictures, but slowly I realized what Griffith wanted me to see. He wanted me to see a man who'd lost a woman and fought a duel immersed, absolutely immersed—not lost, Griffith wasn't lost—in work. And he wanted me to see what was on the screen.

Over the noise of the projector, with Tod Browning asleep and Allan Dwan's head nodding, the Master asked, "Did you like the third better than the fifth? What about the light on Howard's face in the fourth? Could we do something with the shadows in two?"

The Smiths answered. Others mumbled or slept. I watched, gradually less disappointed, less lonely, then caught, entranced, mesmerized by pointing fingers, angry faces, stones, and Howard Gaye playing Jesus. Only . . . Only as version after version rolled over the screen, it wasn't woman-hunting, hilarious Howard Gaye pointing and speaking. It was Jesus.

I watched again and again, amazed. It was Him moving so subtly, so humbly, so royally. I saw those long hands, the infinite peace of the eyes in different light, different shadows, different angles of waving spears. There He was on a stone bench, in a stone place, with *The Woman Taken* so wrapped and swaddled in robes, so wrapped and swaddled in sin, you couldn't see her face. Was this Edith? Was this me? Was this every person taken in sin?

The mob clutched stones—haughty, bearded men rooted in the vengeful Old Testament, lusting to punish, taunting and sanctimonious. There was the Woman shaking in fear, alone, terrified against dark rock. Griffith made everything stone—stone floor, stone walls, stone bench. Next we saw a solitary robed figure writing on the ground. The camera pulled back, revealing the mob that was in front of Him. To the mob the Woman was sin, and sin required death; that was the law, and the law was their covenant with God, but there, in the swirl and threat, was Jesus, who brought a new law. He slowly raised His hand, pointed and spoke the irrefutable words that have come down the millennia: "He that is without sin among you, let him cast a stone at her." Hands waver. Heads quiver. The mob was face to face with Jesus. Jesus, who brings a new covenant. Jesus, something new under the sun. The haughty, bearded men looked wildly at each other and dropped their stones. They ran. Jesus, by force of character, sent them away to look to their own consciences, then turned the Woman over to herself, and set her on that journey.

Griffith caught all this on a square screen using the face, beard and hands of a sinner. But it wasn't Howard Gaye showing a mob, showing us all, human beings are not their sins. It wasn't Howard Gaye declaring sin is not eternal.

12

Griffith told the assistant directors they could leave, and the sleepy group obliged, pulling themselves up, stopping to wish him luck with the Shot, and then going quickly.

The Smiths were reluctant, but D. W. patted each on the shoulder and said, "You need sleep."

"So do you," said Rose.

~

We were alone in the black room with the folding chairs and leatherette sofa. "Light out, please," said Griffith, and we were in the dark except for a beam of intense light the projector threw on the square screen. Dust in the light produced that hypnotic, machine-like cathedral effect one sees when film isn't running through the projector, when glare and clacking machine are a sign this isn't the theater but a new, hard art. The beam cut the void and there was an unsettling moment, like a warning.

"How do you feel?" said Griffith.

"Tired." I felt alone and abandoned and stared at the streaming light. "Watching that was difficult."

"Why?" Griffith leaned back on the leatherette. It creaked. The thing was cracked and broken like the skin of a rhinoceros. I saw his profile against a steam of violent white light.

"You want me to think about forgiving adultery," I said.

"And?"

I chose my words carefully. "Forgiveness is a powerful act. It's not just turning the other cheek. It's turning away so the person who hurt you has to confront what he or she has done. Live with it. Understand it. You turn and try to understand your part."

Griffith's profile was still in the harsh, moving light. "Will you forgive your wife?"

"I said I did, but that was saying good-bye."

"We didn't forgive each other," said Griffith. "We had to fight."

"Or pretend to."

"The real is revealed in the unreal," said Griffith.

"Yesterday Harry and I talked. We started to get to know each other. That's as much of God as I deserve."

"But will you forgive Edith?" said Griffith.

"That's hard."

"There's nothing easy about the Nazarene."

Dust swirled in the light beams—random, inhuman—no ghosts, no voices. Light cut violent nothingness to a screen the Master didn't control.

"You think I sinned with *The Birth*?" said Griffith.

"I don't like the word sin."

"If we are going to talk, we must use the right words."

"All right."

"How did I sin?" said Griffith.

We sat in the dark with the blinding empty future streaming over our heads. After a while, I said, "A work of art lives in imagination. In the Great Memory. It can't be taken back. It may be the sin against the Holy Ghost that Christ said was unforgivable."

Griffith sat up. "That's the hardest thing anyone ever said to me."

Light blasted the darkness.

"Who am I to say you can't separate yourself from your sin?" I said.

～

We had been quiet a long time when Griffith spoke. "If I had made *The Birth* differently, I would have sinned against my father."

I looked up.

"My father, to use your idea, your words, was form without content until the War. He hadn't been good at anything. He'd been to California and the Gold Rush and got $5,000. The money got as close to Louisville as a river boat on the Ohio.

"He tried politics. The man loved to talk. My father had a booming, wonderful voice. Politics didn't work, so he farmed, but you don't farm with a voice. He got a plantation and named it Lofty Green. Lofty Green didn't have time to fail because war came. Fate, destiny, history, content, all came calling in a Gray uniform, and Jacob Wark Griffith rode away with the men of Oldham County. Kentucky men. Southern men. Then the dream met the horror. The talk met cannons. The Gray met Blue. I wonder how many men's lives seemed hard-scrabble and pointless till then, but now they had a point. Too many points maybe—honor, courage, comrades, killing, starving, arms and legs in a pile by the surgeon's tent so dreadful my father said they moved. And fear. Hours and days of exhaustion, riding, marching, scrounging food wherever, whenever, whatever—all pointing, all leading, all coming together on the day of battle. The unavoidable, fateful seconds and minutes of battle. After Gettysburg, you knew if you won the battle, you couldn't win the War. You just kept fighting. Fighting to keep the Yankees away from your home and county as long as possible. Fighting for the man next to you, then for the memory of the man next to you. Fighting because men depended on you and looked up to you, and wondered how you could keep on so far from home, from victory, from family. They wondered what made you brave. You probably wondered too. Duty? Honor? Oldham County? What was the point of their lives now? Parched corn and bandages? No shoes? No word from home. But they kept on. They didn't have the supplies, population, resources. Most didn't own slaves and some didn't believe in slavery. Their friends were dead. Their families were starving. Their country was thrown to the dogs but they kept going. They kept going.

"My father was wounded many times but most seriously in the retreat from Chattanooga, the north Georgia campaign. He was an officer in the 'Orphan Brigade.' The Confederate Cavalry, the eyes and sword of the South, which by Christmas, 1863, was half blind and badly dented. The War was now counterattacks and hope, though I suspect hope was in as short supply as everything else in '63, '4, or '5, but at Charleston, Tennessee, Colonel Griffith was too wounded to mount a horse, so he had a buggy rigged and led a charge flat on his back. The wound throbbed and hurt with every bounce but that charge broke the Yankee line, and Wheeler's army was saved for a while.

"He was good. He was good when all was lost and wounded. He was good past the time when you ask, argue, or pray. That's who we are, Harrison. What we are. We have to be good past talk, argument, right and wrong, black and white. Long past. That's what *The Birth* is. Something past talk and argument, to be remembered when blacks and whites won't remember the sad days between them. Yes, something good and fine past what anyone says, said, or will say."

13

Tell me about your father," said Griffith, and we talked about Antietam, which he called Sharpsburg.

"My father said the withering fire in the cornfield cut each stalk like a knife. Those forty acres were crossed fifteen times by opposing armies, which left so many dead, dying and wounded, you could walk across without touching the ground."

"The red landscape," said Griffith.

We talked and I realized I was doing what Griffith did. I was telling a story I'd told many times, a story I needed to tell, but never wondered why I needed to tell it, why I constantly polished this creation. I looked at the blinding chaos on the screen and wondered why I kept telling a story my father couldn't tell, when he'd been there and I hadn't.

Griffith talked. For him the subject of fathers and war was inexhaustible, as it was for me, but as the blinding future streamed over our heads, and I nodded close to sleep, a voice kept asking *why*? I understood the need for second-generation glory, the pleasure and pride we took in men who fought, were wounded, did things we try to imagine, but something was not being said. We shared the imagined suffering and courage of a wounded man in a buggy and a twenty-one-year-old in forty acres of blood and corpses, and we shared how much we missed those men, but there was more. I slumped in a folding chair, nodding, and heard that voice.

"The best times," said Griffith, "were when men came for talk and whiskey and I'd hide under the table and listen the whole night. The Colonel must have known I was there. Must have known my ears were burning with curiosity and pride. That's what he gave me. Nights filling up with stories. Hearing about day after day of fighting, starving. The courage. The land. The men of '61 loved their land. They found their place, Harrison, your father and mine. They found their place in time."

What wasn't he saying? What wasn't I saying?

"What was your best time?" said Griffith.

"I went east to boarding school," I said, fighting a yawn. "One day my father appeared at Thayer Academy and told the headmaster we had 'family business' in Boston. The business was at the South End Grounds where King Kelly hit two triples. My father came all the way from Cleveland to go to a ball game. It was the best time. I was away when he died."

He gave me a ball game. Not a story.

"My father died in '85," said Griffith. "I was ten, and just like that, we lost everything. We went to the city and lived in boarding houses. The Colonel lived in his talk, but we couldn't live on it. Harrison, each of us saw a world and saw it go. Each of us knew a man who had his place in time, who gave what he could, but there was much he couldn't."

It's what they didn't give. That's why we tell their stories.

"We are, I'm afraid, our own Orphan's Brigade," said Griffith.

What they couldn't.

"You have a son," said Griffith. "You're lucky." He didn't say anything for a while, then, looking into the dark, said, "I suppose we create our fathers if we miss them too much."

∽

We dozed and I didn't ask if Griffith missed the Colonel while the Colonel was still alive. I didn't ask how much the man back from war was already a ghost. It might be my pain but it wasn't my business. In the relentless light, before he slept, I saw sadness in Griffith. He saw me see and turned into the dark, but not before I saw, in a blinding moment, that his genius was as complex as the future streaming over our heads, and as simple as a child hiding under a table. I didn't ask why Griffith still grieved, didn't ask if he made a motion picture big enough, great enough, daring enough, if he'd stop living in hotels, lusting after child-women, gambling instead of banking millions, or raise a family. Under the hard light, I wondered if Griffith missed a father so much he couldn't be one, because what he missed was a shadow—a storytelling, gambling, con man, charlatan, shadow—so Griffith had to be gambler, story-teller, con man, and was all these in this new world of the motion picture. Falling asleep, chaos reigning on a white screen, thinking of Babylon, the duel, and Jesus trans-formed, I wondered how out of the chasm between child and shadow, man and dream, man and failure, this unedu-cated Southerner became D. W. Griffith. How did the lonely child, failed actor, failed husband and poet, make himself into a pioneer on a frontier that needs rules and artists, not just hustlers and deal-makers? Somehow, inex-plicably, Griffith became the one to show others how to speak a new language, and that meant he was a genius— flawed, grieving, manipulating, blind to what he did in *Birth*, but a genius. An original. A blind man bringing syntax to light. And now, he was taking on the impossible, not only in the scale of this motion picture, but trying to undo the hurt from his masterpiece. It made me wonder.

"Can't love redeem hate?" said Griffith suddenly.

I was jerked awake. "Does it? Does it really?" Unpre-dictable light flew overhead. Random shadows played on the screen. "In our lives, maybe. With friends and children, maybe. In works of imagination? Photoplays? I don't know."

"Can't art redeem art?"

"Klansmen replaced by Jesus?"

Griffith nodded.

"You came pretty close in what I just saw. It was terrific."

"Close enough to appease the Holy Ghost?"

"I'd like to take Harry to Babylon," I said. "He'd like it."

"We can do better," said Griffith, the leatherette creaking as he sat up. "I want you and the boy to be in the Shot. Would he like to be an extra?"

"Very much."

"It will be a day the boy remembers with his father. A great day."

"Thank you," I said. "As long as we don't have to go up high."

"Be there early."

VIII

ANGELS FLIGHT

April 4, 1916
5:30 a.m.

1

We woke about five. I was cramped, bleary, and felt like I'd been hit with the splats of the chair, rather than merely having rested my back on them in a stuffy, black room. Griffith had fared better on the leatherette. He sat up, raised a hand, and the light went on. Billy hadn't left his post, waiting all night for word from the Master. The flash of bare bulb made the room swim in white grit and oscillating black. I rubbed my eyes. Griffith leapt off the leatherette and began to exercise. He reached for the ceiling, touched his toes, twisted his body, arms akimbo, and rotated his neck.

"Bernarr Macfadden couldn't be so energetic in the morning," I said.

"Have your boy here no later than eight. We'll find you a car."

Griffith ran in place, then jumped up and down, simultaneously touching hands over head while slapping his feet together. In the unrelenting light, he looked like a harlequin-cum–whirling dervish. The Master was, indeed, ready for a great day.

"Where do you live, Harrison?"

"Bunker Hill. Edith is there . . ."

"Go with a driver. Not Max. The driver can go to the door if you wish."

"I'll go to the door," I said, reaching for the ceiling, then touching my toes. This was my day too. I could speak to Murphy, if necessary, or anyone. This was Harry's and my day and we were going to Babylon. I watched Griffith and imagined sitting in a theater with Harry pointing at the screen and shouting, "That's us. There we are!"

"Mr. Griffith," I said. "I must ask about Howard Gaye. He's been kind. Is there any chance he might be retained?"

"None," said Griffith, who now dropped to the floor and did forty push-ups. He rose, eyes flashing, white suit hardly rumpled, as if the calisthenics had smoothed last night's wrinkles. "This motion picture is too important for distraction."

"I had to ask."

"I'd have thought less of you if you hadn't."

"No forgiveness for Jesus?"

"Only a higher power can forgive him. The man is a spectacle." Griffith did more push-ups.

∾

Monday morning was still. Patches of mist clung to Mount Lee, and the strange dawn light was on the hills. Griffith told me to wait by the gates and went to the house where I first met Lillian. Babylon was a city of pillars and mist behind damp walls. The elephants sat in cloud and Ishtar looked white as a shroud. Before my car arrived, a Model T whose driver looked made of dawn pulled up in front of Fine Arts.

It was Jesus, of course, the spectacle himself, in clean and pressed robes, looking fresh as milk and transcendently white in the mist. Before I could say, "Speak of the devil," Allan Dwan came running up, a plaid driving cap pulled over one eye, keys jangling at his belt. "I think I have a ride," I said, as Jesus waved me over.

"The Christ chap?"

"I'm in good hands," I said, and walked out to Sunset. "I'll be back with my son in two hours!"

Dwan walked off and I got in the Model T. Jesus held up a finger as he had with the woman taken in adultery. "Do I get to keep my job?"

"Griffith said no."

"The fool."

A different finger went up and then we pulled away from Fine Arts. "Where to?" Jesus asked, and I told him about being in the Shot and needing to go to Bunker Hill.

"So you and Griffith didn't kill each other, after all?"

"No." I didn't tell him about the duel. I didn't want to explain. "We had a hell of an argument."

Jesus started to speak, then stopped. "You're on Griffith's side now, aren't you?"

I nodded.

"Griffith did it. Got the performance he wanted. In this case, from his biographer."

"I did ask for you," I said.

"Thanks," said Jesus and we drove into the dawn.

∾

We went east and the ghost light made the hillsides whiter and more mysterious. The Ford rattled along at the speed at which Our Lord must have entered Jerusalem on his colt. I looked Jesus over. He was as he had been yesterday. Brown hair flowing to his shoulders, robes flowing to Mr. Ford's upholstery, sandals flanking the low, reverse, and brake pedals.

"Since I'm soon to be unemployed, maybe we can find that freckled woman with the cat."

The Model T crawled as we looked for a bungalow nestled in a hill. It was earlier than when we had been here before, and in the hollow light, that bungalow, woman, and cat seemed like an illusion in the Los Angeles dawn.

"I think you're looking for more than women in bungalows," I said, realizing I liked Jesus. "There's kindness in you."

He erupted in a quick, hard laugh—something between a British snort and an American hoot. "Are *you* looking for more than a woman in a bungalow?"

"Someday."

"You're in a ridiculously optimistic mood, Harrison." Jesus peered into a misty line of coast live oaks, forty-footers with hard, holly-like leaves and branches that grew along the ground. "Where are you, little tart? All men seek for thee!"

We drove up and down dark hills as hints of green sneaked onto pale hillsides. I didn't want to hurt his feelings but hoped Jesus would think about what he really wanted as he rode these morning hills.

"What's Griffith like?" Jesus asked suddenly. "You talked to him all night. No one talks to him."

I thought for a moment. "He's lonely."

"Of course Griffith is lonely, Harrison. That's the first true thing you've said. Americans are lonely. The place is too damn big. The night is empty, fill it with women as you may. I fill it, Harrison. I let them not be lonely for a while. I let them dream and when they dream, they aren't so miserable. They're alone. More alone than ever, but not so lonely. A country of dreamers and maniacs, Harrison. All of you. Fucked and far from home. Vulgar and lonely. You feel it everywhere. On Broadway, in Chicago, on endless afternoons in the big West. Down South they sleep with their sisters and beat niggers, but the crackers don't escape. No one can. Not even lovers who fill the night and devour the lunch hour. You're coyotes, Harrison. All of you—howling and running. No one can catch you. You have everything but you're lonely. It's the American condition.

"You need me. Me. The star. The robes. If you really believed, you wouldn't be lonely. But you don't. You shout in church. You confess. But you don't believe. You believe in the photoplay. The Hupmobile. The telephone. Even you, Harrison. You believe in Griffith, though you won't admit it. I thought your Harvard snobbery would protect you, but you're lonely too. The photoplay is the perfect expression of America. You pay, sit alone, and see tricks. America needs wizards. They can crawl out of Kentucky or come across the sea from the smelliest ghetto, but you must have them. That's democracy. New dreams for new solitude. The photoplay is a coyote, Harrison. I am a coyote."

We sped up. Jesus stood. His robes billowed like a

backward spinnaker as he clutched the wheel and yelled, "Where are you, little tart? All men seek for thee!"

2

I told Jesus not to wait and got off at the bottom of Angels Flight, hoping Harry might be riding the cars, but he wasn't. I decided to wait on Third Street rather than bang on the door at six a.m. The sun was up and the light was clear but still white and strange. *Olivet* and *Sinai* sawed their way up and down Bunker Hill.

After a few minutes, someone came out of the house and got on the car at the top of the hill. It wasn't a child, so I paid my nickel and hopped on *Sinai* just as the brass and oak car started up.

The lone figure in *Olivet* bent over. It was no child, and before I saw his face, I knew it was Murphy. He came down as I went up and he was crying. What had happened? Was Harry all right? I looked hard at the man coming down. Tears ran down his reddish face into the little mustache and wet the red beard like the dew on the hill. His collar hung around his neck, soiled and loose. Everything about him had shrunk. Had Edith asked him to leave? Had they fought?

I saw this in the slow time of wonder, when vision is concentrated in a tiny field, and action seems inevitable, as *Sinai* made its three-hundred-fifteen-foot journey.

3

I ran to the back of the house. I didn't want to scare Edith but had to know if they were all right. The door was open and the back hall was dark. I kicked a baseball glove, stepped over Harry's shoes and the thick-handled bat in which he'd carved "Ty Cobb" with a penknife, opened another door, and ran through the dim first floor.

Edith was standing at the bottom of the wide mahogany stairs in the hall. She started. "Henry! Henry! Is that you?"

"Are you all right? Where's Harry?"

"Fine! Upstairs! What are you doing here?"

"Griffith invited Harry and me to be in the Shot! I came to ask if it was all right and saw Murphy. I was worried so I came in."

"Michael's gone," said Edith, and sat down on the steps. She wore the crimson dress with the square neck and garnet lace. "I thought he'd come back and we'd have to go through it all again."

I had no idea what she meant. I wanted to hug her. "I won't ask what happened. It's not my business."

"No," said Edith. "I don't suppose it is." Morning light warmed the stairs with many hues of oak and many hues of Edith's rich brown hair. A stained-glass cactus in the alcove above glowed like an ember.

"I hoped Harry would be on Angels Flight. God, Edith, you look so tired."

She shook her head. "You can take Harry."

"May I sit down?"

"When did you become so polite?"

"May I?"

"Yes."

I sat next to her. I wanted to touch her so badly.

"Hello, Edith."

"Hello, Henry." She looked away.

I didn't say anything.

"What happened between you and Harry yesterday, Henry?"

"We went to Hollywood Cemetery."

"He was so happy when he came back. He couldn't stop talking about it."

"We got to know each other a little."

"Last night," said Edith, looking down, her voice small, not full of its usual hearty confidence, "you said Harry should stay with me. You said I could live where I wanted and be with whom I wanted. That was the first time you gave me anything, Henry."

I still didn't say anything. The light was stronger. I saw white in Edith's hair, lines by her eyes. She was tired. We were sitting close but not touching and I smelled her.

"You gave Harry something," she said. "I didn't think you could."

I wanted to ask about Murphy but it was time for Edith to speak. After a few minutes, when she kept looking at me and looking away, Edith said, "It wouldn't have worked," then neither of us spoke for a long time. The steps and alcove got lighter. It was going to be a gorgeous day.

"I was so angry with you, Henry. So angry. But I missed you. It hurt when Harry talked about you. Say something. You're remarkably quiet."

"It's wonderful to hear your voice."

"I didn't think you could give," said Edith. "To Harry or me."

I held up my hand, and Edith put her palm and long fingers against my palm and fingers, like we used to at dancing school.

"I can't promise anything," she said.

"No one can."

Edith got up and I followed. Light streamed in at the second floor through red and yellow stained-glass cacti and roses as the sun climbed over the continent and lit Los Angeles. We stopped and held each other in the alcove. Edith felt tall and athletic. I closed my eyes and remembered her at League Park. I kissed her softly on the cheek. Edith was trembling and so was I. We held each other, and I thought of Harry asleep in a room nearby, and Tuck, who like Ulysses had to fly to the watery half of the world, and how I had come out of the dawn to find something stranger. I opened my eyes and kissed her again. Edith opened her eyes and closed them. I had no idea what would happen in an hour, tomorrow, or next week. Right there, on those steps, it didn't matter.

Edith stopped at the third-floor landing and stood in clear, slanting morning light. The sun was too high to be mysterious and was climbing toward the light Griffith favors, the clearest light of the morning. I looked at her and said, "I know you and don't know you, but I don't know you better than anyone in the world." Edith smiled, hurt and tentative, and we looked at each other. Edith's nose seemed bigger with age, her skin was large pored, fine lines ran beside her mouth and deeper lines across her brow; I saw the subtle mustache women develop as the sexes come to resemble each other as they grow old, but Edith wasn't old. She was Edith. She held me. So warm, so strong. I knew her and didn't know her, and smelled that indefinable mix of perspiration, soap, and lilac which is like the scent of trees by Lake Ontario.

Edith touched my hair. "Henry, you're not wearing socks."

4

E dith unbuttoned the crimson dress as we walked down the hall under a slanting roof at the top of the house. Light coming in caught dust and announced the morning. Her arm was around my waist, and my hand was on her hip. The funicular banged up and down the hill, and a few blocks away the trolley was taking the first extras to Hollywood and Sunset. Edith put my hand in the crimson dress. She was crying.

Then I knew what dawn was. It's the color of tears.

∾

Our bed was in the high turret overlooking Angels Flight and the Third Street tunnel. We looked at each other in the brighter, clearer, transparent light as *Olivet* and *Sinai* clanked like a loom below the window. Edith touched the stubble on my face and said, "Be quick so you can go to Babylon."

"Let's all go."

"Do you want me to?"

"We'll be together. It will make Harry happy."

"All right," she said.

I kissed her on the mouth.

"I love you when you love Harry." Edith dropped the crimson dress. She undid a white lacy floral camisole. I took off the beige trousers, tweed jacket, and underwear. Edith lay on her stomach and I ran my finger down the furrow of her spine, deep in her freckled back, all the way to the downy hair at its base, where the tops of her buttocks flared out, firm but fleshy.

I looked at her—handsome shoulders, cool to the touch, long arms and big hands, skin beginning to wrinkle between the breasts, a hollow in the outside of her long thigh—muscles soft, stomach a little big and slightly sagging, like mine, breasts fuller, a little heavier. The sun was on Edith's face, and her brown hair was twisted artfully like the turret of the house—a subtle touch of the nineties in the peppy teens carried gracefully, like the lost time and grief we carry. Her hair was combed over the tops of her ears, neatly setting off translucent lobes and coming to a wonderful stop in the hidden hollow nape of her white neck. I touched Edith's face—no words—and she touched mine.

I have never lost my awe at the sight of my wife naked. Her rich brown hair, elegant with white strands, was not the sun, not Lillian Gish's radiant illusion, not youth's rainbow, the little-girl invitation that drives Jesus, Griffith, and Hollywood crazy. Edith's skin, cool on the shoulders, hot in the thighs, wasn't the flawless marble of the screen, that silk of imagination, which belongs to no one. She belonged to this world. Like Harry.

"Henry, Henry." Edith ran the sole of her foot down my leg. She touched the part that grows. She handled it lightly but perfectly and it expanded to an impatient girth. The lonely, limp performance of last dawn was gone. That failure, that wrongness, was back there with the beating, the duel, and Murphy weeping his way east.

I touched Edith's shoulders, the thrilling cool outside of her arms and warm thighs. I touched her face. All that intelligence and large eyes. They were questioning. Asking.

"How do you feel?" I said.

"Better."

"You're very beautiful."

I kissed her face again, taking it in my hands, looking at her. Then I kissed her long-nippled, fine breasts, putting a hand on each side, pushing them slightly together, sucking gently before going to her wonderfully smooth stomach, and then lower for communion with the body of the woman I loved and would try to love again. Take, eat. I missed her body so much.

We lay beside each other and Edith said, "This is different."

"Maybe."

I put my hand between her legs and felt the warm wetness. Edith guided me in, making a small noise, and we were each other's. We moved slowly, tentatively, as if scared, as if asking: Is this right? Is this what you want? How do you feel? But no words. We were so close, but aware of hurt, mistakes, that we could be apart, lose each other, now, tomorrow, anytime. We knew all this and moved slowly in each other's arms.

5

Harry's bed was under a window facing the sun. Light was on his face and his chestnut hair spread on the pillow. Like any sleeping six-year-old, he looked like all the warmth and goodness in the world, all the resilience and vulnerability of the race. The child scratched his cheek in his sleep and unconsciously rearranged the red and blue Apache blanket.

We love each other so imperfectly, even these.

"Watching them sleep is the reward for taking care of them," said Edith. She smiled her particular smile—part care, part vulnerability, amused, adventurous. Open. I saw it at Miss Walker's, in Maine, when Harry was born, and now she gave it to the sleeping child. Then she gave it to me.

Pedro, the twenty-pound, one-eyed cat, hopped on the bed and Harry woke up.

"Dad!" he said, rubbing his eyes. "Where's Mr. Murphy?"

"He's gone," said Edith.

"Will Mr. Murphy be back?" said Harry, petting Pedro.

Edith touched the child's face, pushing a strand of brown hair away from his eye. "No, Mr. Murphy won't be back."

"Then I don't have to clean my plate before leaving the table and clean my room before going outside and say 'Yes, ma'am,' and 'No, sir'?"

"No," said Edith.

"Harry," I said, smiling and trying to imagine the battle over eating and manners that must have alienated Edith and Harry at the moment Murphy thought he'd won. "Get up. We're going to be Babylonians. We have to be early to get costumes."

"Babylonians?" said Harry slowly. "With beards?"

"Griffith asked us," I said. "We're going to stand under the goddess."

The child rubbed his eyes. "The naked statue?"

"We won't let you look," said Edith. "Now hurry, sleepy one."

"Mum, are you coming?"

Edith picked him up and hugged him. "Yes, now hurry."

IX

BABYLON

April 4, 1916
7:30 a.m. to 11:00 a.m.

1

Sunset was full of cars, trolleys, jitneys, taxis, chariots, pedestrians, and onlookers. Los Angeles was leaving Bunker Hill for Babylon. We left at seven thirty when the mysterious light had become its clearer descendant, as the sun walked the eastern sky, the air warmed, and the morning headed for the Griffith light. When Harry couldn't hear, Edith said, "I'm not sure about us."

"It's your choice," I said. "I'll be here. I'll be near Harry."

"We'll see," Edith said.

The car started with the first crank. Edith sat in the passenger seat, brown hair streaming down her long back over a simple green and yellow dress. Harry tried to sit on the backseat but was so excited he kept jumping up, got put down by bumps, and let loose little shrieks of delight.

We were to dress on the lot, but hundreds, maybe thousands, dressed at home, so the road was a caravan of Babylonians, many holding beards, some singing. Women in jitneys waved, soldiers marching in ragged formations shook spears, five priests of Bel whipped by in an Oldsmobile, and we saw a cloud of dust raised by a speeding Model T going up Glendale, Jesus' hair and robes flying. Harry wanted to know who everyone was. Were they soldiers or ministers or bad men, and what did the pretty girls do?

"Was being pretty a job in Babylon?"

"It seems to be in Los Angeles," said Edith.

Harry waved to everyone. We saw an Orthodox Jew. He waved. People stood by bungalows and waved. A redheaded woman with freckles across her nose waved so hard Edith thought she was trying to flag us down.

"She's looking for Howard Gaye," I said.

"You mean Jesus," said Harry.

"Everyone's looking for Jesus," said Edith.

"Jesus is over on Glendale," said Harry.

I was getting the hang of dodging cars and passing jitneys, and got neatly around a chariot, receiving a salute from the charioteer I'd yelled at yesterday, when a large car, raising dust like the pillar of cloud that led the Israelites by day, bore down on us. It scattered all who shared the road, and for a second I thought we might end up in a ditch, but we came to a church, and I pulled over, trying to appear nonchalant. Harry wasn't fooled and said, "Good thing Dad got out of the way." The pillar of cloud stopped beside us.

A black chauffeur stepped out of the enormous Fiat and opened the rear door with brisk formality. Lillian, wearing a gorgeous white dress, and then Griffith stepped into the sunshine. D. W. wore a fresh, fine white suit and removed his yellow coolie hat with a bow.

"Mr. and Mrs. Harrison and Master Harry, I presume. Together on this fine day."

"We'd all like to be in the Shot," I said.

"Of course," said Griffith shaking Harry's hand. The child stood on the backseat. "It will be my pleasure."

"I promise I won't look at the naked lady," said Harry.

"We'll see how long you keep that promise," said Griffith. "You're not afraid of heights, are you? You're going to stand at the base of a column. Fifty feet up."

"No," said Harry, "that's my dad."

Cars and a jitney stopped. D. W. spoke to Edith, and Lillian, after saying good morning to Edith and shaking Harry's hand, stepped around the rear of the Fiat and I followed. The world began to stop around us. Traffic was backing up. Horns blew. The minister, in a black suit, stood in the door of his church, and I stood with Lillian Gish, as Los Angeles snarled in a traffic jam, on the way to Babylon to be in a motion picture D. W. Griffith thought might change the world.

"What happened?" Lillian said.

"It was a strange night."

"You're together?"

"For now. Maybe longer. I don't know."

"And you and Mr. Griffith are friends," Lillian said, with a knowing smile.

"No thanks to you."

"With complete thanks to me," said Lillian, and took my hands in her hands. "Thank you, Henry. Everything is as it should be, as it must be. We're all friends now and everything will be all right. I know it."

I didn't know it, but smiled. Lillian Gish was so vividly beautiful in the morning light, it was hard to look at her.

Griffith bowed to Harry and Edith, Lillian and me. He

seemed to be saluting the world. "The Harrisons shall stand together!" he said. "Lad, would you like to ride in the big car?"

Harry looked at the Fiat and driver. "No, I'll ride with Dad."

The Master bowed again. His suit was so sharply creased and perfect. The Fiat gleamed in the early sun. The sky was cloudless, and Babylon stood over the hills against the green world.

2

We rode behind the pillar of cloud, trying to keep up with the turns, bumps, and horn-blowing intimidation of the Fiat. When drivers, marching Babylonians, chariots, everyone but a sullen teamster in a delivery van, saw who was barreling down Sunset, they turned aside, waved, and looked dumbstruck at Lillian Gish. We raced through a dusty, crowded wake.

"You seem to know Miss Gish quite well," said Edith, as she waved at the dust with a green handkerchief.

"Not that well," I said, blowing the horn and waving at Jesus, who was paralleling Sunset, raising dust, pointing at Edith and raising both arms in celebration.

"You seem to know him, too," said Edith.

I nodded.

"Griffith seems to have gotten over your calling him a

Confederate charlatan and Colonel Chucklehead."

We flew over a bump, and Harry howled with delight. The Fiat blew its horn to clear a path to the gates of Babylon as Sunset turned west, and we came to the plain where the hills open. Fine Arts Studio, Griffith's city, sat south of Sunset, and Babylon, the Great Memory's city, rose on the north.

"Griffith's trying to undo the hurt of *Birth,* Edith."

"How?"

"By making a different kind of photoplay."

"Is that enough?"

"What else can he do? What can anyone do but start over and do it differently?"

"Henry, you like anyone who likes you."

We pulled in behind the Fiat. Griffith hopped out and began shadowboxing in front of his corps of assistant directors. Harry climbed out of the Ford and joined the crowd. I took Edith's hand and said, "Let's judge what he does, not what he did."

3

Joe Henabery led us up the seventeen steps by couchant lions and black-haired, scantily clad, gleaming Denishawn Dancers, who smiled and waved at Harry, then up purple and yellow steps to the base of the wide, elephant-supporting pillar under Ishtar. We all sneaked a look at the enormous goddess. Behind the pillar was a platform covered with coiled rope, stacks of boards, hammers, a saw, boxes of nails, a few cans of paint, and several brushes for last minute touch-up. A monocled Stroheim talked with Babylonian priests, musicians, and women in white tunics, who were taking a break at the bottom of a ladder, which rose at a steeper angle than Angels Flight, sixty feet to the balcony above the capital of a wide, fluted, red and yellow pillar, topped by a trumpeting elephant. The ladder was actually a pole with footlong rungs for hands and feet, which looked like crosses going to heaven. Everywhere, out of sight of the camera, were wires, ropes, and carpenters. From behind, Babylon was a motion-picture set, a trick, with all the conjurer's wires, secret pockets, and false bottoms revealed. It was a theater, not the sacred place where Griffith and I heard voices. The magic would be in the dimension of photoplay. In the morning light the Great Hall was the Master's illusion.

We were to stand in front of Ishtar at the base of the pillar, but Harry suddenly ran to the ladder. He took off and started to climb. Edith gasped and Henabery froze. The boy was ten feet up before anyone could react. He yelled, "Come on!" and scrambled up and up, stretching his whole lithe, small body between crosses. His little sandals—the props people found a child's pair—pounded the rungs, and his tiny hands flew from cross to cross.

I got to the ladder first and started up. The boy was twenty feet above me, and the pole slanted up another forty feet to a lion and god-painted orange balcony.

"Get him, Harrison!" yelled Stroheim. Everyone else was silent, and I climbed fast, immediately high enough to be alone with the rising terror of height. I didn't look down. I couldn't. Whatever actors, carpenters, Edith, Henabery, Stroheim might yell or plead, I was in a vacuum of terror. My only hope was to keep moving, looking up at the small sandals, the waving white tunic, and the little gold dagger in Harry's belt.

In the rush of altitude and fear, I knew this was a test. Harry looked down and climbed harder, little feet churning, glancing off wooden crosses. He had to know I'd follow. I pulled, breathing hard, arms aching, sandals slipping when I pushed too hard, but the little body kept rising over me. If he fell, could I catch him? If he stopped? Nothing was real but the dagger, tunic, and tiny feet.

Prove you won't leave me no matter where I go.

Harry slowed but still climbed. How long could he keep going? I was close and yelled, "Go up. Down is harder. I love you."

"To the top?"

"Yes."

We were high, and a vertiginous sense of unreal deadly nothing crept up my spine. Did Harry feel it? What if he stops? He didn't stop. Why wasn't he afraid? Was he more afraid of losing us? People shouted from the next platform, but I didn't look and could barely hear.

Harry stopped and looked down.

"Don't look down," I said.

"I don't like it so much."

"Look up. It's not far."

I squeezed the rung over my head—the world was a foot long. I prayed I could catch him if he fell.

"How are you?" I said.

"I'm tired."

"We'll rest."

Across Belshazzar's crowded court, ladders sent men and women into the sky. On the back wall, rising over the curved, sky-defining S-trunks of the elephants, was a quivering line of men making a horizon in the air.

I climbed under Harry and touched his foot.

"Just a little more," I said. Actually there were twenty feet, angling up, higher and higher.

"I can't. I'm scared."

"Don't be scared. I'm here."

"Are you scared?"

"No," I lied. Acting.

"My arms hurt."

"OK," I said. "I'm going to climb over you, then you grab me around the neck. I'll take you up."

I didn't know if this was possible. Do it before he panics!

I got over him. It wasn't easy. I had to look down—the wooden crosses were tiny and we were terrifyingly high. People on the platform urged us on, even offering a rope, but I waved it off. I had to do this quickly. I wanted to close my eyes, squeeze Harry, and never move again, but I had to get him to hold on to me. I couldn't get us up the ladder with one arm.

"I've got you." I put my right arm under him, between his warm little body and the ladder. "You've got to turn over and grab me. I've got you. You won't fall."

Harry, all thirty-six pounds of him, didn't move.

"I can't." He squirmed.

"Close your eyes and let go. I've got you."

Harry tightened his grip. I didn't know what to do. "I love you. Try." Slowly, very slowly, Harry released his grip, and with my arm cradling him, he closed his eyes and turned as neatly as Irene Castle executing a spin, throwing his arms around my neck and wrapping his legs around my waist so hard I almost couldn't breathe. The ladder shook.

"Easy now. You've got me."

Harry held so tight.

I grabbed a rung with my right hand. My left arm felt numb. I shook it, then squeezed the rung with both hands, adjusted for Harry's weight, and feeling his warm breath and arching my back to carry the precious burden, started up. Thank God Edith had strapped my sandals on tightly.

I climbed and Harry held. To say it was twenty feet or fifteen or ten means nothing. It was an eternity of placing one foot on a rung, one hand on a rung, then one foot, one hand, one foot, one hand—feeling the child's warm body and hot, frightened breath—and doing it again, again, again.

I climbed. I didn't think.

At the top I heard noise. It was clapping and shouting. We were in the sky.

4

Strong hands pulled us over the top, and Harry wouldn't let go of me. We sat by the base of the elephant and I held him, saying, "It's OK. I love you. It's OK." He kept his head on my tunic until ropes were tied around our waists, then said, "OK," but didn't let go. We rested by the elephant until a carpenter said Edith was coming up. A rope went over the side and was tied around her waist, then tied to a man above and below her, and Edith climbed steadily until she was pulled over the edge, white as her tunic, eyes wide as the sun, and kissed Harry, me, held us, cried, and tried not to cry. We were roped together and sat in the sun. Edith kissed Harry's ear and he said, "Will Dad leave?" and Edith said, "No one will leave."

Finally we moved to the edge and stood with other Babylonians, a hundred and fifty feet up in the air. Harry was calm. Edith and I were shaking but held each other and held him. "You did it," she said. "You did it."

I had one arm around Edith, the other around Harry, and looked out at Hollywood Boulevard, Sunset, and Los Angeles. We were in front of small, fat pillars connected by a red plank that provided a modest barrier. We carefully tucked our ropes under our tunics, breathed easier, though

Edith and I were pale, and our arms and legs ached. Harry kept looking at me. Edith looked at me and I looked at them. We were frightened but we were proud.

I saw everything. Extras nimbly climbing ladders; the Hanging Gardens motionless in the perfect morning. The tower elevator ready on its glistening tracks. Ishtar, serene and gigantic. Babylon, magnificent and chaotic. We were in a moment that defined us, and I realized that Ishtar and Babylon, like the Virgin, Son, and Father are something always with us. Something more powerful than lust, sacrifice, or anger. It's what Griffith was trying to photograph and what drove me up the crosses to the sky and pulled Harry, Edith, and me together. Griffith and Gish tried to harness it. A millennium ago it made cathedrals as men housed the invisible and found community with God and sanctuary from each other. Now it made a spectacle of wire and plaster and dollar-a-day-plus-lunch extras who will live in a silver-nitrate eternity. One millennium cut stone, the next light. Harry, Edith, and I cut our own millennium.

We faced south, looking directly at the railroad tracks and tower where Bitzer aimed the Pathé, and Griffith, dazzling in white, and Lillian, dazzling in white, sat in canvas chairs surveying the great set. What was Babylon for them? A new kingdom or new loneliness? Did it matter?

"They look like figures on a wedding cake," said Edith.

We saw Babylonians dancing, musicians blowing long horns, carpenters testing wires to make sure they were secure and invisible, and assistants barking directions for the Shot—this gamble of thousands of extras and dollars—this dice roll to see if Babylon could be caught in Bitzer's camera: inhuman scale made human, past made present, present made immortal. The Babylonians by us, hard-looking specimens, newly minted second-chance Californians, stood tall.

Harry, Edith, and I were like royalty on a balcony. We looked from the Baldwin Hills to Bunker Hill to Mount Lee to the arroyos of the Hollywood Hills. I looked all around the green rim of the world, which seemed to explode in a trance of unreal, lethal ecstasy—it was a new heaven and a new earth—and I looked at Harry, so intent, so rapt in fascination, so swept up in vision, and he smiled. I looked at Edith, who smiled at Harry, then me, and it was that smile again—the smile that is our life, with its flaws and pain and loneliness, and what we have, however flawed and painful, that isn't lonely—and I saw that what Griffith made with hawsers and plaster, we could make with pain and closeness.

Babylon: part mystery, part trick, part magic. Sanctuary.

∾

We felt a rush of wonder under the elephants and behind an orange plank, fifty feet over Ishtar, twenty feet over the Hanging Gardens, over dancers and extras, actors and builders, Griffith and Gish.

"We have to act," said Harry, with the seriousness of a child doing something important.

We were over the world. We could see Mack Sennett's tower—perhaps the comedian was bathing—we could see the roof-dotted Los Angeles basin, Hollywood High School, red trolleys climbing Mount Lee. We saw oil derricks sprinkled over the horizon, automobiles crawling on Sunset, a Model T and white figure parked in the hills. Jesus stood behind the wheel, arms extended—if not invited to Babylon, at least blessing it, and speaking to a crowd. Harry trembled with the importance of being a Babylonian child. Edith squeezed my hand.

After what seemed like an hour, the tower began to move. The orchestra hidden behind the set started playing, and women on the steps, sparkling with bangles and bare arms, danced as if welcoming a god. Men in shirtsleeves pushed the flatbed, and the rails gleamed in the high sun. Griffith pointed like Columbus. Bitzer aimed the tiny box that Karl Brown so delicately prepared and now cranked from the lower floor—the essential box, as important as Babylon. Lillian Gish, hair a miniature sun, rode the sky.

∾

The place lived. The moment lived. The men and women around us stood taller. The dancers threw themselves at the air—supplicating and inviting the camera: god of the hour, god of the future. Charioteers restrained horses. Men surreptitiously scratched fake beards. Men looked at women and women looked at men and we looked at Griffith. This was no picture, no frieze, no sculpture but a tableau—living, breathing, baking in the sun, and I felt, we felt, *knew*, we were part of something immortal.

The tower moved, and the Master sat on a folding

chair a hundred and fifty feet in the air. The taped, worn essential Pathé was grinding. Lillian beamed with excitement, flush with concentration—Griffith, Gish, and camera. An unbreakable triangle. Neither could have one without the others, and D. W. seemed to abide it. No, he wanted it. Even a hundred and forty feet in the air, over his thousands, the breathing, flirting, dancing, concentrating thousands, you could see it. Griffith was free and Lillian was never more beautiful. They were their chosen selves.

I looked at Harry and Edith. They looked at me and we looked at each other; then faced the camera, uniter of here and hereafter.

ABOUT THE AUTHOR

Luke Salisbury is professor of English at Bunker Hill Community College in Boston, where he teaches English and film. He is the author of the nonfiction *The Answer Is Baseball,* which the *Chicago Tribune* called "the best baseball book of 1989," and two previous works of fiction, *The Cleveland Indian,* nominated for the Casey Award in 1992 as best baseball book of the year, and *Blue Eden.* He has contributed to numerous baseball anthologies and wrote the Krank column for *Boston Baseball* from 1996 to 1999. He is past vice president and past national secretary of the Society for American Baseball Research.

He attended the Hun School and New College and received an MA in creative writing from Boston University. He lives with his wife, Barbara, and son, Ace, in Chelsea, Massachusetts.

For more information about Luke Salisbury, visit his Web site at www.lukesalisbury.com.